A Matter of Trust

Radclyffe

ISBN 1-930928-87-4

First Printing 2003

9 8 7 6 5 4 3 2 1

Cover design by Sheri

Published by:

Renaissance Alliance Publishing, Inc.
PMB 238, 8691 9th Avenue
Port Arthur, Texas 77642-8025

Find us on the World Wide Web at
http://www.rapbooks.biz

Printed in the United States of America

Acknowledgements

Athos, Jane, JB, Laney, and Tomboy—despite life's changes and challenges, you all keep hanging in. Thanks—cause I need you.

Much gratitude to HS (P,TB), for the verse and the friendship and the tremendous gift of the Radlist.

Stacia, once again, provided sensitive, thorough, and painless editing, for which I am exceedingly appreciative.

Most especially, there aren't enough words to describe my good fortune in having Lee, who understands why it is I need to do this.

— Radclyffe

For Lee
Everlasting

Chapter
One

J. T. Sloan tucked in the borrowed white T-shirt and was about to close the buttons on her fly when warm lips caressed the back of her neck, stilling her motion. All too aware that the woman pressed against her was naked, she murmured, "Hey."

"Hey, yourself," a low sultry voice replied as deft fingers lifted the T-shirt and slid underneath to play over Sloan's abdomen in slow, suggestive circles. "What are you doing? I thought you didn't have anywhere to be this morning."

"I didn't," Sloan affirmed, stiffening as the questing hand moved lower, dipping beneath the waistband of her jeans. "Until fifteen minutes ago when I checked my messages."

"Can't whatever you have to do wait a little longer? If I'd known we wouldn't have the morning, I would've kept you up all night. I'm not *nearly* done yet."

Sloan turned, stepping back from the embrace and catching the other woman's hands in hers. She wasn't in the mood, but if those fingers strayed much lower, she would be. "Sorry, I'd stay if I could. Emergency meeting—it sounded too important to ignore."

"I'll take a rain check then," the brunette answered, her dark eyes searching Sloan's face. "Until next time?"

"I'll call you." Sloan wondered if she would, but she didn't have time to ponder that one way or the other at the moment. "Thanks for the clean shirt, by the way."

As the woman leaned naked against the bathroom door, watching Sloan gather her jacket and briefcase from the bureau in the bedroom, she answered with a slow smile, "It's the least I could do after practically holding you hostage last night."

Sloan grinned. "Believe me, it was no hardship." She crossed the room and kissed her with practiced deliberation, only drawing back when she began to feel the sharp edge of arousal. She had work to do, and she couldn't afford to be distracted, even by something as pleasant as this. "Thanks again," she whispered and walked quickly from the room.

Within minutes, she was on the expressway and punching in the number to her office on her cell phone.

"Sloan Security," a familiar male voice answered.

"I'm running late," Sloan said sharply by way of greeting.

"Good morning to you, too. What's your ETA?"

"I don't know. I'm sitting in a two-mile jam-up on I-76. Is the client there yet?"

Hearing the edge of annoyance in Sloan's voice despite the telltale crackle of the cellular connection, Jason McBride glanced across the room at the glacially cool countenance of the 9:00 a.m. appointment. "Uh-huh."

What he thought was *uh-oh*. His associate did not like surprises, and it was his job to prevent them. He seemed to have dropped the ball, and his timing couldn't have been worse. There was something about the expression on their prospective client's face that suggested the upcoming meeting would be anything but routine. "Look—"

"Damn it," Sloan snapped, slowing for yet another bottleneck on an expressway that hadn't been express for twenty years. "There's not much I can do about it. Get him a donut or something." With that, she disengaged the cell phone, tossed it onto the passenger seat of her Porsche Carrera next to her battered leather briefcase, and tried for an end run around the long line of nearly stopped traffic in front of her. *Just what I get for not driving home last night.*

But the dinner meeting had run late, her companion had been charming, and the invitation to stay the night had been *so* eloquently phrased. Plus, the physical enticements had been too hard to ignore. With the project nearly completed, all systems up and operational, she saw no reason not to mix a little pleasure with her business. Not exactly routine, but hardly out of the ordinary either.

And, she thought with a grin, *I could hardly complain about the hospitality.*

Unfortunately, she hadn't planned on an early-morning appointment, expecting instead to drive home, shower, and change before going in to her office. Being her own boss had many advantages, not the least of which was setting her own hours. However, when, out of habit, she'd checked her messages from Claudia's bedroom phone upon awakening, Jason's cheerful tenor informed her that he had scheduled an appointment for her first thing that morning.

So, instead of a leisurely breakfast and another few hours of very enjoyable sex, she'd settled for a hasty shower and rush-hour traffic. And now, here she sat, breathing exhaust and getting hotter by the second.

"Son of a bitch," she growled. With a quick turn of the wrist, she angled out and around a stalled SEPTA bus, riding the shoulder until she passed most of the congestion. Being late was not acceptable. This client had requested an urgent consultation, and even though it usually took Jason weeks to find an opening in her schedule for a new project, this time he'd made an exception. He hadn't even had time to send a fax to her laptop with the usual summary he prepared before an interview.

"High-profile corporation, big-time connections, and money is *not* an issue," was precisely how he had phrased it in his *do not argue with me* voice when he'd informed her of the meeting. She trusted his judgment completely, which was why she let him manage everything about her business except the work she actually did. He handled the details behind the scenes and occasionally assisted her with larger projects on site. He was an able technician himself, and they didn't need a large staff. *She* was the talent they brokered, and any additional help she needed was subcontracted out.

"You'll want this one," was the final part of his message.

She couldn't help but wonder what made him so sure.

Michael Lassiter looked up from the *New York Times* business section as the office door banged open and a black-haired woman in a well-cut leather blazer, snowy white T-shirt, and blue jeans hurried in, halting in front of the reception desk on the other side of the room. In one appraising glance, Michael took stock. *Well built, five-ten, one forty or so—probably a couple of years younger than me. Twenty-nine, maybe?*

The slender blond man behind the wide walnut desk swiveled away from his monitor toward the commotion, a mixture of faint disapproval and reluctant fondness playing over his elegantly attractive face.

"Sorry," the woman called to him, turning in the middle of the room to face Michael. An instant's confusion skimmed over the surface of her sculpted features, then she stepped forward, her right hand extended. "Ms. Lassiter? Sorry to keep you waiting. I'm J. T. Sloan."

The unexpectedly low melodious voice, the piercing deep violet eyes, the strong clear planes of her striking face startled Michael for a second. Just as quickly, she recovered. She stood, automatically smoothing the slight creases in her navy silk skirt. "No trouble, Ms. Sloan."

"Just Sloan," Sloan replied with the devil-may-care grin, deep dimples and all, that had melted many a heart. It didn't seem to have much effect on Michael Lassiter, however. Her ice blue eyes and perfect features showed not the slightest hint of warming as she returned the handshake.

"Why don't we get comfortable in my office?" Sloan suggested, pointing toward the double doors at the far side of the reception area. She looked at Jason, who was watching them with the attention of a Phillies fan at the World Series.

"Coffee?" she queried, her tone indicating it was not a request.

He sighed and rose to brew a fresh pot. *She's aggravated because she isn't prepared for the meeting...or the client. How was I supposed to know that Michael wasn't a Michael? All I had time to do was check the corporate profile—that was more than enough incentive to schedule the damn appointment. Hell, I didn't even have time for the usual deep background searches.*

In the private office beyond the reception area, Sloan settled behind the antique oak desk that she had painstakingly moved from her parents' home almost a decade previously. It had gone with her first to Washington D.C., then into storage while she'd dropped out of sight for several months, and finally to her company's central office in the section of Philadelphia traditionally known as Old City.

The district had once been dominated by factories but had recently become the focus of highly publicized renovations. Now there were trendy restaurants and much sought-after loft apartments interspersed with warehouses and historic landmarks. Her building was a four-story converted warehouse, part of the second and third floors serving as office and work space, the top floor as her living area. "Please, have a seat. I just need a minute before we begin."

"Fine."

Michael Lassiter chose a leather swivel armchair facing Sloan. Large floor-to-ceiling windows to her left gave a panoramic view across the Delaware River into the state beyond, but neither woman looked outside. The office was comfortably functional, a deep blue carpet warming the high-ceilinged space, but Michael didn't get the feeling that the dark-haired woman seated behind the desk spent much time in the room. The desktop was unadorned by any personal mementos, its surface free of clutter, and the off-white walls were decorated with stylish yet oddly impersonal-appearing black-and-white photographs. There was nothing to give her a sense of the woman who headed Sloan Security, other than she seemed all business. *Which is just exactly why I'm here. If she can do what her reputation says she can, I don't need to know who she is.*

Sloan glanced at the open file folder that Jason had placed on her desk. It contained the data intake sheet for new clients—basic information such as name, company address, reason for initial interview, and a box for notations at the bottom of the first page where any unusual or particularly salient information could be added for quick review. She noted that the company name was Innova Designs. In the notation box Jason had typed "CEO, Michael Lassiter."

Nowhere on the page did Sloan see any indication that Michael Lassiter was a woman. Not that that fact mattered per se, but she liked to have as much background as possible when she was interviewing a prospective client. Information was power, and she was the one deciding if the client was worthy of her attentions—not the other way around. Another advantage of working for herself—she could choose her projects, and answered to no one.

When she looked up from the paperwork, she found the woman in the impeccably tailored suit observing her with unapologetic frankness. Deliberately, Sloan stared back. The double-breasted jacket was open to reveal a creamy silk shell that was fashionable without being flashy. She checked Michael Lassiter's hands, which were folded loosely in her lap. *No wedding ring. In fact, no rings of any kind.*

What jewelry she did wear was understated and tastefully elegant. A small gold hoop in each earlobe reflected the highlights in her naturally golden, exquisitely styled collar-length hair, and gray pearls accentuated the smooth pale skin of her neck. Sloan's gaze moved upward until their eyes met.

"I'm sorry to have kept you waiting," Sloan heard herself repeating, wondering what it was about this woman that had put her off her stride. She was used to corporate types, although usually they were men. Aggressive, arrogant, habitually engaged in one-upmanship. She wasn't easily impressed and was even less easily intimidated. And she was neither at the moment, but neither was she completely comfortable. Michael Lassiter was beautiful, like a precious *objet d'art* sequestered in a museum—separated from the observer by velvet ropes, bulletproof glass, and discreet but formal signs reading "Hands Off" posted nearby.

"That's quite all right. These things happen," Michael conceded with a small shrug.

But not to you, I'll bet. To break the silence that felt strangely hypnotic, Sloan pulled a lined yellow legal tablet from a stack near her right hand and picked up her fountain pen. "Tell me, what is it, precisely, that you need?"

Michael Lassiter smiled, a small tight smile that did not reach her eyes. "I believe that's what *you'll* need to tell me."

"Fair enough. Why don't we start with a little bit of background? This involves your company, I presume?"

For the first time, her client appeared uncertain. A brief flicker of something that might have been pain rose in her eyes and then was quickly extinguished. The CEO straightened slightly and met the questioning violet eyes squarely.

"Six years ago, my husband and I founded Innova Designs. We were fortunate to have a number of our early pilot projects picked up by several international corporations, and the collaborations turned out to be gratifyingly successful. The company has...grown, shall we say, rapidly over the past three years. We now employ several hundred people and have satellite offices in New York, Chicago, and Washington."

And you're threatening to break into the Fortune 500 if you keep escalating at your present rate of growth. While Michael Lassiter had been talking, Sloan skimmed a recent prospectus

Jason had managed to find on short notice, along with synopses of public financial reports for the firm. Innova Designs was a think tank—an array of the brightest and the best minds from industry, technology, the arts, and many other areas. The purpose of such companies was to analyze market trends, predict potential growth, and assist—or convince—others to finance and build new products. Success for a firm like Innova depended on the accuracy and ingenuity of the designers' vision. They didn't make products themselves; they created futures.

A knock on the door interrupted Michael's explanation, and both women waited in silence as Jason brought cups of coffee on a tray.

"Go on," Sloan prompted after Jason left, reaching for her pen to continue with her notes. "What kind of problem are you having?"

"May I assume this meeting is confidential?"

Sloan raised her head slowly, noting for the first time the subtle signs of strain—the too rigid posture, the slight clenching of a very lovely jaw, the faint lines of fatigue around searching blue eyes. "I'm not an attorney, Ms. Lassiter, or a priest. But client confidentiality is my business. If, at the end of our discussion, we decide our needs are not compatible, whatever you tell me now will be forgotten."

It was Michael's turn to scrutinize. She knew of Sloan Security by reputation, of course, which was why she had chosen the firm. Endorsements from previous clients and various official institutions had all been favorable. Now she studied the woman behind the desk, noting her imperturbable expression, her inquiring eyes. Sloan herself was known to be extremely efficient, resourceful, and highly capable. There were also those who suggested she was competitive and ruthless, but that did not concern Michael.

Personal information regarding the head of Sloan Security was more difficult to ascertain. Sloan's past was a cipher, and even those who purported to know her well had no knowledge of her history prior to her first appearance in the city several years ago. Rumors abounded, with speculation that she had been everything from a CIA agent deep undercover to a criminal engaged in nefarious underworld dealings.

Although young for her position, she was reputed to be at the top of her field. And Michael had a feeling she would need the best. She had no doubt that the woman watching her with faintly hooded eyes was capable of providing the service she required. The question was whether she could be trusted with the confidences.

The silence lengthened, each watching the other carefully. Violet and blue, fire and ice—they each sought something in the other's gaze. Finally, Michael spoke.

"This is not yet general knowledge, but in the very near future, I intend to divorce my husband and dissolve our business association."

It was not at all what Sloan had anticipated. Corporate cases like this were almost always about low-level security breaches— web site defacements, denial-of-service attacks, or internal glitches. But the urgency of the appointment and this unexpected introduction warned her that this was not going to be an ordinary case.

"Does *he* know?"

"Not yet." Michael kept her eyes on Sloan's face, waiting for some reaction. All she saw was attention. "Innova is currently in the midst of negotiating several new long-range contracts with businesses in both the public and private sectors. Because of that, the next few months are a critical time for us. Obviously, I am concerned that Innova continue to be perceived as a stable enterprise. No one wants to invest in a company that is in flux, and if information such as this were made public before the company has been restructured, we could lose important clients. Businesses have gone under with less reason than this."

"I can see why you're worried about a leak," Sloan agreed, beginning to understand the reason for the emergency consultation as well as the signs of stress in the woman seated across from her. Even the rumor of destabilization of a fast-growing company such as Innova would have a major negative impact on Lassiter's ability to secure new market acquisitions. What Sloan had just been told did not require further comment. The significance of the revelation spoke for itself.

Nevertheless, she had a feeling this was only part of the issue. "I understand that you need to accomplish this transition with as little fanfare as possible." Waiting a beat, she added, "What else do you need?"

"You mean, why am I really here?" Michael asked with a slight smile, very aware that Sloan was waiting for her to reveal the true cause of her concern. *Most people would have taken my explanation at face value. Certainly most men would have. But she knows there's something else. I'll have to be very careful with her or I'll have no secrets left.*

"The reasons for confidentiality are obvious. However," Michael continued smoothly, "the reason that I need to engage your services is that I expect my husband will attempt to take control of the company—by any means available to him."

"Physical means?" Sloan asked quickly, her eyes narrowing. "That's not the kind of security I provide."

"No, I'm sorry," Michael replied just as quickly. "I don't even think in those terms. I am..." She hesitated, trying to describe what she very rarely thought about—herself. "I am a theoretician, Ms. Sloan. I deal in ideas, concepts. I need to ensure that my current projects and future proposals are protected. Without them, I have no value and Nicholas, my...husband, may very well be able to convince the board of directors that I'm replaceable."

No value beyond her ideas. Odd way of describing yourself. Sloan dropped her fountain pen on the legal pad and leaned back in her leather swivel chair. She steepled her fingers in front of her chest and thought for a moment. At length she said quietly, "Let me see if I understand this. You're presently CEO of one of the country's most rapidly growing design technology firms. Your husband, Nicholas...Lassiter?"

"Burke."

"He's...what? Chief operating officer?"

At Michael's affirming nod, Sloan continued. "You intend to divorce him and keep the company on an even keel in the process...until you replace him with someone you trust, I presume." She raised an eyebrow, and again, Michael nodded. "You need *me* to ensure that your internal systems are secure and that your operations are tamperproof. And you expect me to do this without rousing suspicion while you execute this coup?"

Michael smiled thinly, her blue eyes troubled. "I'm not sure I'd call this a *coup,* Ms. Sloan," she said somewhat testily. "This company was my conception and was primarily funded from my personal resources. It's just that I've always been much better at theory than management. The vision, I suppose you could say, has been mine. My husband's natural talents have been in recruitment and marketing. I can assure you, I'm planning nothing illegal or even particularly underhanded. I intend only to protect my work from assault, which is exactly what I anticipate will happen as soon as my attorneys contact my husband."

Sloan leaned forward, picking up the pen again. "What's the timetable?"

"I believe that may very well be up to you." Michael shrugged. "I don't want to proceed until I'm certain that ongoing projects and the blueprints for future growth cannot be pirated or compromised in some way. Until that time, I intend to continue with the status quo."

At that, Sloan looked up in surprise, studying the cool, composed woman across from her. Despite the small signs of tension, the blond was remarkably controlled. What she had so calmly outlined amounted to nothing short of war within the arena of the financial world. It was the kind of confrontation that could lead to personal ruin and, indeed, had in many instances. The fact that she was married to the man she was about to engage in an all-out conflict did not appear to trouble her. Sloan wondered briefly if Michael Lassiter would also continue the personal relationship with her husband as if nothing were amiss. "Are you still...living with him?"

When Michael hesitated, color rising in her face, Sloan added quickly, "I'm sorry. I only ask because I'm trying to get a sense of the playing field here. Hostile takeovers can get messy, and—"

"No, that's quite all right," Michael interjected, her mask of imperturbability firmly in place. "We are still together, yes."

"Thank you," Sloan replied, oddly disturbed by the information. It gave her pause to think of this woman compromising herself privately for the sake of eventual financial supremacy. It also struck her as merely a form of prostitution and somehow much too demeaning for this obviously accomplished woman. *I'd better just stick to business. And what Michael Lassiter does in her private life is most definitely not part of my business.*

Closing the file folder, Sloan added, "You'll need a cover story as to why I'm spending so much time in your corporate headquarters. I'll also need to visit each of your branch divisions; I'll have to meet with your present systems operators; and I'll need unrestricted access to all levels of program applications and data acquisition."

"Am I to take it that you accept?" Michael Lassiter seemed to relax infinitesimally, letting a small sigh escape.

Sloan shrugged. "We haven't talked about the contract conditions or costs yet. Depending on the current state of your system, the software and consultant fees could run into five or six figures."

"Those details are inconsequential to me." Michael stood and stretched out a slim elegant hand. When Sloan rose, taking it wordlessly, she added, "What I require is your discretion and your talent."

"Of that I can assure you," Sloan responded. The hand in hers was remarkably warm, and she felt a slight reluctance to relinquish it. When she did, Michael Lassiter turned and left the room without another word.

An hour later, a knock drew her attention away from the reports she'd been rather unsuccessfully reviewing. Her mind kept returning to the meeting she'd had with Michael Lassiter—bits of conversation and fleeting images kept obscuring the data she was trying to absorb. She couldn't quite put her finger on what it was about the woman that affected her so strongly that it interfered with her concentration. Because nothing ever did.

Maybe it's the mixture of determination and discomfort in her eyes. She's going to do what she needs to do, but it's hurting her just the same. Jesus, why do I care? It's all just part of the game.

"Permission to enter?" a lightly mocking voice requested, accompanied by another knock.

"What?" Sloan responded irritably.

Jason stood in the open doorway, leaning one slim hip against the doorjamb, his arms crossed over his chest. His tailored trousers, monochromatic shirt and tie, and glossy European loafers screamed aspiring businessman-on-the-rise. His model-perfect, blond good looks verged on being too pretty for a man, but his intense blue eyes and tightly muscled physique added just the right amount of masculine flavor. "Time to compare notes."

"Come on in," Sloan replied in a tone that suggested she knew she had no choice in the matter.

"Sorry about the unexpected meeting."

"No problem."

He regarded her with one eyebrow cocked. "And should I even ask where you spent last evening?"

Sloan fixed him with a stony glare as she tossed the report

aside. "No, I don't think so."

"Talkative, aren't we? Testy, too," he observed dryly, walking further into the room. "Must be sleep deprivation."

He tried unsuccessfully to hide a frown, because he hadn't really intended to browbeat her about her private life. It was just that he'd hoped by now she'd show signs of settling down, but she never did. With each new woman in her life she seemed even less interested in anything serious. It wouldn't have bothered him so much if it weren't for the shadows in her eyes that had nothing to do with fatigue. He managed to hold his tongue, reminding himself that he wasn't doing much better in that department himself.

"Can we save the lecture for another time?" She rubbed her face with both hands, aware for the first time that she *was* tired. It wasn't just the lack of sleep. If anything, sex usually relaxed her. Unfortunately, she'd learned through bitter experience that such pleasures often came at a price. Claudia Carson had made it very clear that she wanted to see more of her. That idea wasn't an altogether unpleasant one by any means, but the intensity in Claudia's voice had set off alarms.

I will have to be very certain that the ground rules are clear before things became unnecessarily complicated. Sex is one thing, but—

"What about the client this morning? Did we at least get the new contract?"

"Yes, *we* got it," Sloan answered somewhat churlishly and then immediately regretted it. She saw the hurt in his eyes and reminded herself that they were friends. "Look," she sighed, "I'm sorry. You're right. I really *didn't* get much sleep."

"And I suppose that's *my* fault?" He flopped down in the chair Michael Lassiter had occupied earlier that day, deciding from the homicidal look on her face that it would be safer to change the subject. "So tell me about the Ice Queen."

Sloan skewered him with another stare meant to do damage. When he squirmed a bit and mouthed a silent *Please,* hands clutched to his heart, she finally laughed.

"She's a client, Jason, not a date."

"Oh please, like there's a big difference," Jason retorted, but this time his tone was uncritical.

Sloan shook her head, still smiling. "So now and then I see one of our clients...ah...socially, shall we say? It's never interfered with business. And besides, I can assure you that won't be happening with this one."

Jason wondered if he didn't detect a slight hint of regret in Sloan's voice, but he wisely chose not to comment upon it. Instead, he asked playfully, "And why exactly is that?"

"First and very foremost, she's straight," Sloan said with finality. Although she probably deserved her reputation as someone who never lacked for female companionship and never made a long-term commitment, she did have some limits. Dating straight women was definitely one of them.

"Things can always change," Jason commented.

"Not this time."

It was clear to him that for the moment at least, the matter was closed. He also knew that if he continued to push the issue, Sloan was likely to lose her famous temper. He'd been on the other end of that enough times not to want to provoke her. "Okay, I yield. No more business talk. Are you coming to the show tomorrow night?"

"Of course I'm coming," she said emphatically. "You know I love to watch Jasmine perform."

After almost five years, she still found it hard to believe that the buttoned-up, straight-laced man she had first met in the esteemed halls of Justice in D.C. was actually the sultry, sexy siren he became on stage. His transition was so complete that she sometimes wondered how he managed to keep Jasmine under wraps as successfully as he did. She was one of the few people who knew them both, and, secretly, she had to admit to a slight bit of sexual provocation when Jasmine flirted with her. It was bad enough that Jason was a guy; the fact that he was straight made it even more confusing.

She grinned. By now she should know better than to try to sort out all the conflicting reactions Jasmine incited. "Besides, I haven't seen Jasmine in weeks."

"Good," he said as he rose and carefully shook out the perfect creases in his trousers, "because she just bought a new dress." He winked and for a second, Jasmine's beautiful face flickered beneath the surface of his good-looking male countenance. "And I just *know* you'll like it."

Sloan laughed again. "Why don't you go pretend to work for a while and give me a break? Don't we have something—a background check on someone, a network to hack into—*something* that needs your attention?"

"I suppose I could start the file on Lassiter," he admitted, and finally left her in peace.

She sat staring after him, her mind returning once again to the interview with Michael Lassiter. It wasn't the most difficult job she had ever undertaken. Now that all the major corporations and most small businesses were computer dependent, computer hacking, software piracy, and network disruptions were becoming daily occurrences. Corporate espionage was one of the largest financial drains on most international organizations, mostly because it went unreported for fear of undermining public confidence in the company.

It never ceased to amaze her that most people who were critically dependent upon computer networks knew almost nothing about them, and even those who did rarely took the time to ensure that they were totally tamperproof. She had recognized the need for Internet security services well ahead of the pack. Now that there were almost daily news reports detailing the ease with which systems could be entered and altered, computer security was a hot area. She had foreseen the need, and her previous experience made her perfect for the work.

What both intrigued and troubled her about this particular assignment was her employer. Michael Lassiter struck her as a woman who was completely capable of living with the consequences of her decisions. But once or twice, Sloan thought she had seen a flicker of fear in the other woman's eyes. For no reason she cared to explore, that bothered her.

Chapter
Two

Michael swiveled her chair to look out the window of her twenty-first floor office. It was after 7:00 on a Friday night and just getting dark. Her Center City offices overlooked the financial district with a view beyond the skyline to the river. Had she been looking, she would have been able to see for miles across the broad expanse of water as commuters crossed the Walt Whitman and Ben Franklin bridges heading home. But her gaze was unfocused, and what she saw was only the ghost of an image in her mind.

Usually what occupied her mind were visions of the future; what excited her were concepts—possibilities—the ideas she formulated for others to implement. More and more companies were looking outside their own spheres for advice on product development, market trends, and emerging technologies. It paid to be the first on the block with the newest creation, items to facilitate how humans worked and played and communicated. And the bottom line was, companies were willing to pay for that advantage.

She and her central core of designers worked with corporate executives to put their businesses not on the crest of innovation, but ahead of the curve. Everything she had accomplished, and everything she hoped to accomplish, lay stored in the far-from-unassailable memory banks of the company's computer system.

However, Michael was not envisioning the future now, at least not the future she had formerly imagined. Until recently, she had had no reason to contemplate her own life. Work occupied her mind almost constantly—that and what she and Nicholas needed to do to accomplish their shared dream. She had met Nicholas

Burke almost fifteen years ago when she'd been a precocious freshman at the Cambridge Institute of Design and he had been a worldly graduate student at MIT. Barely 17, she had been socially inexperienced, despite her privileged upbringing, and intellectually too intimidating for most boys her age. But when she had met Nicholas in a theoretical design class, he had appreciated her ideas and had been supportive and encouraging. Together they had spent hours talking, dreaming, and finally forging their common vision into the formidable enterprise it had become. Along the way, it seemed only natural that they should wed.

It had never occurred to her that their relationship lacked passion or romance. It was not something she was aware of needing. She probably would have ignored those moments when she felt a loneliness so acute it was physically painful had she not finally become aware of Nicholas's affair with a young female graphic artist in their firm. She was less hurt than baffled.

Although she didn't consider herself particularly inventive or adventurous in the physical department, she wasn't aware of ever refusing Nicholas's advances either. It was a part of their relationship that left her strangely unmoved, but she had assumed her performance had been adequate. Clearly, however, Nicholas required something additional.

She supposed that she could have simply ignored his affair, but, once she became aware of it, she rebelled at the idea of continuing a relationship so false. When she confronted him with her desire to divorce, she felt quite certain that he would seek greater control of the company. She intended to preempt that event, and one way she could be prepared was to ensure that her unique contribution to the company was safe.

Leaning back in the contoured black leather chair, she was alone in the polished, elegant office that was so perfectly appointed it deserved a center spread in *Architectural Digest*. After so many years, however, she was immune to the physical manifestations of her success. She didn't see the room; she didn't even see the spectacular sunset. What slowly came into focus just behind her nearly closed eyelids was J. T. Sloan's face. Strong, certain, a hint of aggression—the head of Sloan Security certainly inspired confidence.

Sighing, Michael hoped that her assessment of the woman she had hired the day before was correct. She indeed was going to need help.

"I'm leaving," a soft voice behind her announced, mercifully interrupting her introspection. "The agenda for Monday's meeting just went to Development."

"Yes, fine." Michael swiveled away from the window to face the door. She smiled tiredly at the brunette in the doorway. "Thank you."

Michael's executive assistant studied her. "You look beat. Why don't you go home?"

"I will, soon," Michael lied, appreciating the concern in the other woman's voice.

Why should I? Nicholas probably won't be there, and if he were, I wouldn't want to see him. It's easier to relax here.

Michael was suddenly more conscious of being alone than ever before. It wasn't because of the imminent loss of her marriage, but the absence of the intimacy that she and Nicholas had never truly shared—an intimacy that until now she hadn't been fully aware of missing. She forced a smile and waved goodnight, waiting only a moment before turning down the lights and closing her eyes in the welcoming darkness.

"Damn, I'm sorry," Sloan exclaimed, watching Michael jerk awake and blink in confusion. She automatically brushed the dimmer switch, muting the lights she had turned up full when she walked into the room. It was nine o'clock at night, and she hadn't expected anyone to be in the office. Certainly not the CEO of the company, alone in a darkened room on the deserted floor of her office building. Sloan couldn't help but see the fatigue, merely hinted at the day before, much more apparent now in the blond's face. Faint purplish shadows bruised the perfect skin under her eyes, and there was a weariness in the way she pushed herself upright in her chair.

"It's okay," Michael assured her, rubbing her eyes and trying desperately to orient herself. She glanced out the window. *Dark. Nighttime.* She sat up straight, brushing her hair back with both hands. "What are you doing here?"

Sloan grinned her trademark lopsided grin. "Working. When we spoke on the phone this afternoon, we agreed I'd get started by running a preliminary systems review, remember?"

"I didn't realize you meant tonight," Michael said dryly, firmly in control again.

"No point in waiting. By the way, *computer* security isn't your only loose end around here. The guard downstairs let me in at the mere mention of your name and kindly directed me to your office. Never even asked for ID."

"I'll speak to him about that."

"Good," Sloan answered easily, setting a large leather brief-case down on the floor. "So...I figured I could get an idea of what I'm up against when most of your staff was absent—less traffic on the network, fewer people around. That way I can cover some of my tracks when I need to start pulling the system apart."

"I understand that," Michael said a touch impatiently, "but what are you doing in *my* office? The IT center is at the other end of the hall."

Sloan leaned one jeans-clad hip against the arm of an expen-sive leather couch and took inventory. A low glass coffee table occupied the space in front of the sofa with other butter-colored leather furniture flanking it. Directly across from the seating area, Michael sat behind a huge pedestal desk that held the usual array of phones, folders, and stacks of papers. The woman behind the desk looked sleek and stylish in an ocean green silk pants suit and low-heeled pale leather shoes, her blond hair looking only mod-estly disarrayed from her recent finger combing. Her momentary disorientation when Sloan startled her awake had been replaced with a calm expression now, but, for an instant, she had appeared vulnerable, and very young.

Ignoring the slight pulse of attraction, Sloan hastily averted her gaze. The room was huge, windowed on three sides, with a small alcove kitchenette/bar arrangement to her left and to the right, beyond the seating area, an impressive workstation with several computers, large flat-screen monitors, and drafting boards. *Impressive. The corner office, indeed.*

She realized that the CEO was still waiting for a further explanation. *"Your* computers are the logical and easiest place to start. I need to see how secure you are. Plus, I can't very well look for tampering if I don't look here. It's where the money is...so to speak."

"Of course." Michael watched Sloan grin that damnable grin again. Irritated to find herself smiling back, she rose to gather her papers into a small portfolio. "You'll need the passwords."

"I'll find them. It's a good way to test how adequate your cur-rent safeguards are."

Michael looked up sharply. "No one knows mine. Not even my executive assistant."

"How often do you change them?" Sloan asked mildly, crossing to the console.

"I have no idea." Michael shrugged dismissively. "Whenever the system prompts me to. I've never paid any attention to the way the network was constructed. It's just a tool to me—I know as much about it as I do the engine in my car."

"You're not much different than most business execs in that regard," Sloan observed, completely without censure. Settling into the molded leather chair, she spent a few seconds with the keyboard and mouse, and the 19-inch flat-screen monitor leapt to life. After downloading a program from the web designed to crack passwords, she began routing through the files, muttering absently. "Information is almost never truly deleted, merely layered over. This is a little like archaeology—you just have to dig down to it."

"Wonderful," Michael commented acerbically. "I should at least be happy that Nicholas doesn't have much more interest in the finer points of these things than I do."

"He doesn't need to." Sloan looked over her shoulder at the woman behind the desk, thinking once again how damned lovely she was, even with the lines of stress etched a little deeper around her eyes tonight. "He can hire someone."

"Yes. Exactly as I did." Michael worked not to let her uneasiness show. She didn't like the idea of drawing battle lines with Nicholas, or of living in what could amount to an armed camp until their affairs could be disentangled, but she had to protect her business. It was all she had.

"What you should be pleased about is that you hired me first," Sloan joked. She frowned at something that appeared on the screen, clicked through a few items, then pushed back in the chair to look at Michael again. "Is this where you do most of your project designs?"

"Here or my laptop at home. I just synchronize the files when I come in. The division heads get summaries of future lines of development, but no hard details. I work them out alone." *Like I do almost everything,* she thought, but had no reason to voice.

She had been an insular child, an awkward teenager, and a reclusive student until Nicholas had taken the time to listen to her. Somewhere in the last fifteen years she had grown up and, in turn,

outgrown her simple need for his validation. And when that had
happened, they had little left to bind them. *A shell of a marriage,
and now, not even that.* She was suddenly aware of Sloan's deep
voice. "What? I'm sorry, I was...wandering."

"I was saying that one of the first things we need to do is beef
up your personal security."

"How?"

"Encryption, for starters."

"Which will do what?"

"Plenty," Sloan muttered, still mentally cataloguing her work
list. "It can authenticate user identity, protect e-mail transmissions, assign cryptographic document signatures, and verify
authorship. When you're interfacing with multiple systems, user-
to-server security is key. Plus, it adds one more layer around your
sensitive data that a hacker needs to wade through."

"Okay," Michael murmured. On the surface it sounded good.
The details eluded her, which was precisely why she'd hired an
expert.

Sloan stared at the monitor, scanning through files, looking
for traces of tampering or unauthorized entry. This was what she
loved—the hunt, the chase. The thrill of finding the hidden
secrets. Some of her less kind critics had said that was what she
loved best about women, too. The hunt. Had she cared at all about
public opinion, it might have bothered her.

"And," she said at length, "we really need to get you an ID
chip to lock down your hard drive, too."

Michael raised an eyebrow. "Meaning?"

"An electronic chip keyed to a unique identifier like your fingerprints or an iris scan, for example, so that you can be positively
identified, and anyone else is locked out. A few companies are
working on prototypes but they're still a little buggy," she continued absently, arranging a work strategy in her head. "We need
something similar to prevent anyone else from doing just what I'm
doing now—breaking into this drive. It will dissuade hands-on
intrusion from inside. It won't protect you from outside hackers,
but that's going to take me a bit longer. I'll see what I can come up
with."

"Can you tell if someone's been in here?" Michael asked,
watching Sloan work. "Figuratively speaking?"

"Sure. Given enough time."

"And this ID chip is still in the prototype stage," Michael

remarked, feeling oddly violated just thinking about someone tampering with her work. "How are you going to get one?"

Sloan was silent as she searched around in her tool kit for a temporary fix. When she had the intrusion detection program loaded, she looked up. "I have my ways," she answered, an amused glint in her eyes.

"Legal, I presume?"

"Oh, but of course." A grin now.

"How did you get into this?" Michael asked, fascinated by the topic, but more so by the woman, who exuded an intriguing combination of startling candor and secrecy.

Sloan shrugged, offering her automatic explanation—all of it true, just not the whole story. "The Internet is the new frontier, and we are woefully unprepared to confront it. It is fast becoming the foundation of communication, commerce, even culture. And it's wide open, lawless. There are no rules, no methods of enforcing any if there were, and few means to detect or deter crime. I saw the possibilities, and I had the experience."

"And you got that experience where?" Michael probed.

"Cal Tech, then later..." she hesitated, aware that she was revealing things that she rarely discussed, "uh...industry."

Warning bells started clanging loudly in Sloan's head—Michael Lassiter was easy to talk to, and even easier on the eyes. *Oh man. Not good, not good at all.* She shut up and concentrated on the monitor.

Sloan stretched and looked at her watch, surprised to find that she and Michael had been sitting wordlessly fifteen feet from each other for over an hour, each silently working. She looked over at her companion, unaware of both the pensive smile that Michael quickly hid and the fact that the CEO had been watching her for the better part of the last quarter-hour.

"Done for the night?" Michael inquired.

Sloan nodded.

"So, you're a cyber-cop?" Michael asked, still curious and genuinely interested.

"Hardly." Sloan laughed harshly, thinking of how she had once been called that by condescending colleagues, another lifetime ago. "'Incident response expert' is the latest jargon. Mostly, I guess, I'm just a technogeek, without the glasses and pocket protector."

Whatever you call yourself, you're far from that, Michael
thought. It had been a long time since she had lost herself in conversation with someone when it hadn't been focused on sales or
development or some other aspect of her work. Perhaps as long
ago as those early years with Nicholas, when they had stayed up
half the night fantasizing about a world that was now coming to
be. *Had it been this easy then?*

"Somehow I can't see you in the nerd role," Michael laughed.

Sloan laughed with her. "You should have seen me when I
was twelve."

"So this was what you always wanted to do?"

Sloan's immediate impulse was to change the subject. Her
past was not something she discussed with anyone, even her
friends, and she didn't have many of those. She looked into
Michael's eyes, prepared for evasive maneuvers, and discovered
something she hadn't seen in a long time—simple interest, unac-
companied by innuendo or pretense. Often when women inquired
about her personal life, it was a prelude to seduction. Not that
attempts at seduction were unwelcome, by any means, but she *had*
learned to subtly direct conversations away from revelations that
could put her at a disadvantage.

From this woman, however, the questions seemed merely
friendly, and Sloan dropped her guard. There was no need to protect herself from Michael Lassiter, because nothing was going to
happen between them. There was no danger here.

"I was into computers before most of my peers, when I was
still a kid really. It just came easily to me. Pretty soon I was hacking into places I probably shouldn't have been, but it got me
turned on to the possibilities very early. One thing led to another."

"We have that in common," Michael noted.

Sloan regarded her with surprise. "What?"

"An early fascination with something other people don't
understand." Her face took on a distant expression, and she continued musingly, "It sets you apart. It can be hard."

"Yes."

Their eyes met, and Michael sensed that there was more that
Sloan wasn't saying. There was a harsh undertone in her deep
voice that hinted at pain, and Michael had the distinct impression
the security specialist was censoring her replies. She wondered,
too, if Sloan had felt the same numbing isolation that she had

experienced before Nicholas.

With that thought, she suddenly realized how wrong she had been about Nicholas, perhaps from the very beginning. At seventeen, what she believed to be a partnership of equals had very likely only been youthful dependence spawned from aching loneliness. Now, when she thought of Nicholas, she saw only a remote, calculating stranger. Not someone who loved her. And not someone she loved. *My God, has my whole life been a lie?*

The flicker of sorrow in Michael's expressive eyes didn't escape Sloan's notice. It bothered her, and she had no idea why. Impulsively, she asked, "Have you eaten?"

"No," Michael replied cautiously, wondering where the conversation was headed. She was surprised by the question, realizing she hadn't even been aware that she was hungry, and surprised even more so that Sloan was inquiring. The other woman didn't seem the type for easy familiarity any more than she was.

"Actually," Sloan began hesitantly, still uncertain why she was doing what she seemed to be doing. Maybe it was because they appeared to share some of the same disaffected past; maybe it was nothing more than that they had been able to talk so easily. She shrugged. *Nothing wrong with being friendly, right?*

"I'm about to catch a show in Old City. A friend is performing, and the food there is serviceable. Want to come along?"

Normally Michael wasn't impulsive, but when she thought of the long night ahead, this seemed like a harmless enough diversion. "Why not?"

Michael almost backed out a dozen times.

We're virtual strangers; what if we have nothing to talk about?

Unfortunately, she had agreed to let Sloan drive, which at the time seemed to make sense. She hadn't thought about the fact that she wouldn't be able to make a hasty retreat if the evening turned into a disaster.

She sat in the front seat of the sports coupe, staring out the window at the busy city streets. It was close to 11:00 on an unseasonably warm Friday night in April, and an unusual number of people were still walking about, taking advantage of the weather. She realized that she was rarely out at this time of night, unless it was to travel home from the office. And at those times, her mind was on automatic, busy constructing answers to questions most people hadn't yet asked. That was one of her strengths, her ability to see both the problems and the solutions inherent in a project before they developed. She sorely wished that ability extended to her private life as well.

Beside her, Sloan drove with quiet concentration. She was efficient, aggressive without being reckless, and intensely focused on maneuvering the powerful sports car through the narrow, crowded streets. Michael was surprised to find that she wasn't uncomfortable, even though she was doing something completely foreign to her. She rarely socialized outside the obligatory business meetings, and when she and Nicholas had been forced to entertain, she had done so reluctantly. She simply didn't feel comfortable making casual conversation with near-strangers. When she tried to remember the last time she and Nicholas had been out alone together, she couldn't. How on earth she had ever allowed herself to be drawn into *this* strange outing escaped her.

"You needn't stay if it doesn't please you," Sloan said as if reading her mind.

Michael looked at her sharply, studying the angles of her face in the flickering light from overhead street lamps and passing cars that illuminated her features briefly before darkness descended again. In those brief patches of light, she could make out the strong chin, sculpted cheekbones, and straight fine nose. She couldn't see the color of her eyes, but she didn't need to. That deep violet was something already etched in her memory.

Despite the odd turn of events, Michael reminded herself that she had spent the last few hours in this woman's company, in far more than casual conversation. Contrary to being awkward, it had been amazingly easy.

"I'm accustomed to looking after myself, Ms. Sloan. Please don't worry about me."

"Just Sloan," Sloan repeated again. She glanced briefly at Michael, then returned her attention to the road. "I have absolutely no doubt that you are entirely capable of looking after yourself. I only meant that it might not be the kind of entertainment you're used to."

"You said a show—down here I'd guess a jazz combo or a piano bar." At Sloan's faint smile she asked cautiously, "What exactly does your friend do?"

Grinning a little wider, Sloan deftly maneuvered into a parking space on the street. She cut the engine and turned in her seat to face Michael, carelessly draping her right arm over the back of the passenger seat. There wasn't a great deal of room in the interior of her Porsche, and her fingers glanced unintentionally over Michael's shoulder. "It's a drag show."

Michael jumped slightly, more from the unexpected contact than the unanticipated answer. She swallowed, then answered steadily, "Of course, a drag show. Exactly what I was expecting."

Sloan laughed, appreciating her companion's aplomb. She released her seat belt and pushed open the driver's door. "Come on. I have a table reserved up front."

Michael waited on the sidewalk, watching the unquestionably handsome woman come around the car to join her. *What in God's name am I doing?*

Chapter
Three

Backstage in the dressing room shared by all the performers, Jasmine sat before a light-encircled mirror at a long table that ran along the entire length of one wall. She finished applying the last touches of mascara and reached for the lip gloss to seal the dark crimson shade she had chosen to highlight the subtle sweep of blush along the crest of her cheekbones. Carefully, she used a fine brush to shade the edges of her upper lip and then checked to ensure that any hint of shadow along her jaw line had been obliterated with a light foundation.

As the door to the dressing room opened and one of the other performers entered, she turned on her chair and smiled up at the newcomer. "How's the crowd?"

"Full house." The statuesque brunette in the form-fitting red dress eased into the adjoining chair. She studied her reflection in the mirror and, after assuring herself that everything was in order, swiveled to face Jasmine. "You should get a load of Sloan's date," she remarked too casually.

Jasmine arched an eyebrow in surprise. "Oh really? Sloan never said anything about bringing someone."

"Well, she's at her usual table, and she's got a gorgeous blond with her. Even by Sloan's usual standards, this one's a show-stopper."

"Blond, as in natural?" Jasmine inquired, feeling a faint stirring of anxiety. "As in perfect size 6? As in Ingrid Bergman elegant and Sharon Stone sexy? That type of blond?"

Crystal stood, smoothing out nonexistent wrinkles in her dress, looking into the mirror again as she made a subtle adjustment to the very expensive body-sculpting brassiere she wore and squeezing her lips together in a slight kissing motion. "That would be the one."

The new client. Jasmine closed her eyes briefly, then muttered, "Oh, fuck. That's a first even for her."

"Problems with the randy partner again?" Crystal was always eager for any gossip about Jasmine's secretive associate. She could never get Jasmine to tell her the dirt, but she kept trying. *Everyone* wanted to know Jasmine and Sloan's story.

"Sloan's reputation is greatly exaggerated," Jasmine remarked at length, her sense of loyalty overcoming her irritation. *If Sloan wants to risk losing a client by breaking her heart before the deal is closed, I won't be able to stop her. Maybe she'll learn something.*

"That's not what I hear around town," Crystal prodded.

Jasmine reached for the black sheath dress, lowered it over her head and smoothed it down her body, reminding herself that it was not her problem—and none of her business. "She just needs to settle down with someone."

Carefully, she fitted the expensive wig over the thin skullcap that contained her own blond hair. *Better for business, better for my nerves, better for her. Especially better for her.*

"Sloan? Settle down?" Crystal laughed. "Oh, I don't think so. Honey, that one is not the marrying kind."

· Jasmine followed Crystal out of the small, harshly lit dressing room toward the shadows at the edges of the curtained stage. She knew better, but it was not her story to tell.

Glancing surreptitiously around the room, Michael edged her chair closer to the small circular table, unsuccessfully trying to avoid being bumped by the bustling wait people and harried latecomers. It was crowded and noisy. The patrons displayed such a contagious exuberance that it made her smile. It was a partylike atmosphere, and she felt herself relaxing despite her initial misgivings.

"Drink?" Sloan shouted, her shoulder brushing Michael's while she steadied the teetering pedestal table with one hand. With the other, she accepted a plate of surprisingly good-looking sandwiches from a waiter and settled it in the center of the tiny tabletop.

"Wine?" Michael shouted back. Whatever the seating capacity of the club, she was certain it had already been exceeded by a wide margin. If the fire marshal happened in, they'd all be out in the street.

"I wouldn't chance it here." Sloan pulled a face. "It's most likely something that comes with a screw cap in a gallon jug."

"Vodka tonic?"

Sloan nodded as she rose. "Safer," she called as she moved off into the crowd.

Michael watched her impromptu escort wend her way effortlessly through the throng of shouting, jostling people. Sloan moved gracefully, with a subtle air of confidence that suggested she was used to others stepping aside for her. Some people might find that kind of self-assuredness off-putting, but Michael merely found it compelling. Sloan's natural graciousness seemed to temper what on the surface might appear to be arrogance.

Alone, without Sloan's charismatic presence to distract her, Michael had to wonder at her *own* behavior. She didn't know this woman, had never been in any place remotely like this before, and worried that she would say or do something to embarrass herself. And yet, despite her anxiety, she also felt a surge of excitement. She hadn't been away from the office for anything other than business trips in months. This was as far from her usual routines as she could get, and just the diversion she needed.

"Hi, I'm Sarah," a slender redhead in soft tan chinos and a white cotton turtleneck announced as she pulled a chair over to the already crowded table. At the look of perplexity on Michael's face, she added, "I'm a friend of Sloan's."

Michael held out her hand. "Michael Lassiter."

Sarah regarded her carefully for a moment, noting the perfectly styled hair, understated but flawless make-up, and the suit so expensively tailored that it looked casual. "If you're a drag queen, you're the best I've ever seen."

"Ah..." Michael stared, struggling for any reply that would be remotely appropriate.

"Ms. Lassiter is a business associate, Sarah," Sloan said smoothly as she wedged herself into the remaining chair at the cramped table, depositing Michael's drink and her own. Looking at Michael, she tried to hide her amusement. The beautiful face showed faint signs of numb shock. "Sarah is a doctor of Oriental medicine, Michael."

"Oh, I see." Not that she did. But it might explain the slight fragrance of spices that clung to the redhead and the quiet contained expression on her smooth, even features that Michael found oddly companionable. It didn't explain, though, who Sarah was, or why she was there, or how she knew Sloan.

But then why should anything about this experience make sense? After all, I'm here, and I'm not entirely certain how that came about. I don't know these women at all, but I feel comfortable with them. Clearly, the rhyme and reason of it is inconsequential at the moment.

As if sensing Michael's thoughts, Sarah laughed and laid her hand briefly on Michael's arm. "Sloan never has gotten over being cryptic, even when she doesn't have to be. We met ages ago when we both did a stint in Thailand. I ended up staying behind and studying there. We've just recently reconnected since I got back to the States, but you might say we're best friends."

"I see," Michael repeated, nodding as if that cleared everything up. When she saw the look of discomfort pass over Sloan's features, darkening her gaze for a moment, she didn't ask for clarification. *She's certainly entitled to her privacy and her secrets.*

"Then," Sarah continued as if oblivious to Sloan's glowering expression, "she invited me to see Jasmine perform, and now I hate to miss one of her shows. Have you seen her in action yet?"

"No," Michael answered, seeing no point in adding that she had never in her life seen so many women who might *not* be women, and how did one tell anyway? Mercifully, the lights went down signaling the beginning of the show, sparing her from any further response.

And then she was too engrossed to talk.

Michael could scarcely remember two hours that she had ever enjoyed more. She wasn't certain what was more entertaining— the costumes, the music, or the genuinely talented performers. To her amazement, the voices of the half-dozen or so female impersonators were marvelous. Throughout the show, she was aware of Sloan beside her, laughing softly at some joke, applauding enthusiastically for every performer, and bending close during breaks in the entertainment to fill her in on some of the background of the Cabaret. Once, she had disappeared for a few moments and returned with a fresh drink for Michael, setting it before her with a warm smile. She was considerate, attentive, and altogether charming. Michael had never met anyone quite like her.

As the lights came up, Michael found herself pressed against Sloan at the tiny table. The noise level had not abated, and if anything, the raucous crowd had become even more celebratory as the evening progressed. She and Sloan had to lean almost forehead to forehead to hear each other.

"Well, what did you think?" Sloan inquired, her eyes alight with enjoyment.

"It was amazing," Michael replied enthusiastically. "They sound wonderful, and they're so beautiful to look at. The costumes are gorgeous, too. They remind me of birds of paradise."

"The flowers?"

"Yes."

Sloan laughed and nodded. "I'll have to remember to tell Jasmine. She'll love that."

At the sound of Jasmine's name, Sarah leaned forward to join their conversation. "Jasmine has a wonderful singing voice, don't you think," she declared, more a statement than a question.

"She's incredible," Michael agreed.

Sloan caught the tone of admiration in Sarah's voice and saw that her face was flushed with pleasure, her eyes bright with excitement. Her friend appeared altogether effervescent, and Sloan had a feeling that she knew why.

Six weeks before, she had brought Sarah to the Cabaret for the first time, and since that night, Sarah had been at every one of Jasmine's performances. Sarah's eyes never left Jasmine, whether Jasmine was on stage or enjoying a drink with them at their table after the show. The attraction was unmistakable, and Sloan was worried. She knew for a fact that Jasmine never saw anyone socially outside of the club and wondered if Sarah really appreciated Jasmine's story. She said nothing, however, for she made a point never to involve herself in the personal affairs of other people, particularly her friends.

She simply nodded her agreement and said, "Yeah, Jasmine's fantastic."

At that moment, the subject of their conversation appeared from the hallway behind the stage, threading her way carefully between the crowded and disorderly tables toward them. Sloan gallantly rose and offered her chair at the table. Jasmine thanked her with a quick kiss on the mouth. Sloan couldn't help but grin, rubbing off the faint smudge of lipstick with her finger.

"I'm so glad all of you stayed," Jasmine said, taking the offered seat. She crossed her legs, the hem of her dress riding up to expose trim smooth legs beneath sheer stockings. A stiletto-heeled satin shoe dangled from her foot. "You all looked as if you're having such fun, and I didn't want to miss a minute of it."

"We were just saying how wonderful your performance was," Sarah remarked, her attention totally focused on Jasmine.

As Sloan pulled over another chair from a nearby table and settled again next to Michael, she was certain she saw Jasmine blush, even in the dim light of the smoky room.

"I'm Jasmine," the performer said slowly, extending her hand to Michael. "Did you enjoy the show?"

"Michael Lassiter. And yes, I did, very much."

Sloan smiled, pleased that Michael was having a good time. She was still surprised at herself for having impetuously invited her. It wasn't something she generally did—inviting near-total strangers, particularly straight married strangers, out on the town. She'd just had the feeling, while working in that cold, glass-enclosed high-rise office late on a Friday night, that Michael Lassiter was lonely. Why exactly she should care was another question altogether, and not something she wanted to consider too closely. The fact that she was very aware of Michael's arm against her own at the crowded table was also making her uncomfortable. She glanced at her watch and saw that it was after 1:00 a.m.

With something close to relief, Sloan said to Michael, "It's getting late. Would you like me to drive you back to your office, or may I take you home?" It wasn't until she had said it that she realized it might be misinterpreted as an invitation to something more personal. Hastily, she amended, "I mean...if you don't feel like driving, I could drop you anywhere you like."

Michael smiled faintly, pretending not to notice Sloan's discomfort. "Actually, I took the train into the city this morning. At this hour, I'm going to need a cab."

"Nonsense," Sloan said firmly, ignoring the quick rush of pleasure that accompanied the thought of a few more minutes with the lovely new client. "I'll take you home. It's no trouble at all. Are you ready?"

Michael glanced over and saw Sarah and Jasmine engaged in animated discussion, Sarah's hand resting lightly on Jasmine's forearm. Most of the patrons had begun making their way toward the door, and with some regret, she realized that the evening had come to an end. "Yes, of course," she said, quickly rising.

They called goodnight to Sarah and Jasmine and got rather absent-minded waves as the two of them continued their intense conversation with scarcely a break. Sloan smiled at her two friends and lightly took Michael's hand to lead her through the crowd.

"They seem to be very good friends," Michael remarked casually as she and Sloan stepped out into the street. She was still holding Sloan's hand, and it was surprisingly strong—smooth and warm against her skin. It wasn't at all unpleasant, that firm, sure touch.

"They just met not long ago," Sloan informed her, "but they hit it off right away." She didn't ordinarily discuss Jason and Jasmine's connection. That was for Jason to reveal, and, although she thought Michael might understand, she redirected the conversation to a safer topic.

"I'm really glad that you enjoyed the show." As she spoke, she released her grip on Michael's fingers, disengaged the alarm on the Carrera with her remote, and opened the passenger door for her guest.

"Oh, I did," Michael replied, settling into the front seat and then strapping on her seat belt. She shifted in the seat so she could face Sloan as they drove. "Thank you for inviting me."

For a moment, Sloan was uncomfortable, very aware that only the day before Michael had contracted her to do a job, and that she didn't know her very well. Usually when she was alone with a woman, she felt a little more certain of her moves. Tonight had been different. Michael Lassiter was not someone with whom you indulged in a casual dalliance. Sloan had a feeling that Michael wouldn't even know the rules. Glancing at her passenger, she was surprised anew by her quiet elegance and composure. Grinning suddenly, she said, "Sorry if the evening took you a little by surprise."

"Not at all." Michael laughed. "Once I figured out that most of the beautiful women were men, and many of the handsome ones were really women, I wasn't confused in the slightest."

"Well, that's the first time I ever heard it put quite that way, but it does seem to sum it up." She looked at Michael and added without thinking, "Except for you. You're very beautiful, and most definitely not a man."

Michael stared, her skin flushing hot at the compliment. If Nicholas had ever called her beautiful, he'd never said it in exactly that tone. There was something slightly sensuous in the way Sloan said it. Watching the moonlight flicker across the other woman's face, she realized at that moment that handsome was exactly the right word for J. T. Sloan. Lean and well muscled, with features too chiseled to be anything but androgynous, she was not exactly masculine, but "beautiful" was not a strong enough word for her attractiveness either. When Michael realized she was staring, she forced her gaze away.

"Thank you," she said softly, not knowing what else to say.

"You're welcome," Sloan replied just as softly, surprised at her own uncensored admission, and even more surprised by how inadequate the words seemed. "Beautiful" did not come close to describing Michael Lassiter. Most disturbing of all was that she had no words for how good being with her made her feel.

As the Carrera hurtled through the night, each woman was very aware of the other, neither of them feeling the need to break the silence. Eventually they entered one of the older, wealthier sections of the city, and Michael directed Sloan to her home. When Sloan pulled into the circular drive in front of a large stone mansion, Michael was strangely disappointed. She glanced up at the familiar edifice and realized how cold and impersonal it now seemed.

Lights were lit in strategic windows, turned on and off at irregular intervals by the electronic timer. This gave the semblance of an inhabited home, when in fact she and Nicholas were rarely there at the same time. Often, their separate business obligations took them in opposite directions across the country for policy or marketing meetings. Days would pass when one or both of them were out of town, or they would simply be coming and going at different times.

They rarely shared a bed, and she noted with relief that his Ferrari was not in the drive. She also realized for the first time how much she did not want to lie down next to him and wondered why she hadn't felt it sooner. They had been estranged emotionally for years.

Sloan came around the front of the car and opened the passenger door. As Michael stepped out, Sloan said, "I was planning on spending some time in your offices tomorrow. Can you notify security in the morning and let them know to expect me—just in case the guy on the day shift is a little more cautious than the one tonight?"

"You don't need to worry about that. I'll be there working. Just tell him to call up for verification when you come in if there's any question."

Ignoring the slight surge of pleasure that the thought of seeing Michael in the morning provoked, Sloan simply nodded. "Good night then, Ms. Lassiter," she said softly, her deep voice oddly husky. She resisted the strong urge to brush her fingers across Michael's cheek.

Michael hesitated for a moment, leaning forward almost imperceptibly, drawn by the quiet intensity of Sloan's tone. Finally, she simply smiled and walked away.

Sloan climbed back into her car, but she did not drive off until the massive front door had closed firmly, eclipsing Michael Lassiter's figure. Even then, the memory of that parting smile lingered in her mind.

Chapter
Four

At 9:00 the next morning, Sloan walked down the brightly lit, cavernous central corridor of Michael's high-tech corporate complex. Small warrens of offices, conference rooms, and lounges branched off the main hallway at irregular intervals. The passage terminated on the east side of the building, with Michael's corner suite occupying a large part of that section. A woman stood behind a large horseshoe-shaped reception desk sorting through a deep file cabinet, her back to Sloan.

"Excuse me," Sloan called, assuming that this was Michael's secretary. "Ms. Lassiter is expecting me."

The woman turned, glanced at Sloan, and then uttered a small startled cry. Her eyes widened and a faint blush stole across her attractive features. "Oh my God. Sloan. What are you doing here?"

"Hello, Angela," Sloan replied calmly, hiding her astonishment with a cool expression. "I'm working," she answered briefly, hoping that explanation would suffice. She wasn't certain exactly how much Michael had confided with members of her staff about her plans to restructure the company, and she didn't want to go into detail. "I didn't realize that you work here."

"Considering that I haven't talked to you in almost two and a half years, how would you know?" Angela shrugged, a slightly bitter smile tugging at her lips. "Of course, even before, you were never particularly interested in the details of my life. As I recall, your *interests* were somewhat more limited."

Sloan thought she probably deserved that jibe, considering that she had rather abruptly ended her liaison with Angela Striker.

They had dated a few times after meeting at a local political event. Angela, however, demanded a degree of exclusivity from her romantic partners that Sloan found impossible to provide. At the time, she'd thought the better part of valor was to end the relationship quickly before both of them regretted it.

Nevertheless, she said nothing now. She had learned over the years that attempting to defend her actions where bruised egos and dashed dreams were concerned was futile. It was simply easier to let others believe that she didn't care.

"So, is she ready for me?" Sloan questioned, indicating the closed door behind Angela.

"I don't know. Let me check with her and see," Angela replied, a look of irritation flickering over her face. *I see that nothing's changed. You always were good at deflecting anything personal by using work as an excuse.*

A minute later, Sloan strode once again across the wide expanse of luxurious office space toward Michael, who was looking casual that morning in beige slacks and a cashmere V-neck pullover of darker rust. Sloan tried hard to ignore the subtle signs that Michael wasn't wearing anything of substance underneath the delicate sweater.

"Hi," she said, absurdly pleased to see her.

Michael smiled in welcome. "Good morning."

Sloan deposited her briefcase next to the computer console, then glanced over her shoulder at Michael. "Have you been here long?"

"A while." Michael looked away uncomfortably. "I had trouble sleeping."

"I'm sorry," Sloan said, meaning it. She'd had a rather hard time getting to sleep herself and had walked aimlessly through her fourth-floor loft apartment, the lights out, patches of moonlight the only illumination. Inexplicably restless, she had endlessly replayed the evening and the drive to Michael's in her mind.

It had been a long time since she had spent so many hours with a woman when at least one of them wasn't bent on seduction. But it hadn't been like that with Michael. There had been something in the air—her skin had tingled with it—but it hadn't been sex. Not the simple, pheromone-inspired attraction she was used to. It might have been something as simple as the fact that she liked this quietly self-contained woman and didn't like to think of her alone in the night, awake and worried. She straightened her shoulders and blew out a breath. "Well, let me get to work, and maybe I can give you a little peace of mind about this stuff at least."

"There's fresh coffee," Michael offered.

"Thanks, I'll get some in a minute," Sloan mumbled distractedly, already seated and rapidly typing in commands.

Michael watched her for a moment, enjoying the look of utter concentration on her face. She was also thinking how relaxed and at home Sloan looked in her faded jeans and slightly frayed at the cuffs white button-down shirt. The battered brown boots were decidedly lived-in and completed the picture of someone who couldn't have cared less about making the usual professional statement. No power suits in appearance *here.* She wondered if Sloan had any idea what an appealing image her obvious confidence projected. After a moment, she got up and filled two ceramic mugs with coffee and carried one over to Sloan.

"Black okay?" she asked, setting the mug down near Sloan's right hand.

"Huh?" Sloan replied, not looking away from the monitor. Then the aroma of very good French Roast caught her attention, and she glanced up at Michael over her shoulder. "You aren't supposed to be waiting on me," she admonished with a winning grin, "but thanks."

Michael returned the smile. "It's the least I can do to repay you for last night."

"You don't need to repay me." Sloan swiveled on the chair to face her, her violet eyes serious. "I enjoyed every minute."

"I'm glad." Michael blushed. She had no idea why that pleased her so much. Turning away, she said softly, "I'd better let you work."

It was some minutes before Sloan could concentrate on the diagnostics she was running, and even then she was acutely aware of Michael across the room, sketching something out on her drafting table. That undercurrent in the air that made her skin tingle was back again. She diligently determined to ignore it.

"Well, well, well," Sloan remarked almost to herself a few moments later.

Michael looked up from her work, noting the slight frown on Sloan's face. "What is it?"

"Hang on." Sloan held up one hand, indicating for Michael to be patient while she perused several windows she had open on the screen. "Last night before we left, I added a second-level intrusion blocker to the firewall you already had on your system, just to see if there was any activity. It looks as if you've had uninvited guests trying to slip in the back door."

Regarding Sloan intently, Michael put down her pencil and turned on her high drafting stool, her work momentarily forgotten. "Is it something serious?"

"Not necessarily." Sloan shrugged, still frowning. "There are literally thousands of people around the world who are constantly attempting to hack into other people's systems, just for the fun of it. They run programs that search for open networks, either private or corporate. When they find one, a scout program is launched that basically opens files on the system and allows the hacker to read through them. Since your entire system is networked, internally here and between your branch offices, web traffic on port 80 of your server is a big point of vulnerability. And we can't completely close those gateways."

"No," Michael confirmed. "We have so many interdivisional conferences, as well as design overlaps between the various physical plants, that we are constantly sharing files. The financial and personnel divisions are only accessible here, however, at the corporate headquarters, but to be honest, I never inquired as to exactly how they are secured."

"Never mind. I'll be looking at that." Sloan leaned back in her chair and rubbed her face with both hands. She needed another cup of coffee, but she was reluctant to ask for it. She had been a little surprised when Michael brought her the first one. She wasn't used to anyone looking after her in that way.

"It sounds like I hired you in the nick of time," Michael said only half-facetiously. "I had a feeling our system had some serious problems."

"The way your computer consultant set things up probably seemed practical at the time," Sloan continued, "but it makes you more vulnerable as well. What about your home systems? How many people can access the company network from their private computers?"

"Oh God, I don't know." Michael laughed at the absurdity of that thought. "Hundreds, probably. At first, we weren't even networked, and then as our numbers grew and we needed to be able to reach each other, we just cobbled things together. We never had anyone overhaul the entire system. Didn't seem to need to."

As she talked, she slid off the stool and crossed to Sloan's working area, picking up her empty coffee cup. In the small alcove where the very expensive little French bistro coffeemaker was located, she poured them each another cup, then returned to stand by Sloan's shoulder. She deposited the cup and stared at the monitor. "Can you tell who it is?"

"Given enough time, probably," Sloan acknowledged as she reached for the coffee. "Thanks," she said quietly.

"I suppose it's not the best use of your time at the moment," Michael mused. "I'm afraid if there's a sudden, obvious change that locks others out of the system—particularly Nicholas—it will merely raise his suspicions. I don't want to do that until you have my critical data safe."

Sloan nodded, understanding but not liking that the urgency for security had to be balanced against the larger issue of Michael's personal situation. "I'm sorry, I don't mean to pry, but what do you think he's likely to do?"

"I don't know." Michael edged her hip onto the corner of the broad workstation that held the array of electronic equipment and sighed, her blue eyes troubled. *I should, shouldn't I? But I don't know him very well anymore. Or maybe...I never did.*

Sloan looked up at her, confused. How could a woman not have some idea what her husband would do when she left him? Could it be possible that she knew so little of him, or he of her? Suddenly, she had a very uneasy feeling. Situations like this could provoke the worst in people, and Michael was vulnerable in more ways than just financially. "I know what you said earlier, but are you certain he won't become..." she hesitated, then asked softly, "physical?"

For a moment, Michael looked uncertain, then she blushed faintly. "I'm sure. He has something of a temper, though generally when he's angry, he simply becomes cold and remote. I believe he thinks that the worst thing he could do to me is to abandon me, shut me out."

There was just a hint of pain and bewilderment in her voice, and Sloan had the feeling that Michael's husband was correct. He knew exactly what to do to hurt her. For a moment, she despised him. "I'm sorry, I shouldn't have asked that."

"It's all right." Michael placed her hand lightly on Sloan's shoulder. "It doesn't matter to me anymore."

Sloan nodded and turned back to the computer. She needed to

concentrate on what she had been hired to do and stop worrying about Michael Lassiter's personal life. It wasn't up to her to erase that shadow of unhappiness in Michael's eyes or to ease the sadness that was so often present in her voice. "Let me work on this a while and maybe I can give you some kind of answer to this problem at least."

Michael silently returned to her drafting table, aware that she had been dismissed. She was a little surprised that it hurt. When Sloan failed to look up again, she forced her mind back to business. They did not speak again except to say goodbye.

After Sloan left, Michael sorted file folders and downloaded the work she intended to finish at home onto disks and put them into her briefcase. As she closed the office door behind her, she was surprised to find Angela still at her desk. "What are you doing here this late?"

"Foster sent in the summary for the telecommunications project late yesterday afternoon. I knew that you'd want the portfolio to go out to Marketing first thing on Monday, so I thought I'd get started on it. I'm collating the information now. It should be ready to print soon."

Michael smiled, shaking her head in fond admonishment. "You know I don't expect you to work on Saturday afternoons unless it's an absolute emergency." She glanced at her watch. "And it's officially afternoon now. I appreciate it, and you're right—I will need it on Monday. But it can wait until you come in Monday morning."

"Say no more—I'm on my way," Angela said with a grateful smile. She had a date that night and a million things to do before Karen picked her up. She tilted her head and studied Michael carefully. Her boss looked weary and, strangely, sad. "Is everything all right?"

"Yes, of course." Never comfortable discussing herself, Michael stiffened slightly. Even though Angela had been her executive assistant for three years and knew her about as well as anyone, they were not friends. She trusted Angela, but she did not confide in her. "I'm fine."

Angela accepted the automatic response, knowing there was no point in questioning Michael further. Besides, she was curious about something else. "By the way, I've noticed you've got a new computer consultant. Is Mayfield leaving?"

Michael hesitated, wishing she could explain. She had confidence in Angela's discretion, but it didn't seem fair to burden her with knowledge that she would have to conceal. Angela rarely worked directly with Nicholas, but they certainly came into contact frequently enough that it could be uncomfortable for her.

"No, it's not about Mayfield," Michael said casually, referring to the systems administrator they employed to handle their ordinary computer issues. "Sloan is just doing some personal work for me."

"That's definitely Sloan's strength." Angela snorted slightly. "Up close and personal kind of work."

Michael looked at her assistant in slight confusion. "I beg your pardon?"

Angela only shook her head. Sometimes Michael could be so naïve. "J. T. Sloan is a very smooth operator," she remarked, not bothering to hide her bitterness. "She tends to mix business with pleasure, if you know what I mean, and women are her specialty. Although I guess that's not likely to be an issue with you."

For some reason, Michael blushed. She knew Sloan was a lesbian, but she hadn't given it any thought the previous night. Perhaps she had been hasty in accepting Sloan's invitation to the Cabaret, although she seriously doubted that J. T. Sloan would take any notice of *her* in that way. It had seemed harmless enough and had turned out to be one of the most enjoyable evenings she could remember in a long time.

"I hardly think that Ms. Sloan would have any interest in me in that regard," she said dismissively.

Angela stared incredulously at her, wondering if it were possible that Michael really did *not* know how attractive she was. In addition to being stunningly beautiful, she was intelligent, accomplished, and kind. Definitely a rare combination for a successful businessperson. Angela had struggled with her own attraction to Michael for months. She knew a romantic relationship was impossible, not only because her charismatic employer was married but also because Michael Lassiter seemed to have no clue as to the possible interest that others might have in her. Angela had seen any number of men, and several women, too, make fruitless attempts to entice Michael into an office dalliance. Michael simply didn't recognize the overtures. She was always too preoccupied with whatever idea consumed her at the moment, literally lost in her own world.

"With Sloan, any woman is a possibility. Just don't take anything she says or does seriously, and you'll be fine," Angela
advised, getting up to gather her things.

"Thanks," Michael said dryly. "I'll remember that."

Resolutely, she waved goodbye to Angela and headed for the
elevators, pushing the lingering sound of Sloan's voice and the
fleeting images of that remarkable profile outlined in moonlight
from her mind. As she did so often, and so unconsciously after
these many years, she turned her thoughts to her latest project.
She was unaware that the hollow sound of her footsteps echoing
in the deserted hallway matched the ever-deepening emptiness in
her life.

Chapter
Five

"I need you to dig out some background for me," Sloan said as she inched her way through the early-afternoon traffic on the cross-town expressway.

"Oh yeah? Who are we investigating?" Jason asked on the other end of the phone.

"I want to know what you can find on Michael Lassiter and Nicholas Burke—family and background checks."

"I haven't turned up anything with the usual corporate search so far. You want personal info, too?" Jason inquired, obviously surprised by her request. It wasn't typical, particularly with their jobs in the private sector. But then, despite Sloan's reputation as a playgirl, it wasn't typical for her to date a client either, at least not before the account was completed. She had caught him unawares showing up at the Cabaret with Michael. Of course, there was always the chance that he had been wrong about the way Sloan had looked at the new client the night before, and she wasn't really taken with her after all. "Is there something off with the assignment?"

"No. No problem. I just have the feeling that the time might come when I'll need to know everything there is to know about the two of them." She didn't see any point in explaining to Jason how uneasy she felt, since she couldn't explain it to herself. She just couldn't envision Nicholas Burke folding his tent and disappearing without a struggle. Information was often powerful ammunition in these kinds of skirmishes, and if she could lend Michael a hand in the upcoming battle, she would. She told herself it was simply good business, nothing more. Certainly nothing personal.

"Where are you?" Jason asked with a sigh.

"I'm on my way to the gym. I just finished doing the initial scans of the Innova system."

"Sloan, love...it's Saturday afternoon. I bet *you* have plans for the evening, don't you?"

She frowned at the thought. She did, and for some reason, she wasn't particularly looking forward to them. "Dinner later with Claudia."

"Uh-huh. Well, perhaps *I* have plans, too. And they didn't include spending the night rifling through someone else's virtual underwear drawer."

She laughed. "Fine. Monday morning will be time enough." She assumed the deep sigh from Jason's end of the line indicated assent.

"What kind of background are we talking about? Am I going to need to call in favors?" he asked.

"I shouldn't think so. There's nothing to suggest classified information. I just want anything you can find, before and after their marriage, personal and professional."

Jason heard the undercurrent of concern in her voice, and, suddenly serious, he asked again, "Are you sure there's no problem?"

"I'm sure," Sloan said tersely. She and Michael hadn't even talked much the last few hours that Sloan had been there. Then, when it was time to leave, she hadn't wanted to go. She couldn't explain that either. She'd had to force herself not to ask Michael about her plans for the weekend.

Impatiently, she brushed her hand through her hair, cursed at some fool who tried to cut her off, and continued, "I just want to know exactly what I'm dealing with here, Jason. Is that too much to ask?"

"Oh, absolutely not," Jason said theatrically, a hint of sarcasm in his voice. "I live to serve you, almighty one."

Sloan laughed despite her lingering uneasiness. "Just do it, Jason."

"Your wish is my command." After a second's hesitation, he continued, "By the way, Sarah phoned and left a message for you to call her."

"Oh?" Sloan queried. "Did she say what she needed?"

"No," Jason said somewhat distractedly. "We didn't talk

long."

Sloan found it fascinating that *Jasmine* and Sarah shared an easy friendship that had blossomed almost immediately, and they never appeared to want for conversation. *Jason,* however, seemed awkward and unsure of himself on the occasions when Sarah had called or dropped by the office.

"Okay, thanks. I'll call her when I get home from the gym."

"Try not to offend anyone or break any hearts for the rest of the weekend, okay?" he said semi-seriously.

"Yeah, right," she muttered, crossing three lanes of traffic to a cacophony of honking horns and angry gestures as she exited into downtown traffic. *As if it were always up to me.*

"You should have a spotter," the pleasant female voice announced calmly.

Sloan looked up through her braced arms and saw Sarah's face, bisected by the barbell, peering down at her with an affectionate smile. "Yeah," she grunted, pushing up another rep. "So I've been told. How'd you find me?"

"I called the office again, and Jason told me where you were." Sarah slipped two fingers under the bar, braced her legs, and followed the rhythm of Sloan's arms pumping up and down, ready to take more of the weight if her friend began to tire. "Say, if you really want a workout, we could spar."

Sloan blinked sweat from her eyes. She had been lifting ferociously for forty minutes, and her muscles were starting to hum. She still had the vague sense of disquiet that had plagued her since leaving Innova, and she welcomed the thought of a good bout. She lowered the weights to the upright cleats and wiped the back of her arm across her face.

"I thought you were all *pacifistic* now that you're into Eastern medicine and yoga and the like," she said teasingly.

"I'd consider whipping your butt just another form of meditation, Sloan." Sarah's eyes sparkled with challenge. "Besides, Kung Fu began with monks—that's spiritual enough for me."

Sloan pushed up off the bench. "You're on, Sifu Martin."

Ten minutes later, they faced each other in the adjoining studio, bowed respectfully, then stepped into fighting positions. Sloan faced Sarah full on, her lightly wrapped hands held face high, elbows in, balancing lightly on the balls of her feet in the

typical Muy Thai kickboxing stance. Sarah turned sideways, knees
bent, both hands extended slightly, ready to block Sloan's punch
or pivot away from one of her roundhouse Thai kicks.

It brought back memories for Sloan of the hot, humid jungles
of Thailand, the crowded noisy streets of Bangkok, and the young
naïve agent she had been nearly a decade before. It had been her
first overseas assignment after joining the Justice Department
right out of college, and she had been intermittently homesick and
excited. She and Sarah had gravitated to one another because they
were both Americans, both female, and close in age.

Sloan's area of specialization had been communications, or at
least that was her job description. In addition to developing networks for the government's allies in Southeast Asia, she was also
covertly helping to electronically infiltrate government and corporate systems of interest to the United States throughout the
region. She didn't think of herself as a spy, but looking back, there
hadn't been any other word for it. Sarah Martin was a cultural
liaison with the State Department. The two of them had become
immediate friends and spent much of their free time together.

They had ended up training in the same dojo, and the spiritual bonds they forged went deeper than blood. Then Sloan had
been forced to leave the agency under a cloud of suspicion.
Despite their years of separation, their connection now seemed as
strong as ever. Other than Jason, there was no one she trusted as
much as Sarah.

Sloan's temporary lapse into the past cost her a not-so-gentle
strike on the side of her jaw and a resounding takedown from
Sarah's swift follow-up leg sweep. Fortunately, her reflexes were
still sharp, and she managed to land without rapping the back of
her head against the floor. Converting the fall into a back roll, she
was up in an instant, shaking her head slightly and frowning at
Sarah's delighted laughter.

"You're rusty, Sloan," Sarah taunted good-naturedly. "Getting soft with that desk job of yours."

"That was just luck," she snapped. Circling, she kept a wary
eye on Sarah's lightning fast hands and feet, and, after feinting a
left hook, stepped in quickly to deliver a knee strike to Sarah's
midsection. The air whooshed softly between Sarah's lips at
impact. Sloan grinned in satisfaction.

They sparred continuously for twenty-five minutes until they
were both dripping from the exertion and panting audibly. By

mutual agreement, they stepped back, bowed to one another, and collapsed next to each other on the floor.

"God, I needed that," Sloan gasped when she could catch her breath.

Sarah, lying on her back, turned her head so she could study Sloan's face. "What's up?"

Sloan shrugged. She didn't want to try to explain it—she didn't really even want to know. "Just tense, I guess. Too much time sitting at the computers, like you said."

"Oh yeah, right. Remember to whom you're talking. I've seen you work around the clock and then some without even noticing."

"I was younger then," Sloan said with just a hint of bitterness.

Sarah knew how difficult the subject of Sloan's past was for her, even now, and did not pursue it. Instead, with uncharacteristic hesitancy, she said slowly, "I want to ask your advice about something."

"What?" Sloan shifted slightly so that she could meet Sarah's eyes.

Sarah blushed faintly, but she continued in a steady voice, "I want to ask Jason out."

For a second, Sloan was at a loss for words. It wasn't totally unexpected, and the signs had been there for a while. Sarah seemed to be calling or dropping by the office more and more frequently. And of course, there were all the nights at the Cabaret when Sarah was front and center, watching intently while Jasmine performed. Still, Sloan was surprised that Sarah was taking the next step.

In a fairly normal tone, she commented, "I didn't realize you were interested in him."

"Why wouldn't I be? He's handsome and smart, and he's got a great body," Sarah stated somewhat defensively.

"What about Jasmine?" Sloan didn't see any point in pretending that they didn't both know what the issue was.

"I love Jasmine." Sarah grinned, her eyes sparkling. "But you know me, Sloan, I've never been into women that way."

"I *do* seem to recall that." Sloan had to laugh. There had been a time in those first few months in Thailand when she had tried very hard to get Sarah into her bed. They'd had everything going for them—common interests, similar jobs, and they were thousands of miles from everyone they knew. Finally, one night after too many beers, Sloan had boldly leaned across a tiny table in a dimly lit Bangkok bar and kissed Sarah soundly on the lips.

Sarah had kissed her back, quite thoroughly, and then settled back into her chair and studied Sloan gravely. Her exact words had been, "I've been wondering for months what it would be like to kiss you. You're a damn good kisser, Sloan. I thought you would be. As much as I love you, though, I'm just one of those girls that have a thing for those ridiculous male appendages. I hope you don't take it personally."

And Sloan hadn't.

"Sloan?"

Sarah's voice brought her back to the present. She seemed to be wandering into places she really didn't want to go quite a bit lately. "Damn it, Sarah, I hate to get in the middle of these things. You're one of my oldest friends, and Jason and I not only work together, I'm fond of him...and Jasmine."

"I know; that's why I wanted to talk to you."

Sloan sighed. "How long has it been since you were with someone?"

For a moment, pain shimmered in Sarah's green eyes. "Four years. He was an attaché in Bangkok. *I* thought we had something special. Turns out, *he* didn't."

"I'm sorry," Sloan murmured. She knew Sarah didn't take relationships lightly, and she hated to think of her getting hurt. She also knew Jason had had more than his share of heartache because of the part of him that was Jasmine. Sometimes thinking about Jason and Jasmine made *her* head swim, and she was well used to it by now. She could only imagine what it would be like dating him.

"Look," Sloan continued. "It's up to Jason to tell you how things are with him and Jasmine and everything. All I can tell you is that I don't believe he's ever dated a woman who knew about Jasmine. You might have your work cut out for you in that regard."

Sarah was quiet for a moment, remembering how much she had enjoyed watching Jasmine perform the night before, and how something in her had been excited knowing that Jasmine was part of Jason. It wasn't something she needed to analyze in great depth. It simply was.

"I'm not fooling myself, Sloan," Sarah said quietly. "He's a transvestite. It's not just an act at the Cabaret for him—I know that. But we all have diverse dimensions, sexually and psychologically, that we express in slightly different ways. I appreciate that there are parts of Jason that are best expressed through Jasmine. I don't understand it completely, but it doesn't seem to bother me. At least not so far." She sighed. "I just wanted to let you know before I did anything."

Sloan nodded and sat up. She reached for a towel and tossed one to Sarah as well. She rubbed her face vigorously and then blotted some of the sweat from her hair. "I can't think of anyone I'd rather see with him," she finally said and smiled. She meant it.

"Speaking of that sort of thing," Sarah commented, flashing her friend another grin, "what's the story with you and Michael?"

"There *is* no story," Sloan said stiffly, halting in mid-motion. "There's absolutely nothing between Michael Lassiter and myself."

"Okay," Sarah said softly. "My mistake then."

Sarah thought it prudent not to mention that both Michael and Sloan had spent an enormous amount of time studying each other when they thought the other wasn't watching. It hadn't escaped her notice either that Sloan had been particularly charming and touchingly attentive with Michael. It had also been obvious that Michael, for all her excited interest in what was happening around her, sparkled every time Sloan leaned close to speak to her.

Chapter
Six

Just before 6:00 on Monday morning, Sloan settled into the familiar seat before the computer in Michael's office and booted up the system, hoping to have an hour or so to work before anyone arrived. She preferred to work during the off-hours when there were fewer interruptions, less activity on the network, and more privacy. At the sound of the door opening behind her, she turned, unexpectedly pleased at the thought of company. Especially if that company was Michael Lassiter. Her automatic smile of recognition changed swiftly to concern when she saw, even from across the room, the haunted expression on Michael's face.

Rising quickly, Sloan took several steps forward, her heart pounding. "Michael?"

"I'm sorry, I didn't expect anyone," Michael said, faltering to a stop. Her voice was hoarse with fatigue, and she looked like she hadn't slept in days. She wore no make-up and her face was pale, the shadows under her eyes dark and hollow. She had clearly dressed hastily, her khaki suit uncharacteristically rumpled in contrast to her usual impeccable demeanor. Smiling weakly, she reached one hand for the back of the sofa to steady herself.

"You're shaking," Sloan said softly, moving slowly toward her although every instinct demanded that she touch her immediately. But she wanted to comfort her, not startle her, and the other woman looked as if she was holding on to control by a thread. Stomach churning in a state of near-panic, desperate to assure herself that Michael was not hurt, Sloan asked in a voice tight with anxiety, "Are you all right?"

"What? Oh...yes," Michael replied, looking as if she had just emerged from a dream and was still uncertain if she was truly awake. Hesitantly, she sat on the leather sofa, clasped her hands in her lap, and stared in confusion around the room.

Sloan went to her side and knelt on the carpet in front of her. Slowly, afraid to disrupt Michael's fragile equilibrium, she took her hand. A muscle twitched in Sloan's neck with the effort it took for her to be calm while her mind screamed with anxiety. Very gently, she asked again, "Are you hurt? Can you tell me what's happened?"

Michael ran a weak trembling hand through her hair and fixed on Sloan. Gradually, the confusion in her blue eyes cleared, and she managed a small smile. Softly she said, "I'm so sorry. This isn't like me. I didn't get much sleep, and I can't quite seem to get my bearings this morning. I'm really fine. Thank you for your concern, but I'm quite all right."

It was a valiant lie, and Sloan respected her for it. But she couldn't accept it. There were too many possibilities rushing through her mind, not the least of which was that Michael's husband probably had something to do with her current state. She forced herself not to imagine what might have happened, because the mere thought of anyone harming Michael was physically painful. "Something happened last night. What was it?"

"I'm afraid I made your job a great deal more difficult," Michael said ruefully. Her face became almost expressionless, and Sloan sensed that she was drifting away.

"Michael?" Sloan tried again, resting her fingers on her forearm, hoping to bring her back.

"It's Nicholas. I should have expected—" Abruptly, Michael stood and began to pace agitatedly in front of her desk. She glanced at Sloan, then swept the rest of the room as if seeing it clearly for the first time. "He wants this, you see. I knew he would, but I didn't appreciate just how much. Not this place—he doesn't care about that. It's not this room, this *building*," she said vehemently. "It's not anything that you can touch. It's the ideas, the plans, the hopes and dreams I've spent my entire *life* constructing. It's not me or the money."

Her voice was hollow, her eyes swimming with pain. "Oh, he *does* want the money—don't get me wrong—but that's not the most important thing. He wants what I've created, the very best part of me. He doesn't care if I leave him, as long as *he* takes what I care about most."

Stricken, she stared at Sloan as if just beginning to really understand. "He wants everything I am."

Sloan clenched her hands in her pockets, trying to ignore the almost irrational fury that pounded in her head. *God, if he touched her...* Her eyes dangerously dark, she prompted very gently, "Tell me."

Michael stopped pacing as abruptly as she had begun, standing in the middle of the room, her expression vague and disoriented again. "I was asleep...when he returned last night. It must have been close to midnight." She shivered involuntarily. "I didn't expect him. The light in the hall woke me, and the next thing I knew, he was in the room." She laughed shakily. "I never realized how *big* he is, until just that moment. He seemed to take up all the space."

The memory was undiminished by fatigue—clear and razor-edged, each image etched in her mind.

"Are you awake?" he asked, leaving the lights off and moving about in the faint illumination coming through the windows.

"Yes," she said, sitting up, holding the sheets to her breasts. "I thought you were still in L.A."

He dropped his raincoat over a chair and began to undress. "I finished up earlier than I expected, and I'm damned tired of hotel rooms. I want to sleep in my own bed."

As he approached, naked except for his briefs, she could see enough of his face in the dim light slanting into the room to read his expression. Her heart sank. She recognized his intent, although she hadn't seen that look in his eyes for months. She rarely thought about it until it happened and then gave little thought to it after. It was simply part of their life, part of what had become the routine of their existence together. It was something she neither missed nor desired.

"And I want to sleep with my wife."

There was no tenderness in his voice, only a cold statement of fact.

Watching him reach for the covers, she knew with absolute certainty that she could not sleep next to him, let alone have sex with him. She slid from the opposite side of the bed and reached for a robe from a nearby chair. He stared at her across the bed, clearly surprised.

"What are you doing?" he asked sharply.

"I'm going to sleep in the guest room."

"What?" he demanded, clearly astonished. "Suddenly you're refusing?"

"I can't."

"Why now, all of sudden?" He still sounded confused, but there was an edge of anger rising in his tone.

"I meant to tell you when you returned from this trip," she said quickly. "It wasn't something I wanted to do on the phone. I want a divorce."

He stared at her open-mouthed for what seemed like an interminable length of time, his expression frozen. Then his body went rigid, but whether it was anger or shock she could not tell. When he finally found his voice, it was even, controlled, and exceedingly cold.

"And is this open to discussion or is your decision final?"

"I'm certain," she said in a steady voice.

He nodded once and walked across the room, slipped into his trousers, and pulled a shirt from the closet. She watched him, waiting for something to happen, realizing that she had no idea what he would do. How extraordinary, to be witnessing the beginning of the end of their marriage and to discover that her husband was a stranger. Why had she not known that before? How could she have been blind to what had been missing for a decade? They had been sexual but never intimate. Why had it never mattered before this?

When he was finally dressed, he walked to the windows that overlooked an expanse of gardens. His profile in the moonlight was sharp enough to have been have carved from stone. Without looking at her, he pronounced, "You can divorce me, if that's what you want. But don't think I'm just going to walk away from the company."

Then he made it abundantly clear to her that he would fight for control of the business, despite the legal agreements they had entered into previously. Throughout his entire discourse, he barely raised his voice as he outlined with cold, calculating precision exactly what he intended to do if she made any attempt to contest him.

She said almost nothing as he spoke, not particularly surprised by what he said, but stunned by the way he said it. He might have been talking to someone of so little consequence to him that he couldn't bother to be upset. It was almost as if she weren't human, and she realized that she probably hadn't been a person to him in a very long time. She was surprised that it didn't hurt, but it had been years since she had needed him or expected him to be more than a business associate.

Nevertheless, when he finished his ultimatum, she was shaken, not by what had transpired, but by the knowledge that she had spent nearly fifteen years of her life with someone whom she did not love, and who did not love her. What had begun between them as mutual need had slowly dwindled until they had little more in common than a shared address. She realized how truly alone she had been and wondered why she had never felt it.

Michael fell silent, regarding Sloan with an expression that was a mixture of anger and bewilderment.

"He didn't bother to ask if there was someone else—he must have known there wouldn't be. He *was* kind enough to inform me that I had no worries about any of *his* activities. He had always been careful and had even been tested. For his own safety." She shook her head in disgust.

"He also informed me he had no intention of leaving the house either. I knew I couldn't stay there another minute. By the time I packed and found a hotel, it was almost four in the morning. I tried to sleep but couldn't, and I couldn't think what else to do, so finally I came here." She laughed harshly. "This is the only thing I know how to do, I guess." She walked around behind her desk and slumped into the chair.

When Michael tilted her head back and closed her eyes, Sloan felt her chest constrict so tightly with the desire to comfort her that she couldn't breathe. She swallowed the urge to smooth the furrows from Michael's brow with a caress, steadfastly ignoring the buzzing deep in her stomach. *Uh-uh. No way. Do not even think it.*

"Let me make you some coffee," Sloan suggested when she could get the words out without tripping over her runaway hormones. "It's my turn to get it, I think."

"God, I sound pathetic. I'm sorry." Michael shook her head impatiently, rubbing her hands over her face. "Go back to work, Sloan. I'm all right."

Sloan gritted her teeth until her jaws ached, willing herself to stand still. She wanted so badly just to touch her hand. *That's what I need, but probably not what Michael needs.* Desperately, she sought the words that would help ease the terrible pain she saw in Michael's wounded eyes.

"You're not pathetic. You're just hurt. That's human."

Michael's expression softened. "It's not what you think, Sloan. I'm not mourning my lost marriage. I stopped caring about it, about *him*, in that way a long time ago. I'm just so angry with the mess I've made of my life and how foolish I was not to have seen it years ago. What's wrong with me that I could spend all this time in some *charade* and not even know it?"

This time Sloan went to her, finally trusting that she had her own emotions under control. She grasped Michael's hands lightly, gazing intently into her face, praying that her words would somehow penetrate Michael's anguish and self-doubt.

"There's nothing wrong with you," Sloan said adamantly. "You've accomplished remarkable things, and you're not the first person to make a mistake about a relationship...or to spend years discovering it. It took a lot of guts to face him, and tell him, and to walk out of there. Don't beat yourself up like this." Her voice was thick with feeling. *God, she has no idea how magnificent she is.*

Helpless to stop, Sloan lifted one hand and brushed strands of blond hair from Michael's cheek. Her hand was trembling; she wasn't certain why. She stroked a thumb across the bruised shadow on Michael's cheek, wishing she could soothe the ache from her soul. "Don't be so hard on yourself," she whispered again.

Michael fell into Sloan's deep violet eyes, wrapped in the soothing sound of her words, not really hearing them but sensing the caring behind them. She had no idea why it felt so good for this woman to touch her hand or stroke her cheek, but she felt comforted somewhere beyond words.

"Thank you," she said softly.

They were so close, if Sloan dipped her head just a fraction, their lips would meet. She wanted to, more than she had wanted to kiss any woman in longer than she could remember. She wanted to so badly it was a pain in her chest. It was a hunger that went beyond anything she had ever thought to feel again. What stopped her was her own immutable desire to cherish the tenderness in Michael's eyes.

She stepped back abruptly, more frightened by her own feelings than she could stand. She dropped her hands to her sides,

fists so tight her fingers cramped, her throat so thick she wasn't
certain she could speak.

Stumbling back another step on legs that shook, she swallowed painfully and finally managed, "You don't need to thank
me. You're incredibly brave." Then she grabbed her jacket, made
an excuse about needing to check in with her office, and left hurriedly, leaving Michael to stare after her with an odd sense of loss.

When Sloan got to the gym, she wrapped her hands and
pounded the heavy punching bag until she couldn't lift her arms.
Exhausted, she finally sagged to the floor, her arms around the
gently swaying bag, her sweat-drenched face pressed to the rough
canvas cover, holding onto it with all the desperation of a lover
betrayed.

Chapter
Seven

All the next day, Sloan tried hard not to acknowledge the sudden rush of need that had ambushed her with Michael. Had it been only simple desire—that she would have understood. Michael Lassiter was a beautiful, vital woman—and wanting her was natural. But the ache of need was an emotion long forgotten, and something better left buried.

Work was her panacea, and she sought out Mayfield, the systems administrator at Innova, and introduced herself. She couldn't begin a large-scale analysis of the company's communication lifeline without the in-house expert being advised. He was courteous, but just barely. She wrote it off to professional territorialism and set up her equipment in an unoccupied conference room that Angela directed her to. It had an access port and a coffee machine. That was enough for her.

She saw Michael only fleetingly over the next several days as they passed each other coming and going in the halls, but those brief encounters were enough for her to see that, by midweek, Michael appeared more like her previous self. The shadows haunting her blue eyes had disappeared, and her quick smile was steady and warm. The fragility was gone.

It's just as well we're not working together, Sloan thought after the fourth time they'd seen each other and her pulse rate skyrocketed just from catching the tail end of Michael's smile. The one time she and Michael were actually together while she installed another layer of intrusion blocks on Michael's office computer, she found herself listening to the small sounds Michael made while working, or turning her head just enough to catch a glimpse of her as she bent over her drafting table, or watching her as she talked on the phone. *I can't get anything done when she's around.*

Usually the instant Sloan logged on and started working, she wasn't aware of anyone or anything around her. But the fact that being around Innova's CEO distracted her was more than just a worrisome personal problem. It was a bad time to lose focus—just when she was about to initiate the critical maneuvers needed to change over from the old system to the newer, streamlined, more secure one she had devised. Determined to get a grip, she tried hard to avoid the company of the first woman to really attract her in years.

It was close to 8:00 p.m. on Thursday when Michael opened her office door and walked down the hall to the room where Sloan was working. It hadn't escaped her notice that Sloan had been avoiding her all week, and she could only imagine it was because of the scene she had made in the office that morning after confronting Nicholas. Her own loss of composure embarrassed her still, and she could certainly understand if Sloan preferred to keep her distance.

It was hard to admit, but she missed the casual conversations with Sloan while they worked together, and she missed her quirky grin and quick humor, too. Nevertheless, as much as she respected Sloan's unspoken barriers, she needed an update on the security consultant's progress. Now that Nicholas knew of her intentions to divorce him, her sense of urgency was even greater. She had hoped for a quick buyout and a rapid dissolution of their partnership, but she didn't trust her soon-to-be ex-husband to let the lawyers work out the details. Whatever he might be planning, she wanted to be prepared.

"Can I see you for a moment in my office, please?" Michael asked quietly.

Sloan looked up at the sound of Michael's voice, immediately struck, as she was each time she saw her, by her beauty. Just that simple glance stirred a swift pulse of arousal that was as involuntary as her heart beating. Steadfastly, she ignored it. "Yes, of course. I'll just be a minute."

"Good," Michael replied, suddenly happier than she had been in nearly four days. "I ordered some Chinese, and I always get more than I can eat by myself. If you're hungry?"

"Always."

Sloan walked into Michael's office a few minutes later, closed the door, and looked at her, one elegant dark eyebrow raised in question. Michael stood in front of her desk, offering a brilliant smile that sent the blood coursing hotly through Sloan's veins, and she couldn't stop herself from grinning, too. As always, Michael looked stunning in a forest green suit tailored just enough to accentuate the curve of her hip and the long line of her slender thighs.

"You needed something?" Sloan knew she was staring and hoped that her quick surge of pure lust wasn't obvious.

"A quick update—just to settle my nerves." Michael leaned one hip against the desk, her hands clasping the polished wood on either side of her, apparently oblivious to Sloan's reactions. "How are we doing?"

"Pretty well, actually. I've got a fairly good view of what we need to do."

"Excellent. You can fill me in while we eat." Michael pointed to the glass-topped coffee table in front of the leather sofas, indicating cardboard cartons of food along with wooden chopsticks in paper sleeves, a stack of paper plates, and napkins. "Help yourself. It's the maid's night off."

Sloan occupied herself with the food, grateful for something to take her mind off Michael's body. Eventually she pushed her plate aside and said, "I met with your systems admin, Mayfield. He was cordial, but not overly helpful. I was a bit surprised that he doesn't seem to have set up much of disaster recovery plan. But, I have to admit, even today, when the rate of computer security incidents is up twenty percent over last year, that isn't all that unusual. However, it needs to be done, and it's going to take some time."

"You mean if something goes really wrong, we'll be in big trouble?"

"Theoretically—yes. Most major corporations are woefully underprotected from either external or internal hackers, and if a problem does arise, they're even less likely to be able to survive an assault because of it. Your man Mayfield isn't paying much attention to what I've been doing so far, but it won't take too long for him to figure out I've installed a multi-tiered detection program that reports to an ICEcap server, among other things...if he looks for it."

It was Michael's turn to lift an inquiring eyebrow, and Sloan laughed, then explained, "Think of it as a secondary security checkpoint that accumulates detection data from multiple networked computers, then analyzes and tracks intrusions. It helps you find out who's been poking around your system. The problem with any detection system, though, is that not all Internet transmissions are attacks. Some legitimate applications communicate with your network in the same way that hackers do. However, the more external points of entry to the system you have, such as access from personal home computers or distant office sites, the more holes you have in the system."

"Which means that you can't ever make the system airtight or intrusion impermeable, right?"

Sloan nodded approvingly. "Precisely. So, my job is to make the system as tight as possible and still allow those who need to get in to be able to do so. Mayfield is naturally curious as to some of the changes I've instituted, but I don't think he's particularly suspicious yet. Is he someone you can trust?"

Michael shrugged. "I really have no idea. I'm sure that lines of allegiance will be drawn rather quickly when it becomes generally known that Nicholas and I are divorcing. I think most of the theoretical people will want to stay with me. As to management departments, it's hard to say. Probably the bottom line will be their perception of who can run the company most successfully. And that's where the problem will be. Nicholas has always been more visible on the managerial front. I've been content to work behind the scenes. And...I expect the fact that I'm a woman may decide it for some of them." She made a dismissive gesture. "That I can't change. The only thing I can do is demonstrate that I can bring in the bottom line—new accounts and completed projects. That's where I intend to focus."

"Well, it sounds like you know what you have to do." Sloan thought it was a sound plan, if it was really only money that Nicholas Burke wanted to exact from his wife. She had no doubt that Michael could handle the business challenges to come.

"Right now," Michael added, "I'm just hoping to keep things quiet for a bit longer until my attorney can present Nicholas with a buy-out agreement. Maybe in the end, money will sway him after all. We also have two big projects nearing completion—one with the government and one in the private sector. If I can bring these in on time with no hitches, that will go a long way toward solidifying my position. Obviously, I'll need a good money person as COO, but first I need to be able to show the board that I can lead the entire company successfully, not just the design divisions." Sighing at the thought of the struggles ahead, she asked, "What's your timetable?"

"I'll need the rest of this week at least to tighten things up here. Then, I have to visit your New York offices fairly soon. That seems to be the weakest link in the network. I'll need a few days up there to physically evaluate the system. Meanwhile, Jason is backtracking IP addresses from the analysis engine I've loaded into your personal computer. Most of it will turn out to be nothing, but it's always worth checking. I've got him working on off-site backups for all your critical files, too. You might notice the system is sluggish for a few days while we work out the data transfer."

Michael absently drew a lock of hair off her cheek, tucking it behind her ear. Sloan watched the delicate movement of Michael's slim fingers as she lifted the golden strands, struck by the grace and elegance of the small gesture. She must have been staring, because Michael blushed slightly.

Sloan quickly averted her eyes. *Christ, Sloan, get a grip. You can't keep looking at her like she's lunch.*

"I appreciate how quickly you've been moving on this," Michael remarked. "Since Nicholas and I are now officially separated, the timetable has escalated, I'm afraid."

"Is everything all right?" Sloan asked cautiously. She didn't make a habit of inquiring about personal issues with her clients— or her friends, for that matter—but she couldn't help remembering how shaken Michael had been just a few days before. The memory bothered her even now.

"Yes. At least, I think it is. I haven't heard anything from Nicholas's attorneys yet, although I'm sure I will soon."

"And from him?"

"Nothing."

"Still at the hotel?" Sloan asked, inwardly relieved to learn that Burke had not been bothering his wife. *His wife.* Looking at Michael, she found it difficult to think of her that way. *Maybe because you just don't want to be reminded of the fact that she's straight.*

"Yes." Smiling ruefully, Michael confessed, "The suite of

rooms at the Four Seasons is perfectly adequate for my needs—I have my computer so I can work in the evenings, and I took what clothes I needed when I left the house on Sunday night. It's just...I *am* going a little stir crazy."

It was surprising, really, because being alone was something she thought she had gotten used to. It didn't ordinarily bother her. But at night in the hotel, she found herself restless and agitated— and aware for perhaps the first time in her life of being lonely. She kept thinking of the evening she had spent with Sloan and the others at the Cabaret. Then she had felt lighthearted and excited and somehow so free. *That* was the feeling she realized she missed.

Sloan said nothing, trying her best not to think about Michael in any way at all, except professionally. She definitely didn't want to think about her in terms of dinner at the Monte Carlo restaurant, or a stroll along the riverfront in the moonlight, or perhaps a nightcap in the suite at the Four Seasons. She absolutely did *not* want to think about leaning over and kissing her. Which was exactly what she *had* been thinking about for at least ten minutes. She leaned back on the sofa to break the spell. It didn't work.

"I was just wondering—is Jasmine performing again Friday at the Cabaret?" Michael inquired impulsively, then wondered immediately why in the world she had asked. It must have been just the memory of how happy she had been for those few hours, because it certainly couldn't have anything to do with the fact that Sloan had made her feel so special. Or because the brief touch of Sloan's long, lean fingers seemed to make her skin tingle.

"Actually, she isn't," Sloan said gently, sensing how hard it had been for Michael to ask. The quick flash of disappointment on Michael's face caused her to lose what remained of her better judgment. "She and the troupe from the Cabaret are performing at the annual AIDS benefit at the Franklin Center. I have a table reserved. My associate and Sarah will be going. Would you like to join us?"

"Oh, I couldn't. That's very kind of you, but I'm sure you've already made other arrangements," she said, thinking of the remark Angela had made about Sloan's popularity with women. The idea of spending the evening with Sloan and her date was unexpectedly unappealing.

"No. No particular plans, and there's plenty of room," Sloan informed her, grinning somewhat sheepishly. She didn't think it would be prudent to tell Michael that her date had dumped her after Sloan had explained that she wasn't interested in a serious long-term relationship. The timing had been terrible, but she'd had to find some way of explaining why she hadn't wanted to sleep with Claudia after their dinner date the previous weekend. It was hard enough to come up with an explanation to herself. She wouldn't even consider that it might have something to do with the fact that thoughts of Michael had kept intruding all evening. "There would just be the four of us until Jason has to leave for the performance."

"Jason?" Michael puzzled, searching for the association.

"My business partner."

"Oh, yes." She recalled the handsome young man she had met briefly in Sloan's office and, in almost the same instant, thought of Jasmine's brilliant blue eyes and her elegant but strong features. The two images came together in her mind and she gasped in surprise. "Oh my God, Jason and Jasmine...oh my God."

Sloan laughed. "Amazing, isn't it?"

"Incredible. How ever did you two meet?" she asked innocently. Then she saw that now familiar flash of barely disguised pain flicker in Sloan's eyes and just as quickly disappear. Clearly Sloan's past was off limits.

"Just one of those things." Sloan shrugged and answered carefully, "We both worked in D.C. a few years back. I happened to see Jasmine one night in a bar. She was really hot—black leather pants and a skimpy little top. She was getting plenty of looks. I asked her to dance—God, can she dance. Well, you've seen her."

"Yes," Michael remarked, recalling the confidant way Jasmine moved, as if she just knew that everyone enjoyed watching her.

"Well, one thing led to another...for me at least," Sloan continued, still remembering in vivid detail how turned on she had been after only one dance. It was still a little embarrassing, and then Jasmine had turned her down flat when she suggested they go somewhere a little more private when the number ended.

Clearing her throat, she continued, "I thought it was odd that Jasmine didn't seem to be interested in anything other than a dance, especially when plenty of women were clearly interested in *her*. She was friendly, but she didn't go home with anyone—wasn't even sending out those vibes—but I didn't get it at first. I tried pretty hard, but all I got was a smile and a kind but definite *no*. A couple of days later, I passed this guy in the hall at work. He had the most beautiful eyes, and when he saw me, he blushed. And I knew."

"What did you do?" Michael asked, reaching for one of the fortune cookies in the bottom of the paper bag. She was fascinated. The image of Sloan and Jasmine dancing was unexpectedly exciting. She wasn't certain why—maybe because they would make a strikingly attractive couple. Sloan, handsome and debonair—Jasmine, beautiful and sultry—two women... *Two women.* She drew up short at that thought, then realized that Sloan was speaking. "What? I'm sorry."

"My first reaction was to be pissed off," Sloan repeated. "I actually wondered for a minute if he was some kind of undercover agent gathering dirt on government employees."

Michael was about to laugh, but one look at Sloan's face told her she was serious. "Does that sort of thing actually happen?"

"Not so much anymore, but it certainly did in the past." Sloan shrugged, a bitter expression in her eyes. "And Washington is a very paranoid place. But I had danced with him, and I knew he was the real thing, not some kind of vice cop. He was the best transvestite I had ever seen. Everything—the way he moved, the way he spoke, hell, even the way he *felt.* Jasmine is as real as it gets. No agent would have been able to pull that off. So, when I saw him that day, I turned around, followed him down the hall, and pushed him into the men's room."

She grinned a little ruefully at the memory.

"What the fuck is going on...Jasmine?"

Jason turned pale and looked frantically around the restroom, as if searching for someone to help him.

"Fuck," Sloan cursed, when she saw that he thought she was really going to hurt him. With a sinking feeling in her gut, she realized that he expected it because someone probably had. She stepped back from him, put her hands in her pockets, and looked him up and down. He was wearing a Brooks Brothers suit, polished loafers, and a tie with a perfect Windsor knot. He looked like a cover model for GQ. Then she said, "I liked you a lot better in those leather pants."

"I liked you a lot better in yours, too," he responded softly. "And that wasn't me, actually, it was Jasmine."

"Yeah. Jasmine..." This time when Sloan said the name her

tone was not accusatory, but appreciative. "I suppose you know you...she...had me going the other night."

"I know." Jason blushed. "I didn't mean to lead you on. I thought a dance would be okay. I'm sorry."

"It should have been okay," Sloan admitted. "It wasn't Jasmine's fault that I jumped to conclusions. A dance is a dance—not foreplay."

"No," he said. "I should have realized, but it was so good— just to be able to relax. I forgot how Jasmine would seem..."

Sloan remembered how quietly he had said that, a slightly wistful tone in his voice. She had no idea why he'd trusted her, but he had. She glanced at Michael, wondering if she would understand. Michael's sympathetic smile encouraged her to continue.

"He explained to me that he was straight, which is why he didn't go dressed to a men's bar like most of the drag queens. He wasn't interested in picking up men and was afraid there'd be trouble if he refused someone's advances. At least in a mixed bar, where there were women, too, Jasmine would fit in, and she could always say no if a woman came on to her."

"But Jasmine danced with you," Michael observed, not critically, merely with interest.

"That was unusual, apparently." Sloan grinned, recalling that she had had to ask Jasmine three times before she finally agreed. "I was...persistent. As I recall, I did say to her it was only a dance."

"My God, how difficult that must be for him," Michael murmured. "It would be so much easier if he were gay."

Sloan was surprised at how easily Michael grasped Jason's dilemma. Jason could date straight women, but then how would he explain Jasmine? When dressed as Jasmine, expressing himself as Jasmine, he appeared physically female, but he did not want to attract men. He ran the risk that whoever might be attracted to him would be repulsed when they discovered his particular form of self-expression.

"He hasn't had an easy time," Sloan agreed. She didn't think it was her place to tell Michael that Sarah and Jason were going to the AIDS benefit on their first date. She trusted Sarah to be able to handle the situation, but she wasn't at all certain that Jason could. He was too used to hiding and too used to anticipating rejection. She wasn't certain he would be able to recognize true affection when he found it. "So, Sarah, Jason...*and* Jasmine...and I will all be there."

As Sloan spoke, Michael pulled the small slip of paper from the stale cookie and read to herself, "You will find happiness in the most unexpected place."

"Please, join us," Sloan insisted quietly. "I'd like that very much."

Michael nodded, realizing that she wanted to do that more than she had wanted anything in a very long time. Curling the tiny fortune into her palm, she said, "Yes, so would I."

Chapter
Eight

When Michael answered the knock on her hotel room door at exactly 7:00 Friday night, she was momentarily speechless. Sloan stood before her, dashingly turned out in a finely tailored charcoal pin-striped tuxedo, complete with a pleated white shirt, French cuffs, a navy cummerbund and white bowtie.

"You look...magnificent," Michael stated, laughing as Sloan responded with a small bow.

"And you look..." Sloan searched for words, mesmerized by the vision of Michael in a black silk dress that hugged her sleek figure, thin straps at the shoulders accentuating the low sweep of a clinging bodice that exposed a tantalizing expanse of décolletage. The soft swell of her breasts was just a promise beneath the exquisite material, but it was enough to send the blood rushing from Sloan's head to somewhere much more problematic. Her throat was suddenly dry. She knew that she was staring and couldn't seem to stop as the silence between them lengthened. She was having trouble catching her breath. Finally, she brought her gaze to Michael's, where blue and indigo fused, and they smiled into one another's eyes.

"You're beautiful," Sloan whispered, finding the words completely inadequate.

Michael colored slightly, inordinately pleased. Why did a compliment from Sloan make her heart beat faster?

"Thank you," she said, reaching for Sloan's hand and pulling her inside. "I'll just be a minute. I have to get my things."

Sloan stopped just inside the door, watching Michael move about the room, graceful and sure as she seemed to be in everything she did. Sloan reminded herself that she was a friendly escort only, and that she had best keep her eyes above shoulder level for the rest of the evening. Her inability to control her autonomic nervous system around Michael Lassiter was becoming embarrassing and more than a little physically uncomfortable. Unfortunately, avoiding Michael's body wasn't enough to place her beyond danger, because just looking at Michael's face could devastate her. It went beyond the blond's perfect features and her flawless skin and her breathtakingly beautiful blue eyes; there was a tenderness in her gaze and a gentleness in her voice that soothed Sloan's wounded places.

"Sloan?" Michael inquired lightly, surprised to see her still at the door and wondering at her hesitation to enter the room. It was so unusual for her to appear uncertain. "Do you need anything?"

Sloan shook her head, thinking, *if you only knew.* Quickly, to hide her agitation, she answered, "I'm sorry. No, nothing. I'm fine."

Michael wasn't sure she believed her, but she simply nodded, tossed a light jacket over her arm, and stepped through the door that Sloan held open for her. She was going out with friends, and she intended to have a wonderful time.

As they walked to the elevator, she glanced sideways at Sloan, struck suddenly by her bold strong profile and pantherlike fluidity. She thought again how attractive Sloan was in that dangerous sort of way that wild animals were. She had always been tempted to put her hands through the bars of the leopard's cage at the zoo, just to feel those sleek, stalking muscles ripple under her fingers. It had always made her just a little breathless.

Looking at Sloan was like that; being with her was a little like that, too. No one, male or female, had ever quite captivated her attention the way Sloan seemed able to. Being with her, talking with her, doing something as simple as sharing Chinese takeout in a deserted office building with her seemed to produce a slight shimmer of excitement. When Sloan looked at her with that piercingly intent stare, she made Michael feel as if she was the only thing that mattered at that moment.

Michael caught her breath at that thought, realizing that she had unwittingly been thinking of the evening ahead almost as if it were a date. She laughed inwardly at her own foolishness. She had never been attracted to a woman before, and even if she were, Sloan had more than enough women to choose from without giving her a second thought. *Silly.*

"Michael?" Sloan asked, faint concern in her voice. "Are you all right?"

Michael returned from her unconscious reverie to find Sloan standing by the curb, holding the passenger door of her Porsche open, a slightly bemused expression on her face.

"Yes, of course." She smiled and slid into the sports car, ignoring the slight tingle in her arm where Sloan's fingers brushed against her skin.

As they drove across town, Michael watched the city life through the window. Men and women in elegant evening wear hurried to the theatre; teenagers bedecked in all manner of piercings, tattoos, and outrageous outfits crowded the sidewalks; and tourists watched the other passersby with curious fascination. Everywhere couples held hands, heads bent close, laughing and talking in that intimately exclusive manner that only lovers shared. She was suddenly envious of something she had never before been aware of missing—that unique connection to another human being that defies definition, but is so common to human understanding that poets and writers and composers have tried to capture it for centuries. She ached in some primal place that her rational mind, even with the reminder of all her accomplishments, could not assuage.

"Are Sarah and Jason dating?" she asked abruptly, searching for something to take her mind from the emptiness she had no inkling how to fill.

Sloan was silent for a second, recalling Sarah's excitement when she'd announced that she had asked Jason to go with her to the benefit. Sloan replayed the conversation in her mind, deciding how much to reveal in answer to Michael's question. Sarah had been standing next to her in the locker room before their workout, barely able to contain her enthusiasm.

"What did he say when you asked him?" Sloan questioned.

"He tried to tell me he couldn't go with me because Jasmine was performing, but I knew damn well there were two hours during dinner and the speeches before the Cabaret routine. And then, there's the gala afterwards. I think he actually squirmed when I pointed that out to him." Sarah's eyes twinkled with laughter at the memory.

"That would explain his twitchiness at the office all day,"

Sloan remarked. "Every time I spoke to him, he jumped. I think he might even have spilled his coffee once. For Mr. Perfection, that's unusual."

Sarah's face clouded, and Sloan was instantly sorry she had said anything. "Why is he so nervous, Sloan? We get along so well, and he knows I know about Jasmine."

Sloan tried to ignore the question, hoping Sarah would let it go. She busied herself pulling on her sweats and workout gloves, pretending not to notice the shadow of Sarah's figure standing motionless beside her. Damn. They were both her friends, and her loyalties were conflicted.

"I really like him, Sloan," Sarah whispered softly. "It's the first time I've felt that way in so long."

Fuck. Sloan straightened with a sigh and looked her old friend in the eye. "I told you once that he never dated anyone who knew about Jasmine. That's not exactly true. He dated a clerk in the Justice Department about the time I was...leaving. It was serious. They were even talking marriage. He eventually told her about Jasmine, and she totally decompensated. She actually filed a complaint against him in some kind of weird sexual harassment twist, claiming that he had used his position as her superior to unfairly involve her in an unhealthy relationship."

"Jesus," Sarah uttered in disbelief.

"Yeah. It was absurd and really carried no merit, but even though the allegations were eventually dismissed, it ruined him. I heard about it through the rumor mill, at least the part of it that wasn't busy talking about me. After that I looked him up, and we decided it was time for both of us to disappear. We cleared out and six months later started the business."

Sarah nodded. "I always wondered how the two of you ended up here together. So much has happened while I was away." She didn't need to add that Sloan had never volunteered the details and probably never would.

"There isn't much to tell." Sloan looked away, her eyes darkening for an instant. Sarah's expression said she knew that wasn't true, but she let it go. Sloan had no doubt that the rumors had reached as far away as Thailand, but Sarah didn't press, and she let the subject drop gratefully.

Sloan shook off the memories and looked over at Michael, who was patiently waiting for her to answer. She shrugged. "Dating? I'm not sure if they are or not. They're going out together tonight, and I know Sarah is interested in him. I have a feeling it will all come down to Jason's willingness to trust her."

Michael nodded thoughtfully. "Not always an easy thing to do for anyone, and it must be so much harder for him."

"Yes," Sloan agreed with a sigh, pulling to a stop before the broad entrance to the stately pavilion that stretched for an entire block on the south side of Logan Square. She glanced at her companion, aware of the slight air of melancholy that clung to her. Impulsively, she reached for Michael's hand, drawing her around in the small front seat to face her. They were only inches apart, and neither of them paid any attention to the young man in the short red jacket standing impatiently near Sloan's door, waiting to park her car.

Sloan looked into Michael's eyes, her voice deep and strong. "If there's something possible between them, Sarah will know what to do to help it grow. She's got a gift that way. Now, I am going to take you inside and let everyone wonder how I have somehow managed to get the most beautiful woman in the room to sit at my table."

Blushing, Michael thought that Sarah wasn't the only one with a gift for knowing just the right thing to say. Then her smile erupted like the sun after a long cold winter, and she squeezed Sloan's hand. "Since I could say the same thing about you, I think we should go show off a bit."

Sloan stared at her, warmed both by her smile and the touch of her hand, and then burst into pleased laughter. "Now there's an offer I can't refuse."

As they walked up the broad expanse of marble staircase into the vaulted reception area, Michael slipped her arm through Sloan's, a gesture as unconscious and natural as anything she had ever done. If Michael felt Sloan's quick jerk of surprise or the slight trembling in the muscles under her fingers, she didn't show it.

When Michael and Sloan arrived, the enormous ballroom was nearly full. Magnificent chandeliers, ablaze with candle-shaped bulbs, hung above the dozens of tables that fronted a temporary stage erected at one end. The evening was primarily designed to benefit the myriad city agencies that dealt with the multidimensional challenge of AIDS treatment, but it was also an important venue for the many groups and individuals seeking supporters in the political arena.

Men and women, elegantly turned out, wandered about, greeting friends or taking advantage of the opportunity to network. Some of the women wore tuxedos while others were in designer dresses. Most men were in formal attire, too, although here and there representatives of the leather community strode about in full regalia, offering a striking counterpoint. Were it not for the many women walking hand in hand or the men with arms slung casually around each other's waists, the gala might have passed for any ordinary fundraiser.

Jason and Sarah were already seated at the table Sloan had reserved near the stage. Jason, as always, looked immaculately attired in a black tuxedo, every blond hair in place. Sarah wore a simple dress in flattering tones of blue and green that accentuated her pale skin and emerald eyes. They both greeted Sloan and Michael with enthusiasm.

"God, this is wonderful," Sarah remarked. She looked around the room, continuing, "It's a great turnout." Watching as Sloan pulled out the chair for Michael, she added, "You two look terrific, by the way."

Briefly, she thought what an amazingly attractive couple they were before reminding herself that they weren't a couple at all. But there *was* an unmistakable connection between them that seemed apparent to her, although clearly not to them. Sloan watched Michael with obvious pleasure as Michael slipped into the seat beside Jason, and Michael looked over at Sloan with a soft smile that would have been seductive coming from anyone other than her. On Michael, it merely seemed sweet, and lovely. And Sarah was astonished to see Sloan blush. She thought that might be a first for her very imperturbable friend.

She was also aware of Jason fidgeting, nearly imperceptibly, next to her, and she said to him in a low voice, "Are you nervous about the performance?"

He laughed slightly, but his eyes were tense. "Not Jasmine's," he replied with a hint of sarcasm.

Sarah looked at him for a moment, then touched his arm as she understood his meaning. "Jason, you needn't worry about anything with me. I may kiss on the first date, but that's as far as it goes. I'm looking forward to enjoying the evening with you. I don't have any other designs on the night."

"Sorry," he murmured. "I don't think I mentioned it, but I'm glad you asked me."

"Good. Then stop worrying."

Her soft smile did more to set his mind at ease than even her words, though those helped, too. He thought she was quite the most attractive woman he had seen in forever, and he couldn't understand what was making him so nervous around her. She was smart and sexy and kind, and he liked her laugh and the way she had of looking at him with a whimsical invitation in her eyes. And she knew about Jasmine. Then he realized that he wanted to kiss her, and that fact was more frightening than he could imagine. Could she really accept, or even understand, what a part of him Jasmine truly was?

He shied away from her warm welcoming eyes, glancing first at the mass of people milling about between the tables, not really seeing any of them, before his attention finally focused on Sloan. He had always thought her compellingly good looking, but tonight, she looked exceptionally eye-catching. Her wavy black hair was sleekly brushed back from her temples, falling in casual layers to her collar, and a shock or two hung rakishly over her forehead. Her perfectly fitted tux accentuated her tautly muscled body, and he was reminded of the night they'd met.

Jasmine first saw the dark-haired woman leaning against the bar in a crowded club on Dupont Circle—cool and cocky and sexy as hell in tight leather pants and a white shirt that clung to her chest and was open tantalizingly low between small firm breasts. Jasmine was aware that she was looking particularly hot herself, and before long, the handsome stranger approached.

"Hello. I'm Sloan."

"Jasmine."

"Dance?"

"Not just yet."

"Come on, I'm harmless."

"Funny, you don't look it."

"Looks can be deceiving."

Jasmine's heart thudded, but there was only friendly interest in the woman's eyes—not accusation.

"Just a dance?" Jasmine asked without a hint of flirtatiousness.

"Just a dance," Sloan said with a grin, "unless you change your mind by the end of it."

"I won't."

"Okay then, just a dance."

Maybe she should have said no, but Sloan persisted, gently and charmingly. Even though it was dangerous—even though it didn't make any sense—Jasmine wanted to know what it felt like to be held in a woman's arms. This woman's arms.

Then they were dancing, and their bodies fit together like the intricate curves of two puzzle pieces, as easily if they had danced together forever. As they were nearly the same height, it was natural for Jasmine to dip her head and rest her cheek in the bend of her partner's neck and shoulder. Sloan's hand was pressed to the small of her back, the strong muscles of Sloan's shoulders rippled beneath her fingers, and their thighs brushed lightly as they moved to the music. By the end of the song, they were both breathing hard, and Sloan let her intentions be known.

"I was wrong—it was more than a dance after all." *In a voice low and husky, she whispered against the curve of Jasmine's ear,* *"Come home with me."*

And the wonderful fantasy shattered. Jasmine, despite her attraction, could not do that. Sloan, gorgeous and so sexy that just looking at her was a turn-on, wanted the woman she perceived Jasmine to be. Despite Sloan's efforts, Jasmine demurred.

He'd never expected to see Sloan again. When they'd met by chance that day at work, he had initially been terrified by her anger. When she finally understood that he had not maliciously intended to deceive her, she simply accepted that Jasmine somehow existed in her own right, a conscious and powerfully defined element of his personality. It was the first time in his life that anyone had accepted the confluence so easily.

When she had smiled ruefully and commented, "Man, I'm sorry I don't swing both ways, because Jasmine is *fine*," she had freed some part of him to hope that someone could actually know his secrets and not turn away from him.

Now he sat across from her, admiring her still, knowing that the small spark of desire she still ignited was just one facet of his attraction to her. She was his friend; she had saved his career, and his sanity, and perhaps his life that day she had come looking for him in the Department of Justice to offer him a way forward out of the lie. Joining her in business had been the best thing he had ever done.

He jumped slightly when Sloan leaned toward him and said softly, "So, how you holding up?"

"Fine," he responded, coloring quickly. *Jesus, did everyone have to know what was going on?* He noticed gratefully that Michael didn't seem to be watching him at all. She was clearly fascinated by the diverse and colorful crowd. Come to think of it, when she wasn't watching the throng, her attention was pretty much riveted on Sloan. *Oh God, she is way too naïve for the likes of Sloan.*

Sarah pressed close, murmuring so that only he could hear, "They do look good together, don't they?"

"Yes," he acknowledged, watching Sloan bend her head to Michael's and whisper something that made the blond laugh. He couldn't hear the words, but the deep timbre of Sloan's voice carried to him, and something of the warmth in it as well. She appeared taken with the new client, and the knowledge both pleased and, irrationally, irritated him. He'd thought he was long past the confusing feelings Sloan stirred in him.

Sarah rested her fingers on the top of his hand, and the tender gesture made him want to weep. He couldn't cope with all the conflicting emotions and, turning to Sarah, he said quietly, "Would you walk around with me for a few minutes until I need to go backstage?"

"Sure," she said with a quick smile.

He smiled back, inordinately relieved, and surprisingly pleased. Sarah seemed like the only solid ground in a very rapidly shifting landscape. Impulsively, he took her hand, and they slipped into the stream of people passing by.

Michael watched them go, then turned to Sloan. "Jason seems nervous. I'd think it was sweet if I didn't have a feeling that he was actually frightened. I feel for him."

Sloan studied her, finding her an amazing blend of contrasts. She was coolly beautiful, even remote at first glance, and yet there was warmth in the depth of her eyes and the tone of her voice. "You are very perceptive."

"Am I?" Michael asked with just the hint of a tease in her voice. "Am I correct then in surmising that you are a little nervous, too?"

"Nervous? Me?" Sloan replied mockingly, taken aback by Michael's intuitiveness...and by her frankness. She wasn't used to anyone being able to read her so well. It both pleased and worried her. To be known, to be understood, was a powerfully seductive emotion. *It can make you careless, and it can make you vulnerable. And* that's *a place I never want to be again.*

"Yes, you," Michael persisted, her tone still light but a question in her eyes.

"Perhaps," Sloan allowed with a slight inclination of her head. "But I'm not afraid."

"I wouldn't imagine there is much that could make you nervous, nor anything that would frighten you," Michael remarked quite seriously.

Sloan's eyes darkened. "I am not invincible...or even particularly brave." She stared at Michael, forgetting her earlier vow not to look into her eyes. She forgot her intention to be cautious as well. "You are threatening, but in a most pleasant way," she murmured.

Michael leaned closer, so drawn by Sloan's intent gaze that she lost track of the activity and conversation around her. Everything receded from her view except a violet so deep it was a siren's song beckoning her to the cliffs.

"Why?" she whispered.

"Because..." Sloan managed, her throat suddenly tight with desire, *your loveliness captures the imagination, and your kindness soothes the soul.* Head spinning, insides churning, she felt heat and want suffuse her limbs. Barely stifling a moan, she drew a ragged breath and finished, "You are so very beautiful, in so many ways."

"If I am," Michael whispered, stepping closer to the edge, not even realizing the danger, "you're the first who's ever said so."

"Then you've been surrounded by fools," Sloan murmured, reaching a hand to trace the line of Michael's jaw. Her fingers trembled. When Michael leaned forward to accept the caress, her lips parted slightly and her skin flushed. Her pupils were wide, dark, endless—beckoning Sloan to fall into them. In that instant, Michael appeared so vulnerable that Sloan drew back with a nearly audible gasp. *God almighty, what am I doing?*

Unexpectedly, Sarah returned, sliding back into her seat as she announced, "Jasmine is getting dressed for the show. I wanted to stay and watch but she said no."

She stared from one to the other, suddenly aware of the unearthly stillness surrounding them. She might as well have been invisible. Quietly she asked, "You two okay?"

Michael was the first to regain her composure. Her smile was just a bit shaky. "Yes, of course."

Somehow Sarah didn't believe that, but the expression on Sloan's face convinced her not to question the statement. She had never been one to taunt the animals.

Any lingering unease was dispelled as the three of them watched the show. Female impersonators were always popular, and the Cabaret troupe was exceptionally so. It was partly the elaborate costumes that ranged from outrageously flamboyant floor-length gowns bedecked with feathers, sequins, and plunging necklines to stylish evening dresses that would have befitted any performer on a Las Vegas stage.

In addition to the spectacle, the classic show tunes and popular songs were rendered with skill and consummate style. Some of the impersonators specialized in particular performers, such as Cher or Bette Midler or Celine Dion, much to the delight of the crowd. Jasmine, however, did not. She was not an impersonator in that sense. Her specialty was Billie Holiday-type torch songs, and she performed them straight—no jokes, no exaggerated costumes, nothing but talent, a great voice, and exceptionally fine legs. The audience loved her.

Initially, Michael had difficulty reconciling that these women were men. There was no awkwardness of motion in the clinging sheaths and high, thin heels, no hint of beard to mar the flawless make-up, and no subtle shifting to suggest that the full bodices were anything but real.

Tonight she watched Jasmine with particular interest, searching for bits of Jason. The transformation was remarkable. It wasn't the outward things—the different hair color or style, the feminine body, the expertly applied lipstick or eyeliner. It was the sultry way Jasmine walked, confident and more than a little seductive, and the throaty voice that whispered an invitation with a simple hello, and the look in her eyes that said she knew just how hot she was.

"God, Jasmine is sexy," Michael commented to no one in particular.

Sloan looked at her in surprise, and Sarah grinned, exclaiming, "Yeah, and don't she just know it."

"I seem to recall you weren't interested in women," Sloan grumbled to Sarah good-naturedly. "How things change."

"Jealous, are we?" Sarah arched an eyebrow and laughed. "Don't worry, you haven't lost your touch."

That comment got Michael's attention. She had just assumed that since Sarah was with Jason that she was straight. But *she* herself was with Sloan and that didn't mean she *wasn't*...did it? One thing she was quite sure of, however, was that she did not like the idea that Sloan might be attracted to Sarah. She couldn't discern exactly why.

"No point in being jealous," Sloan continued. "Any way you look at it, I can't compete with Jasmine. I could never dress like that, I can't sing, and I'd kill myself in those shoes."

"Plus, there is the issue of Jason to consider," Sarah said, suddenly serious. "I love Jasmine's sense of humor and her outrageous attitude, but what intrigues me is knowing that Jason is there somewhere, too. I really wanted to watch him dress tonight, to see *him* become *her.*"

"I don't imagine he's ever done that," Sloan remarked. "He's very private about it."

"It surely would be frightening for him to be so exposed," Michael agreed.

Sarah was silent for a moment, considering what they had said. "I hadn't thought that he would be threatened by me seeing," she said with a shake of her head. "Not very sensitive of me, I guess. I'm clearly not as tuned in to the subtleties of all of this as I thought."

"I'm certain that he just wants to be sure of your reaction first," Michael said gently, sensing Sarah's self-criticism. "If he cares about you, it must be terrifying not knowing if you can accept this part of him."

Sloan stared. *How is she able to understand so much so easily? It doesn't matter at all to her that I'm gay and Jason's a transvestite or that Sarah is straight and a little in love with Jasmine.*

She watched, fascinated, as Michael leaned forward and took Sarah's hand, then heard her whisper gently, "Don't be discouraged. I'm sure he needs you to keep asking. Once he finally trusts you, he'll let you closer."

The tender warmth in Michael's gaze had softened her features, giving her an almost ethereal appearance, and the image struck Sloan like a blow. As quickly as she had been moved to desire a few moments earlier, now she was touched by an emotion a great deal more dangerous. These glimpses of deep kindness and compassion inspired longing. Michael was beautiful in more than just body, and the depth of her gracious spirit warmed some long-frozen place in Sloan's soul.

She looked away abruptly, desperate to stifle the unwanted swell of emotion. She could never remember being this affected by any other woman, and she was absolutely certain this attraction would only lead to disaster. Michael Lassiter was a woman whose life was in turmoil, and she was not someone Sloan could simply take to bed and forget about the next day. She reminded herself that since Michael showed no inclination toward that pleasant diversion anyway, it was a moot point. Grimacing in frustration, she looked up with relief to see Jasmine approaching. She needed something to distract her from Michael's disconcerting nearness, and Jasmine filled the order nicely.

"Ah, the party is about to begin," Jasmine declared as she rushed up breathlessly. She waved a hand in the direction of the stage, where a band was warming up and workers were clearing an area for dancing. She was still wearing the form-fitting red dress she had performed in, and she looked as elegant as any lady at the ball.

"Wonderful dress," Sarah said by way of greeting.

Jasmine slipped into the seat between Sloan and Sarah, and turned to Sarah with a smile that was just a tiny bit shy. "Thank you," she responded without a trace of her usual flirtatiousness. "I saw it in the window of a little boutique on my lunch hour one day, and I just knew it was meant for me."

Sarah wondered briefly who had purchased it, Jason or Jasmine, but decided that that was a question best asked when Jasmine felt a little more comfortable with her. "Well, you were right."

Jasmine smiled again, her cheeks flushing slightly, and turned to say her hellos to Michael and Sloan. The four of them chatted and commented on the who's who amongst the attendees for a few moments until the band began to play. Then, Jasmine stood abruptly, grasping Sloan's hand.

"Come on, baby. Come dance with me."

For a moment, Sloan looked uncharacteristically disconcerted, then she shrugged helplessly and allowed Jasmine to pull her into the crowd onto the dance floor. Michael and Sarah looked after them for a second, then at each other, and smiled.

"Poor Sloan." Sarah laughed. "Jasmine just loves to tease her. She's the only one I've ever known who could catch Sloan off guard. If I didn't know better, I'd actually say Sloan was flustered."

"I think that's because Sloan finds Jasmine attractive. I can certainly see why," Michael said, turning the idea over in her mind. She thought back to the story Sloan had told her about that first meeting with Jasmine and realized that the two of them had a long and much more intimate relationship than she had initially surmised. Sloan had admitted her attraction to Jasmine the night they had first met in the bar in D.C., but Michael had assumed that once Sloan learned about Jason, the interest would be gone. Now, seeing Jasmine, she appreciated how that might not necessarily be true. Jasmine was seductive, charming, and female to all appearances, so why wouldn't Sloan be affected by her attentions? One did not look at Jasmine and see Jason.

"You're right," Sarah replied thoughtfully, wondering at Michael's insight. "I'm amazed I didn't see it before this myself." Looking at Michael with new respect, she added, "You don't find it odd?"

Michael smiled and shook her head. "This is all so new to me, I have no preconceived notions of how it all works. Sloan is a lesbian, and Jasmine is a sexy woman. Ergo..." She laughed, lifting her hands into the air in mock obviousness.

"Does that bother you?" Sarah asked, curious about exactly what was happening between Michael and Sloan. "Sloan's response to Jasmine, I mean?"

"Why would it?" Michael laughed a little self-consciously, wondering if Sarah was reading her mind. When she had watched Jasmine take Sloan's hand and so effortlessly lead her away, for one instant, she had been jealous. Jasmine was very attractive, and she and Sloan looked great together. Even reminding herself that Jasmine wasn't, well, *exactly* all she seemed, hadn't erased the slight twinge of envy when she had seen Jasmine step into Sloan's arms.

Without meaning to, she imagined herself in Jasmine's place, dancing in Sloan's arms, and somehow she knew it would feel magical. Shaking her head, astonished at the kind of whimsy that was foreign to her, and very aware that Sarah was waiting for her response while her thoughts wandered down paths too fantastic to contemplate, she said as lightly as she could, "It's certainly none of my business whom Sloan finds attractive. Although I couldn't help but wonder if it bothers *you* that Jasmine and Sloan are, well, interested or...whatever."

Sarah looked contemplative. "Actually, I think *Jason* has a little crush on Sloan but has always known nothing could come of it—him being a he and all. *Jasmine,* on the other hand, is free to flirt with Sloan outrageously, which she does at every opportunity." She grinned at the absurdity of the entire conversation but continued on gamely. "That *does* make me a bit jealous, I guess. Since I, unlike Sloan, wouldn't mind taking Jason to bed at all."

"What about Jasmine? Would you take her to bed, too?" Michael asked before she realized she might be overstepping the limits of her brief acquaintance with the other woman. "I'm sorry...that was awfully personal."

"No," Sarah said with a shake of her head. "Don't worry. And don't think I haven't considered that very question. Women in general don't usually turn me on...well, Sloan a bit, maybe..."

"God...is there anyone she doesn't turn on?" Michael blurted, then immediately regretted it as she blushed furiously.

Sarah pretended not to notice her embarrassment and continued, "But Sloan and I resolved that issue years ago. Then along comes Jason, whom I liked the minute I met, as well as thinking he had the nicest butt I'd seen on a guy in years." She grinned at the memory.

She recalled standing in the office waiting room of Sloan Security nearly open-mouthed in amazement while Jason lectured Sloan about being on time for the afternoon appointments and threatening her with bodily harm if she dared put off her final report to Somebody, Somebody and Somebody that was due the next morning. She had expected Sloan to annihilate him at the very least, but Sloan had merely growled something that sounded a lot like *okay* and stomped out. Jason had winked at Sarah, his impossibly blue eyes sparkling with delight, and she had gotten warm and wet in places that didn't usually feel that way at one o'clock in the afternoon.

"Sarah?" Michael asked, confused by the slightly vacant look on Sarah's face and the long silence.

Sarah jumped, then smiled self-consciously. "Oh, sorry. Anyhow, then I met Jasmine at the club and thought she was funny and wild, and I liked her a lot, too. I didn't know at first, and neither of them told me right away."

"Who *did* tell you? Jasmine, Sloan, or Jason?"

"Sloan. Sort of. I asked if Jason would be coming with us one night when we were planning on going to the Cabaret, and she got that secretive smile thing she does, and said he'd be there, but I might not notice."

"I can see it," Michael murmured, following Jasmine and Sloan as they danced together not too far away.

"Anyhow," Sarah continued, oblivious to Michael's preoccupation with the couple on the dance floor, "Sloan wouldn't elaborate but my antennae were up. I kept watching for Jason, and one time, after scanning the room, I'd looked back to the stage while Jasmine was performing, and for one brief instant, I saw Jason looking back at me. It freaked me out and made all the sense in the world at the same time. It all came together in a flash, and when I found out the connection, it was just so amazing...the more I saw of them, the more I thought of them as two people, but not totally separate. So now when I think about Jasmine..." She hesitated, then put into words what she had been avoiding, even in her own mind. "When I think about undressing her and finding Jason there somewhere, it makes me pretty hot."

"It certainly makes the usual arrangements seem pretty boring."

Sarah grinned as she realized that Michael understood exactly what she had been saying. "God, it's nice to find someone who *gets* it. I've haven't known how to talk about it to anyone without having it sound totally bizarre."

"One thing I've discovered in the last few weeks is that nothing that I thought I knew about life, or myself, is necessarily true," Michael said with a touch of regret. "Least of all what being with someone is all about. Or even the why and the how of it all."

"I think what they say about falling in love when you least expect it, and with the most unexpected person, just might be true," Sarah responded quietly. She had heard the edge of pain in Michael's voice.

"I think you're right about that," Michael said as she watched Sloan and Jasmine moving so naturally in one another's arms. Funny, that they should look so good together when it was all illusion. She wondered at her own bewilderment and confusion. Was that what her life with Nicholas had been? All just illusion?

Chapter
Nine

Sloan attempted to hold Jasmine at a decorous distance, her right hand resting lightly at the base of Jasmine's back in the slight hollow just above her very nice little butt. With her other hand, she enfolded Jasmine's, which was surprisingly just a bit smaller than her own, and held it lightly against her own chest. The floor was fairly crowded with couples of all gender combinations, but even so, she didn't think the proximity of the other dancers quite warranted the closeness with which Jasmine moved against her.

"Jasmine," Sloan said softly.

Jasmine tilted her head back and smiled innocently. "Yes?"

"Are you trying to ruin my reputation?" Sloan asked, maneuvering them confidently among the other couples nearby. She was an expert dancer and used to leading.

Jasmine, for her part, followed effortlessly, slowly moving her hips against Sloan's pelvis. A little closer than she needed to but just exactly where she wanted to be.

"Whatever do you mean? Ruin your reputation?" She laughed, settling herself more comfortably against the length of Sloan's well-toned body. She gyrated subtly but enough to feel Sloan's muscles tighten. Her voice low, she continued, "I don't think you need *me* to do that."

Sloan registered the warmth of Jasmine's body pressed against her chest, her stomach, and her thighs. She knew damn well what was underneath that sheer delicate silk of Jasmine's dress, and that it wasn't exactly what fulfilled her fantasies, but those contradictory facts didn't quite penetrate all the way to her autonomic nervous system. The part of her that was physical, and sexual, and totally beyond her rational control, saw and felt a woman in her arms. Jason was only a memory.

There wasn't a single thing about Jasmine that said *male.* She was soft in all the right places, smooth in just the right places, and curved in *precisely* the right places. Jasmine fit against Sloan completely naturally, and if that wasn't enough, she knew exactly how to move to inflame every sensitive spot on Sloan's body. Sloan was well aware that her heart was pounding hard enough for Jasmine to feel it—that and the tremors starting in her legs.

"Damn it, Jasmine," Sloan said through gritted teeth. "This is no place for a display." She glanced over at the table where Michael and Sarah were watching them with faintly amused expressions and felt color rise to her face. She was oddly embarrassed, and she hoped Michael didn't know why.

"Spoilsport," Jasmine whispered, but she finally took pity on her partner and moved away a fraction of an inch. She liked to play with Sloan, and usually Sloan didn't seem to mind, but tonight she sensed not only Sloan's faint desire but also her discomfort. As much as some part of her enjoyed the heady feeling of turning on the handsome and oh-so-unattainable dark-haired Romeo, she knew enough to stop before things got out of hand—for either of them.

Sloan wasn't the only one whose heart was tripping a little faster, or whose stomach fluttered with those first whispers of wanting. While the sensation was pleasurable, their friendship was more important. One night, one hour even, of mutual exploration, no matter how exciting that might be—and she had no doubt that a roll in the sack with Sloan would be wild beyond her dreams—wouldn't be worth the aftermath. They couldn't have a relationship, let alone a life together, and giving in to their physical attractions would destroy what they did have. Too much to lose, and glancing across the room to where the other women sat watching them, she realized there was another reason now, too. Sarah was smiling at her.

Then Sarah winked, and some long-guarded barrier in Jasmine's soul cracked just a bit. Sarah seemed to understand exactly who she needed to be and how she needed to feel. No one had ever come close to understanding her before. It was so overwhelming that it frightened her almost to death. She was afraid that she would get used to how good it made her feel. And then she might begin to dream. Hope and dreams, she had discovered, were the narcotics of a lonely heart, lulling one into believing happiness could actually be attained. The despair that followed when the empty promises were revealed was devastating.

As much as she ached to have Sarah accept her, she rebelled at the thought of relinquishing her defenses. She had done that once, and her life had been destroyed. If she let another woman close, only to be deserted, her soul would crumble. Anger and fear warred with her desire to believe that Sarah could be different. The old hurts still festered, rejection and humiliation still burned, and she wanted to lash out. Her dance partner was in the path of her pain.

Without thinking, Jasmine said, "What's the matter, Sloan? Are you afraid that Michael will find out that you have no self-control? I would imagine she already knows that. You must have taken her to bed by now."

Sloan stiffened instantly, her jaw bunching with swift rage. "Michael has absolutely nothing to do with this, Jasmine. This is about you and me, and the fact that you seem to enjoy offering what you won't deliver."

"I've never offered you anything, Sloan." Jasmine stepped completely out of the circle of Sloan's arms, her anger rapidly replaced by hurt. "You might find this hard to believe, but one-night stands are your specialty, not mine." She turned, head held high, and moved sensuously back through the crowd to the table.

Sloan stared after her for a second, cursing herself under her breath. It hadn't been Jasmine's fault; she knew Jasmine had only been playing. It wasn't the first time in their lives that had happened, and usually she just laughed it off. It had been the mention of Michael that set her off—and the suggestion that she would treat her like...like...

Well, like one of my casual dates. A little bit of company, a little bit of fun, a physical encounter without any real thought to the consequences. It's not as if I ever make any promises, or even plan for it to happen. If, in the course of an evening, the woman I happen to be with chooses to continue our conversation in bed when I offer...what's the harm? We're both adults, and one night in bed doesn't imply a long-term commitment. Why not share a little mutual pleasure?

Sloan looked at Michael, her face in profile as she leaned close to Sarah to share some thought, her hand resting easily on the other woman's arm. She swallowed and looked away, trying to dispel the lingering image of Michael's poignant beauty, knowing she could never take her to bed for a night. One night would never be enough, and that was exactly the problem. She hadn't wanted more than a night, or anything beyond that level of commitment, in many years. She certainly didn't want it now.

Damn. I overreacted badly when Jasmine hinted that I would take Michael to bed for nothing more than a bit of gratification— because I don't *want to. I'd end up wanting much more than that.*

She took a deep breath and started toward the table to give Jasmine the apology she deserved. She was almost there when a voice at her elbow stopped her.

"Now I see why you couldn't bring *me* to this little affair," the tall, attractive brunette said loudly enough to catch the attention of everyone at Sloan's table as well as those seated nearby.

"Hello, Claudia," Sloan said calmly, her face revealing nothing to those close enough to be curious.

She had originally planned to attend the benefit with Claudia Carson. Claudia was a very attractive, intelligent woman, and they got along well. They had also slept together several times to their mutual enjoyment.

But when they'd last been out to dinner, it had become undeniably apparent to her that the other woman was beginning to think of them as a couple, and Sloan had just barely managed to extract herself from an awkward situation before both of them were embarrassed. At the end of the evening, Sloan realized she didn't want to have sex with Claudia, a fact that surprised even her. Her companion, however, had been under a different impression.

Claudia closed the apartment door and grabbed for her, impatiently pressing her mouth to Sloan's, one hand tugging at the belt on Sloan's trousers, her breasts crushed to Sloan's chest. "I've been so hot for you all night," she panted as she moved urgently against her. "Right here is fine. Let's do it right here."

Sloan was up against the door, and Claudia was all over her. Her skin started to burn where Claudia's nipples, piercingly hard, rubbed against her shirt. It felt good, there was no way she could deny that, just as Claudia's thigh pushing between her own made her limbs grow heavy with lust. She closed her eyes, automatically sweeping her palms up Claudia's smooth sides toward her breasts. Nevertheless, even as her body responded involuntarily, her mind protested. She couldn't say why—couldn't think quite clearly enough to make sense of what she felt—but she knew this wasn't what she wanted.

"Wait," she gasped, attempting to step away and having nowhere to go. Ignoring the trembling in her legs as Claudia worked the zipper down on her fly, she repeated, "Claudia, stop."

"Why?" Claudia murmured, her fingers slipping under Sloan's waistband, her voice throaty with desire. She clearly wasn't listening to anything at that moment other than her own body's demands. "Baby, you're hot, too, and I am so ready."

Sloan shuddered, her head pounding, aware that she was throbbing just below Claudia's fingertips. If she moved an inch, Claudia would be stroking her, and no amount of good sense would make her want to stop then. She grasped Claudia's hand, stilling her explorations. "I can't do this. I'm sorry."

Claudia removed her hand immediately and stepped back so swiftly that Sloan nearly stumbled. The look on Claudia's face went from brief confusion and disappointment to anger. "Get out," was all that she managed.

Sloan was happy to oblige, because, for an instant, she thought Claudia was going to strike her.

Claudia hadn't struck Sloan that night in the apartment, probably because the rejected woman had been stone-cold sober. She wasn't at the moment, however.

"You bastard," Claudia said quite clearly as her hand whipped across Sloan's cheek.

With a reflex turn of her head, Sloan absorbed most of the blow, but still it stung, and she tasted the salty tang of blood on the inside of her lip. She kept both hands firmly at her sides and motioned *no* to Sarah with a quick shake of her head when she saw her friend rising to come to her aid.

"Where is your table, Claudia?" Sloan asked, aware that the woman was swaying and that her face was slack with too much alcohol. "Who are you with?"

"I came alone," Claudia said sharply, anger cutting through the haze. "My *date* preferred to plow fresher fields for the evening." She looked in Michael's direction as she spoke.

"Are you driving?"

"*That* is none of your business," Claudia said archly, but her voice slurred as her anger dissipated, and she stumbled as she started to turn away.

"Why don't you sit down for a minute?" Sloan suggested softly, stepping closer and slipping her hand under Claudia's elbow to steady her.

Claudia tried to fling off Sloan's hold but only succeeded in completely losing her balance. She ended up clutching at Sloan's shirtfront instead, her head resting on Sloan's shoulder. "I *hate* that I still want you."

Realizing that Claudia was much more intoxicated than she had first thought, and that there was no way she could send her home alone in a cab, Sloan guided an unresisting Claudia closer to the table. Quietly, she said to Michael, "I'm sorry, but I need to take Ms. Carson home. Would you mind if Sarah drives you back to your hotel?"

Michael looked from the woman leaning against Sloan's side into Sloan's cool eyes and could read nothing. They might have been the eyes of a stranger. She answered just as quietly, "Of course not. Please go ahead."

"Goodnight," Sloan said with a nod to Sarah and Jasmine, then slipped her arm around Claudia Carson's waist and turned to leave.

Most of the eyes in the crowd followed their departure, and voices speculated on the latest romantic escapades of the somewhat notorious J. T. Sloan. Not saying a word, Michael watched them also. She too wondered just what hold the lovely Ms. Carson had on Sloan.

For a moment, the table was silent. Then Jasmine, in a rare show of restraint, said softly, "Well, Sloan handled that nicely."

Both Sarah and Michael looked at her questioningly.

"Claudia Carson was about to fall down drunk and make a spectacle of herself. She would have been humiliated in front of some of the most influential people in the community, and I don't just mean the gay and lesbian community either. There are a lot of political movers and shakers here tonight. Sloan just saved her a lot of embarrassment."

"Who is she?" Michael asked before she could stop herself.

"I don't know her." Sarah raised an inquiring eyebrow in Jasmine's direction. She had been wondering the same thing herself. She hadn't seen Sloan with a lover in a lot of years, but there hadn't been anything in Sloan's face that looked like love to her. She ventured, "An ex?"

Jasmine shrugged delicately. "I suppose you could say that. Claudia seems to think she is more of an *ex* than is probably warranted, but Sloan has that effect on her dates. One night and they want to marry her." She pushed back from the table and stood with a sigh. The festive atmosphere had definitely dissipated. "I think it's time for me to toddle off. I'll send Jason out in a while."

Sarah watched her go, then looked at Michael. "Are you all right?"

"Of course," Michael said a little too quickly. "Just curious."

"Mmm," Sarah agreed. "Sloan does have a tendency to make one wonder." She studied Michael quietly for a moment, trying to read behind the ice blue gaze. "You know, Michael, Sloan is not nearly the Lothario people would make her out to be. It's true that I haven't been close to her these last few years, but I knew her very well when she was younger, and people don't change all that much. She may avoid commitments, but she has a good reason for it."

"I'm sure you're right," Michael said calmly, wondering what Sarah was trying to tell her, and why. What J. T. Sloan did with the women in her life was no concern of hers. Despite the fact that she enjoyed Sloan's company and thought that the feeling was mutual, she harbored no illusion that there was anything else possible between them. She had a company to save and a marriage to dissolve. The last thing she needed was a sexual identity crisis and an involvement with a woman who obviously didn't care to be involved with anyone.

She sighed and began to gather her things. "I'm going to get a cab. Say goodni—"

Sarah grasped her wrist. "Absolutely not! We'll drive you. I'm sure Jason will be here soon."

"I don't think you need me along on your first date with him, Sarah," Michael said with a laugh. "I'll be fine."

"Really," Sarah protested. "It's no trouble. And I have a feeling we'll be calling it an evening, too. Things went pretty well tonight, considering both of them were here. Jason and Jasmine, I mean. But I don't think I'm going to push my luck. Jason's clearly not ready for anything else...and frankly, neither am I."

Michael stopped what she doing, her eyes concerned. "Are *you* okay?"

"It's not as simple as I thought it would be. While I was watching Jasmine and Sloan dancing, I pretty much forgot about Jason. Jasmine is so *real,* you know? I'm not sure how I'd feel alone with her." Sarah grinned a little shakily. "Or what I'd do with her."

"My guess is you won't find that out until you've been with Jason first. That is probably the way he'll feel most comfortable," Michael commented thoughtfully. Watching Sloan and Jasmine together had fascinated her, too, but her thoughts had all been of Sloan. How she held Jasmine—so sure, so certain. Their bodies had fit together so well. For that instant, when she had imagined herself in Sloan's arms, instead of being strange, the notion had seemed completely natural. She'd never even thought to question it.

Standing abruptly, wanting to dispel any image of herself and Sloan, she stated emphatically, "Say goodnight to Jason for me, please. I really need to go."

And then she was gone, leaving Sarah to wonder about the odd expression on Michael's face. She had looked bewildered and a little sad.

"Claudia. Hey, Claudia," Sloan called softly, shaking the sleeping woman's shoulder lightly. "Time to wake up."

Claudia muttered, snuggled a little deeper into the warm leather seat, and tried to curl up on her side.

"Terrific." Sloan got out, walked around the front of the car, and opened the passenger side door. She leaned down and slipped an arm behind Claudia's back. The other she slid under the smaller woman's knees and swiveled her feet out onto the side-walk.

"Okay, here we go," Sloan said, pulling Claudia upright into her arms. "A few steps, a few stairs, and then an elevator...thank God for the elevator. Piece of cake."

Claudia managed to follow Sloan's lead, becoming more alert as she moved. "Where are we?" she asked groggily.

"Your place," Sloan informed her as she pushed the Up button on the elevator panel. She guided Claudia into the elevator and removed her arm from around Claudia's waist. When the tipsy woman promptly tilted left and looked about to fall, Sloan grabbed her and held on. She didn't try releasing her again until they were inside Claudia's bedroom, where Sloan eased her down onto the side of the bed. She stepped back a pace and inquired, "You okay?"

Claudia pushed both hands through her hair, blinked up at Sloan, and grimaced. "More or less. I really conked out in the car, and I'm still fuzzy. What time is it?"

Sloan glanced at the bedside clock. "Just after midnight."

"Thanks for bringing me home." Claudia's speech was still a bit slurred, and when she tried standing, she wavered with a sudden surge of dizziness. "Shit."

Reflexively, Sloan reached to steady her once again. And in the next instant, Claudia was firmly insinuated in her arms with her fingers laced on the back of Sloan's neck and her lips on Sloan's mouth. The kiss caught Sloan completely off guard, and by the time it registered, Claudia's hand had dropped to her thigh and was moving dangerously close to her crotch.

"Mmph," Sloan muttered, pulling her head back and grabbing for Claudia's wrist at the same time. "Cut it out."

Claudia bit the side of Sloan's neck, harder than she might have if she had been totally aware of what she was doing.

"Son of a bitch, Claudia. That's enough." Sloan would have thrown her off but in Claudia's present condition, she'd probably fall.

"Don't lie and say it doesn't feel good," Claudia breathed against Sloan's neck, pushing her hand a little higher up Sloan's thigh.

It *did* feel good, but that was hardly the point. She wasn't in the habit of having sex with intoxicated women even when she *did* want to sleep with them. And despite the fact that the fingers insistently stroking between her legs were doing an excellent job of making her throb, she did not want to sleep with Claudia Carson.

"Okay. You're obviously capable of taking care of yourself," Sloan gasped, pushing Claudia gently but firmly back down on the bed. "I'm out of here." She turned on somewhat shaky legs and started for the bedroom door. Her body was in a state of rebellion that she valiantly ignored.

"You don't actually think that that blond is going to give you what you need, do you?" Claudia called angrily.

Sloan didn't reply. They both knew the answer to that question. She let herself quietly out of the apartment, rode the elevator down, and walked slowly to her car. She slid behind the wheel, leaned back, and shut her eyes. When her head stopped pounding and the ache in her stomach began to subside, she reached for her cellular phone.

Michael tied the pale gray robe around her waist as she hurried toward the door. She peered through the peephole, stared for a second, then pulled the door wide, a question in her eyes.

"I'm sorry it's so late," Sloan began, shrugging slightly as if she wasn't certain herself why she was there. And she wasn't, exactly. All she knew was that she couldn't go home without seeing Michael. "I called Sarah, and she said you hadn't left with them—"

"I took a cab," Michael interrupted.

Sloan sighed. "I'm sorry..."

"You said that," Michael said, a soft smile on her face. She reached out and tugged on Sloan's sleeve. "Come in out of the hall."

Sloan followed, then stood in the elegant, impersonal hotel suite, looking around like she had no idea where she was. She pushed a hand through her hair, leaving the dark waves tousled. "Hell, I don't even know why I came." She looked at Michael, who was watching her with quiet patience. "Are you angry?"

"Why should I be?" Michael asked, unprepared for the question. *Should I be? Do I even have any right to be?*

She'd been restless and unable to concentrate when she'd returned to the hotel. She hadn't even been able to work, which was so rare as to be unheard of. Was it anger that had left her tossing fretfully while sleep eluded her?

Turning, she walked toward the sofa, one of two that faced a large glass coffee table centered on a plush oriental rug, while she considered the question. She sat at one end, drawing her legs up under her, pulling the hem of the robe down to mid-calf, and motioned for Sloan to join her.

"Sit down, please."

Sloan slumped into the deep cushions, leaned her head against the back, and turned her face to study Michael. She hadn't known she was going to ask that, but now the answer seemed to matter a great deal. "Well, are you angry?"

"No," Michael replied at length, choosing her words carefully as she sorted through the odd assortment of emotions the night had inspired. "I was disappointed at first. I was enjoying the evening so much, and I missed you when you left."

As she spoke the words, she realized how true they were. When Sloan had walked away, the enchanted became ordinary again. The sparkling lights lost their shimmer and the hint of magic in the air grew faint. She laughed shakily at her foolishness. "But that wasn't your fault."

"It *was* my fault," Sloan disagreed. "But I needed to take Claudia home. She was a little too impaired to maneuver safely."

"Really?" Michael commented dryly, arching a brow. "She couldn't have been *too* impaired. She managed to bite your neck."

"Christ." Sloan sat bolt upright, a hand to her neck where she felt a slight sting. She looked at Michael, whose face was absolutely expressionless. "Would you believe that there is a totally innocent explanation?"

"No explanation is required." Michael refrained from mentioning the lipstick on the collar of Sloan's shirt or the rumpled state of her clothes. *It is none of your business.*

Searching for calm, Michael stood and smoothed the robe about her hips, fidgeting with the sash for a moment. At that, Sloan stood, too, only inches away.

"Look, Michael, I'm sorr—"

"And no apology is necessary either," Michael continued firmly, looking into Sloan's eyes, thinking her impossibly attractive as she stood there waiting for Michael to damn her or absolve her. Michael shook her head in frustration. "I got home fine. I wasn't your date *or* your responsibility. Please don't worry about it."

"I know I don't *have* to explain. I *want* to," Sloan insisted, her voice dark and intense. It suddenly felt very important that Michael understand nothing had happened between her and Claudia. She rested her hands on Michael's arms, bending just a bit to catch her glance, very aware of the slight tremor in Michael's body. Those brilliant blue eyes answered hers with a faint expression of uncertainty, and with something that might have been desire.

"Oh, hell," Sloan muttered, leaning closer still, her vision tunneling to encompass only pale skin and full moist lips. Those lips parted in surprise, or perhaps welcome, and then Sloan was kissing her.

It was amazing how something so familiar could be so new. Michael's lips were without a doubt the softest she had ever touched—and the warmest, and the sweetest—and she could smell her, fresh from a shower and misted with spring promises.

*OhJesusGod...*Sloan was lost, senses on overload. Michael's body, covered only by the technicality of the supple thin silk, was molten under Sloan's hands, flowing hot to her touch. Somebody groaned. Sloan thought dimly it might have been herself. There were fingers in her hair, pulling lightly, sending currents of excitement directly between her legs. She wavered a bit on her feet, bombarded by sensation, desperate for more of her. Finally, she edged Michael back toward the sofa.

And then what? An irritated voice inquired from somewhere deep in her unconscious. *You gonna lay her down on the couch in some hotel room and lift her skirt? Nice, Sloan. Very nice.*

Sloan wrenched her lips from Michael's, a task so difficult it left her weak. Michael's eyes were nearly closed, her mouth swollen with kisses, her breasts rising and falling rapidly against Sloan's chest. Their legs were entwined, and Sloan felt an answering heat against her thigh as the woman in her arms moved sensuously against her. Rhythmically smoothing her palms over the rich fullness of Michael's buttocks, she ached to be on top of her, inside of her. She was fully aroused and pulsating, painfully hard, ready to burst, and she...could...not...do...this.

"Michael," Sloan gasped, willing her fingers not to stray inside the partially opened robe. The crescent of exposed breast nearly shredded the last remnants of her control.

"Shh," Michael crooned, leaning harder into Sloan until there was nothing between them but old fears and secret desires. She wanted Sloan to kiss her again. *What a remarkable, glorious kiss that was.* It was the only time in her life when she had been totally without thought. She had known absolutely nothing but the incredible freedom and utter certainty of being in Sloan's embrace. It was a place she never wanted to leave. "Just do that again," she whispered.

Sloan continued to hold her, but she did not lower her head for the desired kiss. Looking at Michael, she saw her undisguised hunger and understood in that instant how completely without pretense or guile Michael was. If innocence existed anywhere, it was in Michael's simple request.

I don't deserve that trust. Hell, I don't even want it.

"We'll both regret this in the morning," Sloan said as lightly as she could manage through a throat tight with need. Michael stiffened in her arms.

"Do you think so?" Michael asked softly, a cold ache beginning in her chest. "Would you?"

Sloan took a step back, released her hold on the other woman, and steeled herself. "Yes. And so would you when you had a chance to think about it. I apologize for putting you in an awkward position. I'm sorry, I wasn't thinking."

"Well, I know *I* certainly wasn't." Michael laughed thinly. "I should thank you for maintaining some sense." She pulled her robe tightly around herself, shivering suddenly. "Will you excuse me, please? It's late, and I'm more than a little embarrassed."

Sloan wanted so badly to comfort her. She had hurt her, but it was a small hurt compared to the disaster it might have been. She forced her hands into her trouser pockets, afraid she would touch her again otherwise. "I'll let myself out. I'm sorry, Michael."

Michael watched her cross the room, watched the door close soundlessly behind her. She listened for her footsteps in the hall, but heard only silence. The room was very still as she moved about turning off the lights. In the darkness, she made her way to the bedroom, where once under the covers, alone, she allowed herself to cry.

Chapter
Ten

The phone rang in Michael's office at 6:45 Monday morning. She glanced at it distractedly, a prospectus in one hand, barely taking her eyes off the columns of figures. Ordinarily, she wouldn't have answered her own phone, but it was too early yet for Angela to be in.

"Lassiter," she said abruptly.

"Michael, it's Sloan," the now familiar smoky voice announced.

Michael drew a sharp breath, laid down the folder, and stared across the room at her office door as if expecting it to open and Sloan to step through. Her heart quickened with anticipation even as she chided herself for the reaction. It had been over forty-eight hours since Sloan had walked out of her hotel room, and she had spent most of that time trying to avoid thinking about what had happened between them.

Usually, her work was something that could distract her from everything else in her life. She had only to pick up a sketchpad, or doodle on the corner of an envelope, or lean back with her eyes closed, and she would be instantly absorbed in constructing something or other out of her imagination. That was the beauty of design—it could result in a tangible product or merely a concept that someone else brought to fruition. Her mind was fluid yet enormously disciplined; she lived by her thoughts, and they had always been her greatest panacea for worry, uncertainty, and fear.

For some reason, this cherished routine hadn't worked during the past weekend. Her thoughts had been elusive, streaking through her mind like fast-forwarded images on an old-time movie reel. She hadn't been able to concentrate, primarily because she couldn't stop thinking about the way Sloan's lips had felt against hers. It was true that she had very little sexual experience with anyone other than Nicholas, but she certainly had not been isolated from the realities of physical relationships. What she had experienced with Sloan went far beyond anything she had previously known or even imagined.

That such a simple kiss could set every cell in her body tingling defied her understanding. She had no frame of reference for the way she'd felt in Sloan's embrace, recalling that slight inner trembling that seemed to magnify as it approached the surface of her skin until she feared she might literally shake apart. Being in Sloan's arms was like watching the sun break through the clouds after a week of gray skies and cold rain. *Like when that first brief flash of golden heat suddenly makes you feel alive...and then you realize that until that moment, you had merely existed.*

She thought she understood the difference now between going through the motions and truly living, but she dared not contemplate whether that sensation was borne only on this one woman's kiss.

"Michael?" Sloan said into the silence.

"Yes?" Michael replied, more sharply than she intended. "I'm sorry, I was working."

"Then *I'm* sorry to disturb you," Sloan said somewhat stiffly. "I actually intended just to leave a message. I didn't expect you to be there." She hadn't wanted to speak with her, let alone see her, which was why she had taken the rather cowardly route of phoning to leave a message. She didn't trust herself not to betray how affected she had been by her slip the other night. She hadn't lost control of herself like that in years, and it shook her. Even worse, she kept thinking about the way Michael had looked, had felt, had moved against her...

Don't go there. She cleared her throat, which was suddenly dry, and continued, "I wanted to let you know that I've decided to drive up to your New York City office today to look things over. I think we've gotten the network in fair shape here, and you should be secure within reason. I can't do much more to tighten things up until I check out the other facilities. Then I should be able to make the changeovers pretty quickly if I don't run into any surprises."

Michael was silent. She hadn't really been listening after

Sloan announced that she was leaving for New York. There was nothing she could say, short of asking Sloan if she was going because of what had happened between them. That certainly didn't seem like a very appropriate question. Sloan had made it quite clear that their very brief interlude had been a mistake and that she had no desire for it to happen again. If Sloan wanted distance between them, it was entirely understandable. Michael saw no point in embarrassing herself further or pursuing what could only make them both more uncomfortable.

"That sounds very reasonable. I'll call up there around 9:00 and let them know you're coming. Shall I have Angela make hotel reservations for you somewhere nearby?"

"No. Thanks," Sloan added. "Jason will take care of that for me. An introduction to your administrative manager would be helpful, though. Just don't tell them too much about what I'll be doing. I would rather inform people on a need-to-know basis, especially given the possibility that some of them may end up being loyal to Nicholas if a split should come about."

"You're right, of course," Michael said, ignoring the slight twist of anxiety caused by the mention of Nicholas's name. "I'm not actually personally familiar with many of the people up there, other than in the design arm. They were pretty much hand-picked by me. Nevertheless, it's probably prudent for you to keep a low profile. Will you call me to keep me informed?"

"Absolutely. In the meantime, if you have any problems or need anything, just call Jason."

Jason. Not you. Michael tried to deflect the swift stab of disappointment. "Certainly."

There was silence on the line as both of them listened for the other's breathing, as if loath to break the connection and not knowing what else to say. Eventually, they murmured meaningless goodbyes and hung up.

Michael went back to work, desperately hoping to occupy her wandering mind, silently hoping that Sloan's image would not continue to intrude on her thoughts.

Across town, Sloan set about packing the single suitcase for her trip. She looked around the loft, edgy and restless. The solitude that usually gave her such comfort now seemed merely empty and lonely. Just the sound of Michael's voice on the phone had awakened her senses, and now her body sang with desire. The kiss they had shared was a tangible memory on her lips, and her palms ached with the imprint of Michael's body pressed to their surface. She was hungry for more of her, and she feared it was for much more than just her body. If it had been only that, she might not have hesitated. Michael was an adult, after all, and more than capable of deciding with whom she might sleep. But it wasn't her unrelenting desire for Michael that troubled her so much; it was her deep longing to lie down beside her and simply rest. She was weary, and the promise of succor was far too dangerous. She hadn't sought comfort in a woman's embrace in a very long time, and she wasn't ready to start now.

She finished packing a light bag, locked the heavy metal clasp on the sliding double doors to the loft, and prayed for a clear highway all the way to New York. Maybe a fast drive would erase the images of Michael's softly welcoming smile from her mind. She would just have to live with the constant pulse of need in her depths. That might be uncomfortable, but it wasn't nearly as frightening.

After two hours of struggling to get the images of Sloan driving out of town—convertible top down, dark hair windblown and wild—from her mind, Michael made the call to her New York office. Only then was she finally able to really work, and she forgot about Sloan's voice, and the electricity of her touch, and her hauntingly attractive profile. She was startled as the intercom on her desk crackled once, and a voice filled the room.

"Michael, I'm sorry—"

The sentence was lost in a commotion as the office door banged open, and Nicholas strode in with Angela close behind. Michael swiveled on her high drafting stool and stared, a pencil still held in her left hand.

"I'm sorry, he didn't give me a chance to call you," Angela stated, clearly distraught.

"That's all right, Angela," Michael said calmly. "Just close the door and hold my calls."

Angela looked uneasily from Nicholas' stony countenance to Michael's perfectly smooth, expressionless face and slowly backed out the door. She didn't like it, but she had no choice. She briefly wondered if she should call security. Were it not for the possibility of embarrassing Michael, she would have. There had been something about the look in Nicholas Burke's eyes that frightened her.

Michael remained seated, silent. Nicholas strode forward another few steps, his hands clenched at his sides. A muscle bunched along the edge of his jaw. When he spoke, his voice was tight with the effort to control his anger.

"I met with my attorneys this morning and reviewed your *offer,*" he said harshly. The way he said *offer* suggested that she had highly insulted him. "I assume that was some kind of joke."

"Actually, Nicholas, I spent a great deal of time reviewing the situation with *my* attorneys and several business consultants." Michael stepped down from the stool and stood by the side of her drafting table, one hand resting along the edge of the slanted drawing surface. Her face remained still, although there was a very fine tremor in her hand. "The package we offered you contained a generous buy-out as well as future stock options. It will provide you with ongoing security as long as the company continues to thrive. In addition, there are considerable monetary incentives up front."

Her attorneys had assured her that the future options were a reasonable method for providing long-term recompense for Nicholas's loss of potential income from the company. They had actually argued with her that the cash package was too generous, but she had insisted, hoping to present him with something that he would readily accept.

However, she certainly wasn't surprised he didn't. It wasn't like Nicholas to agree to something that he himself had not orchestrated. Her attorneys had warned that he was likely to reject her initial overtures, however generous, and that negotiations could drag on for a while. Nevertheless, she had no intention of engaging him in a personal dialogue over the details. That was why she had legal counsel.

He grimaced, moving closer still, crowding her back against the drafting table. "On the surface, your proposal may appear generous to others, but I know very well that the potential of this company resides in future design plans. And those will be *your* exclusive property under the current stipulations."

"The design plans have always been mine, Nicholas." She shrugged slightly and said quietly, "You know that."

"Yes, but *I* have been the one to promote them."

She nodded again, wondering at his point. "Of course I know that, and my attorneys have taken that into account."

"I'm not going to let you do this," he said, his voice low and hard.

He stretched an arm out on either side of her, gripping the metal lip that rimmed the desktop, trapping her. The front of his body pressed close, almost touching her. His physical size alone was intimidating enough, but it was more the shimmering rage in his face that made her flinch.

"Without *me,* you never would have been able to accomplish what you have. You were a naïve, unsophisticated, emotional *misfit* when we met." He threw each word at her like a weapon. "You had no idea how to get along in the world, let alone make a success of business. If I hadn't indulged your *sensitivities* and supported your fragile ego, none of this would have been possible." His face was very near hers now. Anyone looking would have thought he meant to kiss her. His voice was low, dangerous. "You owe me, Michael. You owe me *everything.*"

Michael refused to recoil from his physical intimidation, but she was shocked at the depth of his rancor and stunned at his clear and open disdain of her. His vitriol left her momentarily speechless.

He continued as if he expected her to accept his criticism without response. "I can accept that you want to divorce me, and believe me, it will present no hardship for me. Our marriage was convenient from a professional point of view, but it certainly wasn't anything exceptional in the physical department. I'm well aware that you were simply going through the motions in bed, and if you had been the slightest bit physically challenging or even interesting, I might not have looked elsewhere to satisfy my needs."

She was numb, his verbal assault merely reinforcing what she had gradually come to realize over the past weeks. She did not know this man, although she had lived with him for over a decade. If she did not know him, perhaps she did not know herself, and that was much more frightening than anything he could say to her now. Her nerves were exposed—raw—and yet the pain was familiar. She had been living with it for weeks.

"I regret this is happening this way," she said softly, "because I know I had a part in getting us here. I didn't pay attention to the things that were lacking—for both of us, apparently—"

"I don't care what you think now." He made an impatient gesture, as if anything she had to say was of little consequence to him. "I'm warning you, Michael. I'm not leaving Innova, and if you push me, I'll lobby the board for a vote of no confidence, and it will be *you* who will be looking for a new position. There are plenty of people who would support me in replacing you as CEO. Remember, your position is only as sound as your ability to deliver a product, and the bottom line is what determines success or failure."

He grabbed her chin roughly, his fingers pressing unyieldingly into her flesh so that she was forced to stare into his eyes. "You may have the vision, Michael, but you don't have the skill to do anything with it. You never have."

She grasped the wrist that restrained her, but he brusquely released her and walked toward the door. As he reached for the handle, he turned and looked at her one more time, dark fury in his eyes. "You're about as human as a computer. If you were more of a woman, none of this would have happened."

He had regained enough control of himself that when he left he was able to close the door without slamming it. Nevertheless, as Michael brushed trembling fingers over the tender spot his grip had left on her jaw, she was aware of his anger still swirling around her with almost malevolent force. She took his threats seriously, because she knew that he never said anything he didn't intend to do. She wasn't sure exactly how he meant to attack her, but she knew with certainty that an attack was coming. She moved carefully across the room, trying to ignore the quivering in her stomach and the shaking in her limbs.

The door opened, and for an instant, she thought Nicholas was returning for another round. She straightened and took a deep breath; she would not let him see her falter.

"You okay?" Angela asked anxiously as she stepped into the room and pulled the door closed. "The walls are soundproof, but his face spoke volumes."

"I'm all right," Michael replied with a grateful smile as she leaned against her desk. "Thanks."

Angela nodded, turned to leave, and then hesitated. Facing Michael once more, she said, "I've heard things...about a split."

"I'm sure you have." Michael sighed. "We're getting a divorce. The rumor mill must be bustling."

"Not *that* split—well, yeah—some about that. But I meant the company."

"The company is *not* splitting," Michael said emphatically. "Nicholas and I are, but Innova will be continuing as is."

"I'm out of the loop a little," Angela explained, "because everyone knows I'm...loyal...to you. But I've gathered enough of what's going on to know that Nicholas has been calling in favors and offering unofficial promotions if people swear allegiance to him."

"God," Michael said, running a hand through her hair. "I'd hoped it wouldn't come to this."

She was vulnerable now—she knew that—because if he forced the board of directors to choose between them, it was very possible that she would lose. It was true that the company was founded on her ingenuity and intellect, not to mention her funds, but those were things that might be seen as replaceable. If anything occurred to suggest even slightly that she could not carry the company forward, she would surely lose her bargaining power and any advantage that being CEO afforded her.

"I guess I'm going to have to learn how to fight dirty." She regarded Angela with a rueful smile. "And here I thought that all that mattered was doing the job."

"That's all that *does* matter to anyone who you'd really want around," Angela stated emphatically. "And there are plenty of people who will support you if it comes to that."

Michael nodded briskly and straightened her shoulders. "Schedule a breakfast meeting tomorrow for me with all the division heads. It's time to get this out in the open. I'll be damned if I'll meet behind closed doors like I have something to hide."

"You might have to at some point," Angela warned.

"If the time comes," Michael replied resolutely, "then I will."

"I'll get right on it." Angela smiled and reached for the door. "Boss."

Michael waited until the door was firmly closed before sinking into the chair behind her desk and resting her face in her hands. For the moment, all she could do was stay the course with her current plans. If she brought in the existing projects on schedule and presented the board with a sound strategy for transition, her position should be reasonably secure. A few weeks ago that hadn't seemed quite as daunting a task as it did right now.

She wished that there were someone in whom she could confide, and she immediately thought of Sloan. How strange, to find herself at this point in her life with no one that she trusted more than a woman she had met only a short time before. That connection, however brief when measured in weeks, had touched her more deeply than anything in all her years with Nicholas. She tried to convince herself that it was only Sloan's reassurance she wanted, and not her touch, as she stared at the telephone.

Michael listened to the ringing on the line, still questioning the wisdom of her actions. She'd spent the afternoon trying to distract herself by drafting several new proposals to present to the board if Nicholas forced a showdown before she could complete her current projects. She wanted to be certain that she could demonstrate her ability to head the company on all fronts. She had debated for hours, her anxiety level rising, before finally relenting and calling Jason to ask for Sloan's number in New York. Part of her reluctance was that she simply wanted to hear Sloan's voice, and that was personal, not business. But they *did* have a professional relationship, and she tried to convince herself that that was the only reason she was finally calling. Her heart was pounding by the time the phone was answered.

"Sloan."

"It's Michael Lassiter," she said quietly.

"Michael," Sloan exclaimed, sitting up straight on the side of the hotel room bed, instantly concerned by the unexpected call. She glanced at the digital bedside clock. 8:40 p.m.

"I'm sorry to bother you, but it seemed important," Michael said with uncharacteristic hesitancy.

"No problem." In fact, there was no one else she'd rather hear from. Even being in New York City hadn't been enough to make her forget the weekend—or Michael. After a room service meal, she'd been lying down, trying rather unsuccessfully to read. "Is something wrong?"

"No. Well, maybe. I..."

Now she wasn't certain what to say. The encounter with Nicholas had frightened her, and, worse, it had left her unsure of herself. His threats to sabotage her standing within the company were serious, and she knew that he was determined enough and ruthless enough to accomplish his threats. It was his personal assault on her and the life they had shared that had done the most damage, however. It hurt to hear how easily he had discounted everything about their life together, but facing how unaware she had been of her own needs and feelings had left her wondering if some of what he'd said hadn't been true.

You're about as human as a computer. If you were more of a woman, none of this would have happened.

"Michael?" Sloan asked, worriedly running a hand through her hair.

"I'm sorry to disturb you," she began again. Even accepting that her concerns about Nicholas were reasonable, she warred with herself over turning to Sloan when she felt so emotionally unsteady. She did not want to turn to this woman simply as a remedy for her own fears and pain. She took a deep breath, determined to steer their conversation onto a purely professional level. "I thought you should know of some developments here."

"What?" Sloan listened as silence descended once again. She could almost *feel* Michael's struggle. Something was clearly very wrong, and, immediately, she thought of Nicholas. She'd been worried that he would do something rash, and now the fear tore at her. Struggling to sound calm, she said gently, "Michael, I'm *glad* that you called. It's good to hear your voice. Just tell me what's happened. It's all right."

Finally, Michael relaxed, reassured by the acceptance and comfort evident in Sloan's voice. "Nicholas was here at the office late this afternoon." She laughed grimly. "He apparently did not find my attorneys' proposal to his liking. He made it clear that he would resort to almost any means, including undermining my position in the company and my credibility with the board, to preserve his position. I don't know precisely what he intends, but I don't expect that he'll wait very long. I wasn't certain if it would make any difference with what you need to do up there, but it seemed appropriate that I should let you know."

Michael's heart was pounding. The phone call seemed foolish to her now, when she had so little concrete to tell Sloan, but she remembered the cold fury in Nicholas's eyes and the feel of his fingers on her flesh, and she shivered. Her hand on the receiver was clenched so tightly her fingers were white.

With a calm that belied her racing pulse, Sloan asked, "Are you all right?"

She'd heard the faint tremor in Michael's voice and knew she was trying hard not to become too emotional. She recognized the fear, too. All she really cared about was Michael's safety—the business aspects could wait.

"Yes."

"You're sure?"

"Yes, I—"

"Then what aren't you telling me? What did he do?" She was on her feet, her heart racing.

"Nothing," Michael said swiftly. She hadn't meant to involve Sloan in this. "It was nasty, but it was only words."

"Just words?" Sloan probed, searching the silence on the line that followed. "Michael, did he *hurt* you?" Her tone was deadly cold, hard as stone, but her eyes burned with fury.

"No! He...he crowded me a little. Touched my face—"

"I'm coming back," Sloan declared, fighting not to curse aloud.

"Sloan, no," Michael said firmly. "That's not why I called."

"I *know* that."

"Please, you needn't worry. I'm fine."

"If you're sure," Sloan conceded reluctantly. A hundred miles away, she wished desperately that she was there and could see Michael's face. She wanted to assess for herself just how *all right* Michael really was. Instead, she squeezed the bridge of her nose between her thumb and forefinger, tried to focus on the issues at hand, and tried even harder to quell the rising surge of anxiety in her chest. She hated even thinking about Michael being frightened and upset, and when she considered what the confrontation with Burke must have been like, she nearly choked on her anger. It was her turn to take a deep breath and rein in her emotions.

"Okay, if you're *really* sure."

"I promise," Michael affirmed, touched nevertheless by Sloan's reaction. Trying to get the conversation back to business, she asked, "How are things going up there?"

With effort, Sloan replied quietly, "I've spent the afternoon with the computer people here, and we actually made a fair amount of progress. I don't think there are any major problems at this end, and I expect to be finishing up within the next few days. There are always things that are going to need to be tweaked and modified, but I can do most of that by phone. I'll need to sit down with you to go over exactly how I want you to use the new encryption programs, but that can wait until the beginning of the week."

"Thanks, Sloan." Michael sighed, finally feeling calmer. "I probably didn't need to call and bother you, but I have two major deadlines coming up, and I need to make final proposals and presentations by this time next week. These will actually be the first main projects that I've handled with almost no input from Nicholas. He was traveling so much with other ventures that we simply worked around him. It's important that I finish these up without any difficulties. It will solidify my position not only as a theorist but also as someone who can actually bring in the final product."

"I understand," Sloan said. "If there's anything I can do, even if it's just to talk, please call me. I'll probably be here through Thursday afternoon, but Jason can always find me."

Michael laughed, relieved and, she had to admit, simply happy to have talked with her. "I expect I'll be spending most of the rest of the week and most likely the weekend, too, right here in the office. I doubt that I'll need to bother you again. It was good to hear your voice, though." She hesitated, as if wanting to say more. Then, more softly, she said, "Goodnight, Sloan."

The words seemed too final, but Sloan cherished the warmth in her tone. "Goodnight, Michael," she whispered.

Chapter
Eleven

When her mobile phone rang three nights later, Sloan was sound asleep. She croaked, "Hello," and had to look twice at the clock before she could make out the red numerals. Just after midnight. That got her attention, and she sat up, immediately alert. A phone call at this hour could only be trouble.

"Sloan? It's Jason."

"Jason? What's going on? What's the matter?" She fought a surge of anxiety. Something wasn't right, and she had a feeling it was Michael. Her heart was racing just at the thought. It was Thursday—well, technically Friday morning, now—and she hadn't heard anything from her since the worried call Monday evening. She had told herself that meant everything was fine—except she didn't really believe it and had been on edge ever since.

"I'm on my way to Innova." He waited a beat, as if deliberating, then added, "Michael asked me not to call you, but all hell is breaking loose in her office, and I figured that you'd want to know."

By now, Sloan was standing, flipping on lights and tossing her suitcase with one hand onto the bottom of her hotel bed. As she spoke, she pulled open drawers and dumped her clothing into the open bag. "Is she all right?"

For a moment, Jason didn't understand. Hadn't he just told her that there was a major problem? Then he realized she meant was Michael *physically* all right, and he hurried to answer.

"She's fine. I mean, she's not *fine,* she's practically going out of her mind, but she's not hurt or anything."

"Jason, just tell me what the fuck is wrong and stop beating around the bush." Sloan swore, tugging off the sweats she had been sleeping in and reaching for the jeans she had tossed over a chair earlier that evening. She cradled the phone between her shoulder and chin as she pulled up the jeans, forsaking underwear, and donned a clean white T-shirt. She slid her feet sockless into her loafers and looked around the room for her leather jacket.

"Michael was apparently working late on some big project of hers when out of the blue everything started crashing. From what I can make out, she lost data, can't open programs, and her hard drive has crashed totally."

Sloan stood still for a second, an uneasy feeling starting in her chest. "Did you try to talk her through it over the phone and get her back on-line?"

"Of course. No go," he said, clearly frustrated. "It was just by luck that I happened to get her message. Since you were out of town, I had office calls forwarded to my home number, and I checked my answering machine when I got back from a...date. I called Michael right away, but I can't seem to get things up and running again. I have a bad feeling about this."

"No foolin'." Sloan slammed the suitcase shut, tucked her wallet into her right rear pocket, and grabbed the plastic room cardkey off the desk. She scanned quickly around the room for anything she might have left behind. "I've got the same bad feeling you do. I don't believe in coincidences. I'll be there in two hours. You need to be at Michael's office so we can get started as soon as I get in."

Suitcase in one hand and the phone tucked under her chin, she reached for the door. "And Jason? Pack a bag. I have a feeling we're going to be sleeping over."

At 12:30 a.m., there wasn't a lot of traffic on I-95 South. In a Porsche Carrera, a hundred miles was a ride around the block, and in less than two hours, Sloan was waved through by what passed for night security in the lobby of Innova's building. When she knocked on the executive officer's door, the CEO herself answered.

"Hi," Sloan said quietly, rooted to the spot. Somehow she'd forgotten how beautiful the woman was.

"Hi," Michael began. She stood holding the door open, watching the other woman walk in. It was the middle of the night, and J. T. Sloan should have looked like hell, but she was the best thing Michael had laid eyes on in days. Six very long days, to be exact. Mixed with her intense relief was a pulse of visceral pleasure that she couldn't quite explain. And it wasn't something she wanted to examine too closely at the moment. "I'm so sorry to have to drag you back like this."

"Forget it," Sloan said, shaking her head, a faint smile lifting her mouth at one corner. She dropped her briefcase onto the sofa, shrugged out of her leather jacket and dropped it, too, and turned automatically toward the computer workstation. She wasn't aware of Michael's appraising glance gliding over the tight T-shirt and then moving slowly down her jean-clad thighs. "You're not troubling me. This is my job and what you've been paying me to do. Obviously, I missed something, and it's my responsibility to straighten things out." She glanced at her watch and saw that it was 2:10 a.m. "Where's Jason?"

"He's down the hall in Mayfield's office checking something on the main system. He got here about an hour ago. The last time I saw him, he was mumbling colorfully under his breath." Michael crossed to the computer center and stared at the blue screens of death. "I intend to join in on that front soon."

Sloan appreciated Michael's attempt at levity. It was clear how stressed she was. The fine lines around her eyes were deeper, and there was a gaunt pallor to her face that signaled her fatigue. She had shed her suit jacket and was wearing only a light silk blouse tucked into casual slacks. Despite Michael's air of weariness, Sloan couldn't think of anyone more attractive.

Michael turned from the screens to find Sloan staring at her. For a second, she forgot about the disaster threatening to sabotage the critical work she needed to finish and saw only the appreciative glow in Sloan's violet eyes. She colored slightly, but smiled back. "I think you had better let him know you're here, because he looked about as frazzled as I feel."

"I'll do that." Sloan took several steps forward to the coffee urn and poured two cups, handing one to Michael. "Here, you're going to need this. After I see what he's doing, I'll take a look at your machines." She took a swallow of coffee, grateful for the caffeine infusion. "Until I see what's down, there's no way to analyze what's going on. Can you tell me what programs were running and exactly what happened—in sequence?"

With a sigh, Michael sat on one of the sofas and propped her

stocking feet up on the edge of the glass coffee table. She ran a
hand through her hair, smoothing the golden strands back from
her cheeks. Her voice was flat, defeated, as she spoke.

"I was working on the proposals I need for the research and
development division meeting next week—one of the major
projects I told you about?"

"Uh-huh," Sloan said with a nod. *One of the projects you're
counting on to solidify your position at the helm of Innova.*

"Anyhow, I was entering data into one of the graphics programs, finalizing some details for Tuesday's meeting. Let's see—
I'd also checked e-mail from several of my techs earlier, too, so
that was still open. Uh...Word was running...God, I don't know
what else. A web page or two? I wasn't paying attention."

"And then?"

"First the screen display flickered, like pixels were dropping
out, and next the color faded. It corrected after I rebooted, but
then the graphics program froze up. That's not common, but it
happens." She laughed humorlessly. "Mostly when I'm in the middle of something crucial like tonight. I tried the usual things, but I
couldn't get it up again. Then other files simply disappeared.
Finally, the hard drive crashed. When I had exhausted the few
tricks I knew, and it became obvious something major had happened, I called your office and left a message."

"Why didn't you call me in New York?" Sloan asked gently.
"You had the number."

Michael looked away. "Because you were in New York." She
didn't add that she'd already turned to Sloan once that week when
she'd needed help, and she was afraid of what that meant. Because
she knew, even if she didn't want to admit it to herself, that she
thought of Sloan nearly all the time. And it wasn't because she
needed advice. Sometimes, it was because she wanted to hear
Sloan's voice, and sometimes, it was simply because she couldn't
forget the feel of Sloan's hands on her. She bit her lip and
remained silent.

Sloan let it go. She could see how upset Michael was, and it
was no time for interrogations. "Has anything seemed strange the
last few weeks with your system?"

Businesslike once again, Michael gave it some thought and
recounted a few things that in retrospect seemed odd. While she
talked, Sloan took a seat on the adjoining couch and crossed one
bare ankle over the opposite knee. Leaning forward intently, she

quickly assessed, considered, and discarded possibilities.

Eventually, Michael halted, shrugging helplessly. "I just don't know enough to tell the difference between the normal glitches and something really wrong."

She was exhausted, and worried, and emotionally stretched to breaking. And she was angry. Angry at herself for not realizing years before that her life was founded on a lie—an illusion of stability that now put everything she cared about in jeopardy.

"I'm not going to tell you not to worry," Sloan said quietly. "You're much too intelligent to believe that. In fact, I'm worried, too, but meltdowns like this happen, and sometimes the solution can be relatively simple. The problem is going to be narrowing down exactly where the system has failed. Once we've identified the cause, hopefully we'll be able to resurrect and reconstruct your hard drive and retrieve your critical files."

"What about the automatic backups? Isn't the system set to do that?" Michael asked hopefully.

"For the network—yes. Weekly." At Michael's desperate expression, Sloan asked gently, "How much have you transferred to your hard drive that *isn't* saved to the network?"

"Everything I've been working on the last few days," Michael said quietly. "I've been pulling it together from everywhere."

"It's possible that the local backup files are not contaminated, but that's unlikely."

"How long before you can tell?"

"I don't know. I need to see what Jason's found so far." Sloan could see Michael slump with defeat. "Look, at least *some* of what you've lost must be copied to other people or included in company documents—proposals, meeting notes—that kind of thing."

"Probably," Michael agreed glumly. "But digging it out and getting it all back in one piece could literally take weeks." She remembered the look on Nicholas's face—the cold disdain and resolute anger. *And I don't have weeks. Probably not even days.*

"With any luck," Sloan hastened to add, "the encryption program we installed for your personal design portfolio will have protected the information. It may still be there intact and only temporarily inaccessible."

"How can I help?" Michael asked, taking some hope from the confidence and certainty in Sloan's voice. "I don't want to put any more pressure on you than there already is, but I have critical

deadlines in five days. I might be able to postpone them for a short
time, twelve to twenty-four hours maybe, but after that, people are
going to know there's a problem. If I miss these deadlines, I'm
sure that Nicholas will take advantage of that and attempt a major
takeover. If he pushes for that now, and can point to my failure to
complete essential projects, I will very likely lose."

Sloan nodded grimly, her intense dislike of Nicholas escalating. The timing was too suspicious to discount the idea that he
had something to do with what was happening. He couldn't have
done more damage to Michael unless he had physically assaulted
her. Unfortunately, proving corporate sabotage was difficult, time
consuming, and rarely prosecutable. Plus, it wouldn't help
Michael. At the moment, she had little recourse but to attempt to
identify and undo the damage.

"Michael, you're not pressuring me. My business is deadlines," she said with absolute confidence. "The most important
thing you can do is keep working. Jason and I aren't leaving until
the problem is solved, and if I need specific info, you'll be here to
fill me in. I can't give you a time estimate, but if I need to, I'll call
in some favors and bring in additional techs to help. Worst-case
scenario, we'll have to initiate major data retrieval or even repro-
gram parts of the BIOS chip—whatever we have to do, it will get
done. I promise."

"I trust you, Sloan," Michael said quietly as she leaned forward and took Sloan's hand. She squeezed lightly, and when Sloan
slipped her fingers between Michael's, it felt as right as anything
she had ever experienced. Looking into Sloan's eyes, she found the
welcoming warmth she was coming to count on, and for the first
time in days, she felt safe. There was more than just her career in
Sloan's hands. She was slowly losing her heart to the dark-haired,
violet-eyed woman with the tender touch.

Sloan found Jason in the network administrator's office, sitting in a swivel chair staring at a monitor, a legal pad next to his
right hand covered in shorthand notes to himself.

"Do you think it's a virus?" she asked as soon as she walked
in.

"Don't you?" He looked up at her over his shoulder, his blue
eyes dark with worry. "Every damn thing I try to open gives me a
corrupted file message. Christ, until we can be sure of the extent

of the damage, we have to assume that even the off-site backup files are contaminated."

"Yeah, that's what I figure, too," she commented, studying him carefully. Despite the fact that he had not even gotten the few hours' sleep that she had managed before driving back from New York, he looked fresh and immaculately groomed as always. He wore casual pants and a polo shirt. The dark blue shirt was tight enough to show off his nicely muscled arms and shoulders.

"I can tell you right now it's probably armored, because the TSR you loaded should have picked up most known and in-the-wild species," he added.

"I hope it's *only* a virus." She edged a hip up onto the corner of the long counter and nodded grimly. "If it is, I'm willing to bet it's a polymorphic virus that's been hanging around for a while, slowly infiltrating everything on the network. What I'm really worried about, though, is that it's some kind of stealth virus or Trojan horse that was dropped sometime earlier and remotely triggered recently. With the network running all the time and God knows how many people with access, it could be anywhere by now. We're going to have to look at all the backup copies, clean the system thoroughly, and hope there's no permanent damage to critical files. We're looking at days."

He had already turned back to what he was doing, his face in profile stony with anger. "This has the feel of a malicious infection to me, because it has crippled the system very effectively. This isn't someone looking to download data—this is someone looking to make the data inaccessible. Maybe permanently."

"My guess is we'll eventually find that files were hacked before the network crashed. Then the virus was activated."

"Pirates?"

"Could be. Could be someone just looking to paralyze the network."

"If some bastard did this intentionally, I'm going to find out how."

I'm pretty sure I know who. Sloan got up and moved close enough to rest a hand lightly on his shoulder. "First things first, Jason. We need to get Michael back to work. She's got deadlines. Critical ones. Once we can do that safely, we'll start backtracking and hopefully find out how this started. We'll do mail searches, checksum the files, scan the TCP/IP logs—whatever it takes."

"You got it," he said.

"And Jason," she added, "I appreciate your quick response time."

He turned again to stare at her, surprised. "This is war, Sloan. Someone has taken a shot at our client right in our faces. Besides, I really like Michael. She doesn't deserve this."

Sloan smiled just at the mention of Michael's name, but there was a dark fire simmering in her eyes. "No, she doesn't. Sorry about ruining your weekend, though. I have a feeling we'll be spending most of it right here."

Jason flushed and looked at a point over her left shoulder. "Not as sorry as you're going to be when I have to break my date with Sarah tonight." He looked at the wall clock. "In sixteen hours I'm supposed to be on my way to pick her up for dinner at DeCarlo's."

"Oh no, you don't," Sloan chided good-naturedly. "Don't get me in the middle of that one. Sarah likes nothing better than an excuse to beat up on me, and missing dinner at the best restaurant in town is a pretty good reason."

He grinned, but he looked uneasy. Then he asked quietly, "You've known her a long time, haven't you?"

Sloan was taken aback by his question. Despite their long association, Jason almost never talked to her about personal matters other than to reprimand her for what he considered her loose lifestyle. If he was initiating a serious conversation, it must be very important to him. She glanced at her watch, aware of how much they had to do, but he was her friend. She could spare him a few minutes. She sat back down.

"Yes, I've known her a very long time. I think she's the only person in my life, other than you, whom I trust completely."

Now he was the one who was surprised. Sloan had never before said anything that revealing to him. In fact, she never *said* much of anything to him. He had learned to trust her because she had always treated him with respect and honesty. With Sloan, her actions were usually more revealing than her words.

"I've never met anyone like her," he said softly. "She doesn't seem the least bit put off by the fact that I'm a...transvestite."

Sloan raised an eyebrow. "You know, Jason, I've never thought of you that way." It was damn difficult to describe exactly *how* she perceived the two of them—Jason and Jasmine—but she was clear that there *were* two of them. It wasn't a case of multiple personality disorder, because Jason was clearly aware of Jasmine, and Sloan suspected that Jason could suppress that part of himself if he had to. She couldn't imagine what it would cost him to do that, though, and hoped that he would never have to do so. Nevertheless, Jasmine certainly had an essence all her own.

"I guess technically *transvestite* is the best word," Sloan conceded, "but Jasmine is so much more than just an invention of clothing and make-up. She's another dimension of you—I get that. But sometimes I even forget that she *is* you or you are her...or something." She finished with a laugh.

"Don't you think I've tried to explain it to myself?" He lifted a shoulder, grinning. "The only time I've ever tried to explain it to anyone else, it was a disaster. But you know all about that," he added bitterly. "With Sarah, I don't really need to explain it. She doesn't seem to *need* that."

"So what's the problem?" Sloan queried.

"I'm afraid she'll change her mind when she gets to know me better."

"You mean you're afraid she'll change her mind if you let her see how much a part of you Jasmine really is?"

He nodded. "It's one thing to see Jasmine as a performer a couple of times a month. It would be a lot different if Sarah realized that Jasmine is always around, more or less."

"Is she?" Sloan thought about that for a few minutes, realizing that she had never thought about Jasmine anywhere other than at the Cabaret. She hadn't imagined that perhaps it was something Jason did even in private. It was personal and not something she could ask him.

Instead, she said, "I think if you and Sarah really get serious, you're going to have to let her see Jasmine in all those other situations. In fact, maybe it would be a good idea for Jasmine and Sarah to spend some time together outside of the Cabaret." She thought she could actually see him turn pale. But when he looked at her, there was something like hope in his eyes.

"Do you think that could actually work?"

"I don't honestly know, but I trust Sarah to deal with whatever comes up." Sloan shrugged, standing. "I think you can trust her, too."

She left him then, because she was anxious to get back to Michael. Even though the work ahead looked daunting, Sloan was grateful for the excuse just to be in the same room with her.

Chapter
Twelve

"You need to take a break," Michael said quietly. She came up behind the chair where Sloan sat working, glanced at the monitor, and saw nothing that made sense to her. Without thinking, she placed her hands gently on Sloan's shoulders, rested her thumbs against the back of Sloan's neck, and, unconsciously, softly kneaded the tense muscles under her fingers.

"Ahh." Sloan leaned back with a groan, her head just touching Michael's abdomen. She closed her eyes, very aware of the heat of Michael's body so near. The touch of Michael's hands was at once soothing and incredibly exciting, and if she wasn't careful, she'd have a hard time hiding her arousal. She knew her breathing had already taken a quick leap into hyperdrive, and her hands trembled slightly where they lay on her thighs. Silently, she instructed herself to remember the job she needed to do, which helped, but her voice was husky as she murmured, "God, that feels criminally good. What time is it?"

"Just about noon. You haven't been out of that chair in almost nine hours." Michael looked down at Sloan's face, savoring the opportunity to study the other woman as she rested against her, eyes closed and seemingly unaware.

Her face is made for sculpting, Michael thought, barely able to resist running her fingers over the dark arch of Sloan's brow and along the strong angle of her jaw. As she realized that she was enjoying the supple strength of firm shoulder muscles, her fingers strayed to Sloan's neck, and she felt the other woman stiffen at the touch. *Too much. You can't do this.* She forced herself to step back, dropping her hands to her sides. "You should stop for a bit."

Sloan rubbed both hands vigorously over her face, straightening up in the chair, ignoring the sudden disappointment at the loss of Michael's touch. She was getting used to the steady throb of unanswered desire whenever Michael was around. At least now she had something to distract her.

"This is that critical time when everything is about to come together," said Sloan, weary but starting to feel the excitement that preceded a breakthrough. "It's not something you can get up and walk away from once you start tracking these things down. Another couple of hours and I think I'll have a real handle on it. Then I can take a break for a bit."

"What about something to eat?" Michael asked. "We could hit the diner down the street."

"Another cup of coffee maybe. Besides, you've been working just as hard."

"Yes, but I napped for an hour." Michael frowned. She didn't know what she had thought would happen when Sloan showed up in the middle of the night. She had been too glad to see her, and too worried about disappearing files and critical deadlines. Now she was starting to worry about *her.*

"Sloan," Michael continued cautiously, "if I miss the deadline, it's not the end of the world. I'll manage—"

"Are you kidding?" Sloan swiveled around in the chair, staring up at her in astonishment. "Another ten to twelve hours and we'll be able to bring you back on-line. Once we flush the little bastard and start cleaning, I can get started on the security changeovers, too."

Michael looked horrified. "Twelve hours?"

"She's good for a lot more than that," a voice announced from across the room.

Both women turned at the sound.

"Heck, I've seen her go for days on caffeine and junk food. This is a walk in the park," Sarah continued, grinning as she crossed the wide office, then stooped to kiss Sloan lightly on the mouth. "Hi, Michael," she added as she fondly stroked Sloan's arm.

"And you are here, how?" Sloan inquired with a grin of her own.

"Jason called me. Told me that our much-anticipated dinner and dancing date was off because you and he were in the midst of a crisis. I didn't want to miss the fun. Michael's assistant let me in."

"Some fun," Michael muttered, feeling as if she were slipping down the rabbit hole. These two actually seemed to find all this amusing.

"And," Sarah added with a flourish, "I brought bagels and cream cheese and assorted sinful chocolate things that are guaranteed to keep you awake."

"Oh, what a woman. Give—" Sloan begged. "But bring them here. I have to get back to this."

"Patience," Sarah instructed, noting the return of Michael's worried frown.

As Sarah pulled her away by the arm, Michael gave the back of Sloan's head one more concerned glance, but followed Sarah to the sitting area where several bags rested on the coffee table. In a whisper, she said, "She's been at it since two this morning. Maybe *you* can get her to stop."

Leaning close, Sarah said, "Give her another hour or so, and then we'll gang up on her and make her take a nap. I just coerced Jason into stretching out on the couch in that empty conference room down the hall. He looked like his eyeballs were going to fall out. How about you? Get any sleep?" As she talked, she fixed a plate for Sloan.

"Some," Michael admitted. "I drifted off for a while in here on the sofa. I tried to work on some sketches earlier, but I couldn't concentrate. I feel so damn useless."

"I can imagine." Sarah shrugged sympathetically. "How bad is it?"

"I don't think they know yet. Fortunately, we've been able to cover it up by telling everyone the system is off-line for program updates. But if we're not up again by Monday morning at the latest, I won't be able to hide the fact that we have a major system failure. That kind of news is very bad for business."

"These two know what they're doing. It'll be okay. Sloan's the best."

Michael watched as Sarah carried the plate to Sloan, who acknowledged her with a mumble and then a blazing smile. *The best? Yes, she is, isn't she.*

Sarah turned in time to catch the wistful expression on Michael's face as she stared at Sloan. She'd seen that look before and knew it for precisely what it was. She wondered if Sloan realized that Michael had fallen in love with her. And she wondered, too, if Sloan would have the good sense to accept it.

"I feel like such a traitor being outside while they've been up there struggling for a day and a half," Michael said as she took a deep breath of the crisp, clean air. It was mid-afternoon in early May with the temperatures peaking in the sixties, and everywhere that unique, bright spring sun suffused the day in warm welcome.

"Don't worry. If it weren't for times like this, the two of them would be bored to tears. I think both of them miss the fast pace and high drama of Washington."

They were walking the few blocks to Sarah's apartment in what was commonly known as Society Hill. It was an area ten blocks square replete with brownstone townhouses and historic buildings lining narrow streets, many of which still retained their original cobblestones. Sarah had kindly offered to let Michael shower at her apartment and borrow some of her clothes, since Michael had not been out of her office for almost two days.

Michael could have cabbed across town to her hotel, but Sarah's was closer, and to be honest, she wanted to ask about Sloan's past. She was very aware that neither Sloan nor Sarah ever did more than allude to it. She wanted to know the person who was J. T. Sloan. She already knew the kindness, loyalty, and strength, and those were things that attracted her, but she wondered what had shaped Sloan's silences and forged the fleeting whisper of pain in her eyes. Those were the things that made Michael long to hold her, and more. But, when she finally had the opportunity, she could not ask, understanding it was only Sloan's secret to share.

"I'm sorry about disrupting your weekend plans," she said instead.

"Don't even give it a thought. With any luck, it won't be the last time something disrupts my plans with Jason. I only hope we get to that point someday."

Michael glanced at her in mild surprise. "You're really very serious about him, aren't you?"

"I really am. It wasn't something I ever expected to happen again, but now that it has, it feels exactly right. We were going to spend the evening together, and I think we both sort of knew it would mean spending the night together. I have to say that if we don't do something pretty soon, I'm likely to implode."

"Well then, I'm doubly sorry," Michael said with a soft laugh. "I don't think I've ever really appreciated that sensation before."

Sarah looked up sharply. "Before?"

Michael colored, suddenly realizing what she had said. Her first instinct was to dismiss it as a meaningless comment, but in the next instant, she discerned that for perhaps the first time in her life she actually had someone she trusted enough to confide in.

"I've never felt that way about anyone. I mean...the way you feel about Jason. The attraction and the...wanting," she said finally, hoping her keen embarrassment wasn't obvious.

"What about your husband?" Sarah asked gently. "In the beginning?"

"No. Nicholas was my friend first, and then he was my business partner, and somewhere along the way he became my husband. I didn't have any friends, really, because I was different than most of the people my age. It was a kind of salvation when he seemed to understand what was important to me and shared the things that I loved. But it wasn't a union of the senses; it was an intellectual connection. I was never really aware of—" She stopped, struggling for the words. "Sex."

"Ah...sex." Sarah laughed. "If there is anything more irrational and less explainable than that, I can't imagine what it is. There are a lot of reasons to stay in love, but *why* we fall in love remains a mystery to me. The best we can hope for, I guess, is that we fall in love with someone we can continue to love." For a moment, she remembered her last relationship and added sadly, "And sometimes there's nothing we can do except fall and wait for the crash."

"Are you frightened?" Michael asked quietly, suddenly needing very much to know. "About what's happening between you and Jason?"

"A little bit." Sarah heard the apprehension beneath the question and impulsively took Michael's hand. "I try not to think too much about what might happen. It's hard not to, but since we can never really predict, I'm trying to enjoy how alive I feel when I look at him, and how incredibly exciting it is to imagine being with him."

They came to the stone stairs of Sarah's townhouse, and as if prearranged, they sat side by side on a step and leaned back, faces turned to the sky. It was one of those gifted moments when the world seemed to recede, street sounds and sights grew muted, and all that was real was the seductive heat of the sunshine. It was a moment made for confession.

"I'm having a bit of a problem with Sloan," Michael stated, staring up at the soft white clouds in the blue, blue sky.

"Oh? What's that?"

"I can't stop thinking about her."

"Mmm, I noticed," Sarah said, tilting her head back to catch the slanting rays of sunlight against her neck. "I'd be willing to bet she's having a bit of a problem with you, too."

"No, she isn't." Michael's voice was rough with disappointment. "She's not interested."

Sarah turned her head, wondering why Michael seemed so certain. "What happened?"

Michael blushed but continued determinedly. "Last weekend, in my hotel room, we...well, I guess..." She shrugged helplessly, pushing her left hand through her already tousled blond hair. "It sounds like it should be so simple when I say it. She kissed me, but then she made it clear that it had been a mistake."

"Ah." Sarah nodded, suddenly understanding. "Not surprising."

Michael turned to her, her eyes questioning. "I'm sorry...what?"

"You probably scare the hell out of her."

"Me?" Michael was incredulous. "Why?"

"Because I've got the feeling that she *is* interested and doesn't want to be."

"I don't understand."

"Michael, there are things Sloan needs to tell you. Things you need to know to understand her better. She's my oldest friend, and I love her dearly. She's the strongest and most honest person I've ever met. But she's also the most stubborn, and she's been running from something for a long time. Until she stops, she's not going to be able to let anyone close."

"It's funny," Michael said slowly. "I don't know what you're talking about...but in a way, I do. Sometimes when Sloan and I are together, it feels so easy. So...right. It's as if we're connected, feeling the same way. Then, in the next instant, she pulls away and disappears. I don't know why she does that, but I want to understand."

"And you're...attracted to her? Physically, I mean?" Sarah

questioned cautiously, concern for Sloan suddenly surfacing. She liked Michael, but she *loved* Sloan. If this was just a passing thing, Sloan could get hurt. "Because, you know, if she's already kissed you then we're not talking about just being friends here."

"I know that. I'm not having *just friends* feelings, either."

"Does it bother you, that she's a woman?" Sarah asked quietly.

"I guess it's supposed to," Michael said thoughtfully. "But it doesn't. I never expected anyone to make me feel the way she does. Never even thought about it, really. Yet when I look at her..." She couldn't prevent an image of Sloan from entering her mind. She saw her, in her faded blue jeans and scuffed brown boots and tight white T-shirt, and something turned over deep inside. "I think she's gorgeous. In fact," she added with a small, tight laugh, very aware of exactly what that heavy pulsating sensation signaled, "if I don't stop thinking about wanting her to touch me, *I'm* going to implode."

Sarah burst out laughing, her concerns fading in the face of Michael's honesty. After a few seconds, Michael joined her. They leaned close together, shoulders touching, each of them thinking how good it was to share the moment.

Chapter
Thirteen

When Michael returned to the Innova office shortly after 5:00 p.m. on Saturday, she discovered Sloan stretched out on her back on the sofa, eyes closed, a leg dangling partway over the edge, one hand resting on her thigh and the other open, palm up, by her side. Looking at her, sleeping unawares, Michael knew she should simply turn away and let her rest, but she found she could not avert her gaze. It seemed as if every facet of Sloan's face and body was a miraculous discovery, precious details to savor again and again.

She had never noticed before how sensuous the slight rise of a woman's breast beneath a cotton T-shirt could appear, nor how alluring faded denim might look stretched over a long, lean thigh, nor how the flat planes of the abdomen and gentle slope of hip begged for a hand to brush along them. She stepped closer, one hand poised to stroke the sleeping woman, her breath suspended in anticipation. That was when she realized that she needed to escape, because any second now she was going to do something very embarrassing.

But before she could move, Sloan's eyes opened, caught hers, and held. Shimmering violet embers merged into swirling blue flames, bringing Sloan to a sitting position as Michael leaned down, a force beyond volition or even thought drawing them together. A whisper before their lips could meet, somewhere in the deep reaches of Michael's consciousness, she heard Sloan's quick intake of breath, almost a moan. At the same time, she remembered Sloan's words from only days before. *"We'll both regret this tomorrow."*

"Sloan," Michael whispered, her voice so thick with need she did not recognize herself. "Please tell me that it's all right to kiss you. I don't think I can stop."

"All right?" Sloan blinked, appeared to come fully awake, and collapsed back into the cushions. "Fuck, Michael, I don't know...anything."

They stared at one another, breathing hard, skin flushed, bodies shuddering with strain. The air between them hummed with tension.

Michael closed her eyes and stood upright, hands clenched at her side. She couldn't look at Sloan, not without touching her. And she was stunned and a little frightened by what she had almost done. Never had she wanted anyone like this—so badly, in fact, that she scarcely knew what she was doing. She barely recognized herself—yet she had never felt more alive.

"Sorry," Michael whispered as she finally opened her eyes. Trying to avoid looking directly at Sloan, afraid words would fail her, she sat down on the corner of the adjoining chair, letting her hands fall into her lap. "Well, it seems like we've been *here* before," she said, her voice quivering. "This time, it was clearly *I* who was responsible. I apologize."

Maybe it was the forlorn regret in Michael's voice, or perhaps it was only because Sloan had wanted her since the first time she'd seen her—whatever the reason, Sloan's resistance finally crumbled. Kneeling swiftly on the floor in front of Michael, she leaned forward and kissed her before either of them could think or say no.

Firmly, surely, thoroughly—she kissed her the way she had wanted to kiss her for far too many days, the way she had dreamed of kissing her for countless nights.

Sloan's breath caught as she thrilled to the soft brush of Michael's lips against hers, shivering when a tentative tongue searched gently for her own. She kept her hands securely pressed to the chair on either side of Michael, knowing that if she touched her, she would be lost. Already her heart was pounding and her head was light. There was a roaring in her ears that threatened to shatter reason. With every fiber of her being, she wanted Michael's skin under her fingers, wanted Michael's body yielding to her hands, wanted Michael's cries rising to her caress.

Her fingers cramped from holding them tightly against the leather, because she would not do what she was desperate to do—

not now, not here, and not like this. A kiss was just a kiss, and she just needed this one simple kiss, just this *one* kiss to assuage the fire of longing that had been consuming her whole. She ignored the demanding ache that tightened like a fist in her gut, so heavy that just breathing was a struggle. When she could no longer bear the tender sweetness of Michael's mouth, nor contain the searing pressure that poured down her thighs, spiraled into her spine, and hammered into her stomach, she drew away.

"Well," Michael breathed, her eyes hazy, "that was nice."

"Yeah." Sloan grinned shakily, having trouble focusing herself.

Neither of them moved, lest the spell be broken. Sloan was just inches from Michael, outstretched arms braced on either side of her. When Michael slowly brought her fingers to Sloan's wrist, she turned her hand until they touched. The light pressure of Michael's fingertips circling in her palm was enough to make Sloan's stomach clench. When Michael caressed her arm, then along her shoulder to her neck, finally bringing her palm against Sloan's chest, she gritted her teeth to hold back a moan. She was so aroused she feared she might orgasm without even being touched. "Careful," she whispered—to herself, to Michael.

Michael was oblivious to Sloan's plight. She was mesmerized by the feel of Sloan's sculpted muscles, rigid now under her hand, and the soft promise of breast, beckoning just beyond.

When Michael's thumb brushed unintentionally against Sloan's painfully taut nipple, there was no way Sloan could hold back the groan. A pulse beat between her legs—once, twice. She was losing it. "Michael," she gasped in desperation. "Stop."

Michael froze. *Oh no, not again.*

Had she been more certain of the signs and less hurt by the recent rejection, Michael would have done what her instincts were crying out for her to do. She would have taken Sloan's face in both hands and kissed her with all the abandon of fifteen lonely years; she would have driven a possessive hand down that long flat abdomen with all the ferocity of a hunter claiming its prey; she would have answered the simmering want between Sloan's thighs until she satisfied *both* their hungers. Even as she forced herself to be still, she could see the liquid need in Sloan's eyes. She could almost taste her desire.

"My God, what is it?" Michael cried. "Sloan. Tell me."

"Please," Sloan whispered urgently, "I can't take it. You're going to make me...just...give me a second." When she could control her unsteady legs, she forced herself to stand, took a step away, and jammed her hands into her pockets to hide their trembling. "Sorry. I...sorry."

"Are you always this hard to seduce?" Michael asked softly. Her own hands were shaking.

"My sweet Michael...you could seduce me with a smile. In fact, you *did*, that very first day in the office. I've done nothing except think about you ever since. I've wanted to touch you so many times."

"Then what?" Michael persisted, confused and hurt.

Michael's pain was palpable, and Sloan hated knowing that she was to blame. Frustrated, she spoke without thinking. "Christ, I practically came just now from you kissing me."

Although secretly pleased, Michael responded just as heatedly. "Is that supposed to make me feel better?"

"Yes. No. Oh, hell, I don't know." Sloan grimaced, sweeping her arm in a circle to indicate the rest of the room. "I'm supposed to be *working* here, not bedding you."

Michael ignored the edge of anger in Sloan's voice. Whatever the cause, she knew that she wasn't the target. "But that's not it, is it?"

Sloan was silent. She needed to clear her head, make some sense of what was happening. She needed to tell her. *Jesus, tell her what? That I'm scared to death?*

"Just give me a few more hours to get on top of this, and then we'll take a walk...talk," Sloan finally said. *Something, anything...as long as you don't touch me again right now.*

"Deal." Michael nodded wearily, still reeling from the staggering realization of how much she wanted her. She had never dreamed it possible. She longed to say, *as long as you don't go away*, but she didn't dare. She didn't have the right. She would simply have to trust Sloan to come back to her.

"I'm going to find Jason and see how he's doing with the data retrieval. I might be a while." Sloan hesitated; she didn't want to leave.

"I understand," Michael said, fairly reasonably, though she was loath to let Sloan out of her sight. She watched her walk away with a sense of loss, then sat behind her desk and stared at the unfinished work. *How am I supposed to concentrate now?*

To her surprise, Sloan returned just a few moments later, an odd expression on her face. Michael looked up from her desk and asked, "Did you find him?"

"No, not exactly," Sloan said, still trying to dispel the image of Sarah and Jason entwined on a sofa in the conference room, completely unaware of her presence. She was well beyond the point in her life when any form of sexual expression could disturb her, but there had been no doubt that Sarah's hand was on Jason's fly, and that at any moment her hand would be inside his pants. While Sloan applauded their spontaneity, she had no desire to witness this degree of intimacy between her friends. She had hastily retreated. "He was, ah...involved."

Michael gaped at her in astonishment, taking her meaning from her tone. "My God, what is it tonight? Something in the office air?"

"Apparently," Sloan said ruefully. "Carpe diem," she said to herself. She glanced at the computer. *Yeah, right.*

Close to 10:00 p.m., Sloan announced, "I think that might do it for now." She leaned back in her chair, stretching her cramped shoulders and back. "With any luck, you should be able to start work again tomorrow morning. There are still a few things Jason will probably need to finish, and then I can work on tracing where this came from."

"At this point," Michael said from across the room, "I don't care if the whole goddamned system goes up in smoke. You need to take a break. Now."

Sloan nodded her agreement. She was tired, but exhilarated as well with the thrill of having beaten the damn bug.

"I'm taking you to dinner," Michael said, sensing an opening. She had respected Sloan's wishes to let her work, but she hadn't forgotten what had happened earlier. Her body still throbbed. "You've earned it."

"I need to take a shower and change clothes," Sloan amended. "Do you mind stopping at my place first?"

"Anywhere," Michael said. "As long as it's away from here."

They drove the short distance across town in Sloan's car, the silence companionable as both of them relaxed and let the stress of the last few days recede. When Sloan turned onto one of the streets in the heart of Old City and slowed in front of a familiar building, Michael exclaimed, "You live here?"

"Yep," Sloan answered as she keyed the remote to open the ground-floor garage doors in the warehouse where her office was located. "Top floor."

The narrow side street retained much of its historic charm as evidenced by the original cobblestone streets, horse hitches, and hand-laid brick sidewalks. At the rear of the garage, the original freight elevator gave access to the upper floors. When the two women exited on the top floor and Sloan slid open the double doors leading to her living space, Michael gasped in delighted pleasure.

"This is great!"

"Thanks."

The huge space had a high ceiling and was completely open, different functional areas simply delineated by the strategic place-ment of furniture and scattered area rugs. Across the room, floor-to-ceiling windows afforded a sweeping panoramic view of the waterfront and their sister city across the river.

Michael walked to the windows and looked out, enjoying the flickering lights of sailboats and cabin cruisers that glittered on the glass-like surface of the water. "I've seen it so many times, but never like this."

"Uh...I need to get cleaned up," Sloan said, still standing just inside the door. It was so strange, and yet so right, to have Michael there. "There's beer, wine, and sparkling water in the kitchen. Just help yourself."

"Sloan," Michael called impulsively as Sloan started to turn away. "How about if we just order pizza and stay here? The view is so beautiful, and I'm not sure I want to face the crowds."

Michael looked so relaxed and so lovely that Sloan felt her throat tighten. Just that quickly, she was awash with desire again. Swallowing, she backed up a few steps. "Sure. There are menus in the kitchen by the phone. Anything you like is fine with me."

Then Sloan practically fled around the partition that sepa-rated her bedroom and bathroom from the common space in the rest of the loft. Michael stared after her, wondering what had prompted that quick flash of fear in those expressive eyes. What-ever the cause, she was determined not to leave until she discov-ered the answer.

Her hair wet from the shower, Sloan emerged barefoot from

her bedroom in a clean shirt and jeans. Michael was just opening the pizza, which she had placed on the coffee table in the living room. She looked up with a smile.

"You're just in time."

"God, that smells great," Sloan exclaimed, flopping down gratefully on one end of a large leather sectional facing the windows. "I didn't realize before how hungry I am."

Michael handed her a plate and sat down beside her. She poured two glasses of wine and handed one to Sloan. "Bon appetit."

Sloan took the glass, saluted Michael, and grinned. "Amen."

They attacked the food with enthusiasm, and neither spoke more than a few words until the box was nearly empty.

"That was terrific," Sloan said as she leaned back contentedly.

"I know I promised you dinner, but I didn't have pizza in mind," Michael said with a laugh. "On the other hand," she indicated her borrowed clothing, "I'm hardly dressed for anything elegant tonight."

"I think you look incredible," Sloan said appreciatively. Though Sarah's jeans and blouse were slightly big on Michael's taller, more slender form, she still looked casually lovely. "Besides, it's the company that counts, and you more than make up for anything we might be missing at Les Deux Cheminees."

Michael blushed and looked away. After a moment, she asked softly, "Are you this charming with every woman?"

"Oh, Michael—*no.*" Sloan stared at her in astonishment, hating for her to think that. "Don't you know how very beautiful you are? And so incredibly sexy—Jesus, you practically make my heart stop."

"Then what is it?" Michael looked at her steadily. "Is there something here I'm missing? Something I'm supposed to do or say?"

"It's not *you,*" Sloan said vehemently.

Michael's disbelief and lingering hurt shadowed her blue eyes, but she said nothing.

"I'm sorry," Sloan said bitterly. "It's never been because of you, and if I've made you think that for one minute..."

She got up abruptly and went to the windows, her back to the room and the woman on the sofa. Though she gazed out, she was not seeing the waterfront or the lights flickering like stars fallen to earth; she was remembering the sounds and sights of the nation's capital. It seemed like only yesterday, the pain was still so fresh. Finally she turned, leaned against the window casement, and began to speak.

"When my tour in Thailand was over, I came back to Washington and was assigned to the Justice Department. I had a lot more experience than most of the other people working in computer crimes at that time. They moved me up fairly quickly even though I was young, and pretty soon I was heading a new unit that was similar to an internal affairs division in a police department.

"I was testing our own internal security measures, looking for leaks. I answered directly to a member of the Justice Department—a special prosecutor assigned to deal with computer crimes. That included prosecuting members of government agencies as well. It was publicly very low profile, because obviously evidence of security leaks within the government does not produce confidence in the administration. By the same token, any government employee found to be responsible for, or even remotely connected to, breaches in security was dealt with swiftly. Since it was a fairly new area of investigation and prosecution, overreaction was common when it came to dealing with individuals suspected of a crime. The prosecutors often brought charges first and got the details later."

Sloan returned to the sitting area and poured herself more wine. With effort, she controlled her agitation enough to sit down on a portion of the sectional adjoining Michael's. For a moment, she stared into the wine, aimlessly turning the glass between her long fingers. God, she hadn't thought about it, not consciously, in so long. But it was still so raw that her mind reeled from the memories.

"And then I fell in love with the special prosecutor," she continued, her voice harsh with anger. "She was twelve years older than me and a career government attorney. I think she had already set her sights on the attorney general's office. She was very paranoid about anyone discovering our relationship, although I'm not convinced it would have made a difference. Nevertheless, I was young enough to believe her when she said we had to keep our relationship secret. And I was naïve enough to accept her disavowal of me whenever it suited her." Sloan sighed. "And of course, I believed her when she said she loved me, too."

She drained her glass and set it carefully on the glass-topped coffee table next to the pizza box. She searched Michael's face for a reaction. What she found there was the compassion and comfort she had longed for but had abandoned any hope of finding. It gave her the strength to finish the story.

"I wasn't completely inexperienced. I'd had affairs, but nothing really serious, and I was still foolish enough to believe in the power of love. I would have done anything she wanted. She actually pretended in public to have a long-standing relationship with a male attorney, and she attended official functions with him now and then. She said she never slept with him, but I guess I'll never know. At the time, I trusted her implicitly."

She smiled bitterly, casting Michael an apologetic glance. "I'm sorry. This sounds like every other relationship-gone-bad story I've ever heard. I didn't mean to subject you to this."

"No, don't stop," Michael said quickly and firmly. "I want to know. Please."

"I've never said all of this out loud." Sloan took a deep breath and steeled herself for the rest. "We'd been together almost two years, and for the last six months of that I had been spearheading an investigation of a division of the National Security Agency attached to the Joint Chiefs. There was a lot of highly sensitive information lying around, so to speak, as well as a 'locked room' with classified military armament codes, all stored on a number of hard drives. My people didn't actually have access to those areas, but we were trying to determine precisely who did.

"To make a long story short, an independent internal audit came up two hard drives short, and when the information leaked to the press, someone needed to take the fall. My lover knew that I had no direct or even indirect responsibility for that particular area, but my name was the most identifiable. She cut a deal with someone, probably a senator on one of the powerful subcommittees who promised to advance her career in exchange for avoiding public embarrassment of the NSA, and she offered them me as part of the bargain." Sloan shrugged. "End of story. I trusted her; she wanted a career perk more."

Michael studied her face thoughtfully. She could hear the pain and betrayal in Sloan's voice, and her heart ached for her. But there was something else she saw in her eyes, something that went far beyond the pain of an imperfect love. There was something bitter and hard in their violet depths.

"Tell me the rest," Michael said gently.

Sloan jerked in surprise, staring at her. After a moment's deliberation, she continued. "They came to my office at Justice in the middle of the day and took me away in handcuffs. News of the impending arrest had been leaked to the press. A mob of reporters was waiting when the police brought me out of the building. Cameras, news teams, people surrounding me...shining lights in my face...strangers shouting at me. I had no idea what was happening." She grimaced briefly at the memory. "She let them do that to me, when an internal review board should have handled it before charges were even delineated. It was Friday afternoon, and I couldn't get an arraignment until Monday morning. I spent the weekend in the D.C. lockup. I was the next best thing to having a cop in jail." Her voice broke on the memory. "It was a very unpleasant weekend."

Michael struggled not to let her horror show. She swallowed painfully, nearly choking on her anguish. "Did they...hurt you?"

"No," Sloan said quickly. "Not that way. Oh, they pushed me around a little bit, but nothing serious. It was more the humiliation of being strip-searched—treated like an animal. They take your clothes; they take your name; they take your entire identity. When you're physically helpless and isolated—defenseless, you lose sight of who you are pretty quickly. The justice system is not kind to the accused."

"I'm so sorry," Michael said in a hushed tone. *How confused you must have been—and how terrified. How could anyone do that to you?*

"It's okay." Sloan saw no reason to tell her of the deep sense of loss and self-doubt she had suffered when she had realized that the woman she loved, whom she trusted with all her soul, had abandoned her in such a heartless way. Worse, perhaps, along with losing her dignity, she had lost faith in her own judgment during those seventy-two interminable hours. Knowing that she had been partly responsible for what had happened every time she had let her lover deny her in public and lie to her in private only added to her self-loathing. She was ashamed, and worse, she didn't even trust herself.

"By Monday morning, my attorney had talked to the Justice Department, and when it became clear that there was no evidence to indict me, they apologized, expunged the record, and offered me a transfer. I didn't resign until a few weeks later, just after I heard what had happened to Jason with the sexual harassment suit. We both left, and six months later we started the business here."

"And there's been no one serious since her?"

"No." She couldn't imagine being that vulnerable to anyone again. With love came too much potential for pain, and she could not pay that price more than once.

Michael was silent, wondering if Sloan still loved this woman. That would explain her affairs, and her unwillingness to make a commitment. She did not ask; she was afraid of how she would feel if Sloan admitted it was true.

Finally, Sloan broke the silence. "Would you like me to take you back to your hotel?"

"No," Michael said very quietly. "I would like you to take me into the bedroom."

"Michael," Sloan began, "I don't thi—"

"Wait," Michael interrupted. "I don't need you to explain or make promises or reassure me. I know what I'm saying. I've been going out of my mind today. I just need to feel you. Tonight, right now. Tomorrow is another lifetime away." As she spoke, Michael moved the few feet to stand in front of Sloan. "Please."

Sloan rose, put her hands on Michael's waist, and held her tenderly. She was instantly aware of the fine trembling in Michael's slender body as she rested her head against Sloan's shoulder with a soft sigh. Pressing her face gently to Michael's hair, breathing in that faint spring scent she remembered from the night in Michael's hotel, Sloan whispered hoarsely, "I want you...so much."

Michael turned her cheek, pressing her lips to Sloan's neck. "Yes."

Chapter
Fourteen

Sloan took Michael's hand and led her gently into the bedroom. Moonlight streamed through the windows, illuminating
them in its soft pale glow. They stood by the bed, faces highlighted
in the silvery luster, the air around them as still and filled with
promise as a bird about to take flight. Her eyes never leaving
Michael's, Sloan slowly and carefully worked each button free on
Michael's blouse. Her hands were shaking, and as she parted the
fabric, she heard Michael catch her breath sharply. Instantly, she
stopped.

"Are you afraid?" Sloan whispered, knowing how new this
was for her. *New for me, too, but in a different way.* She dared not
consider all the ways that being with Michael was extraordinary.

"No," Michael answered immediately and smiled. "Are you?"

"Terrified." The corner of Sloan's mouth lifted in a faint echo
of her usual grin.

"Please don't be, and please..." Michael pressed her palm
lightly to Sloan's face, her fingers playing softly down her cheek.
"Don't stop."

"I can't remember ever wanting anyone like this.
I...I'm...practically paralyzed," Sloan confessed. She was afraid to
go too quickly, afraid her passion would explode, afraid of frightening Michael, afraid of losing her chance to savor each precious
second. These were moments she wanted to burn indelibly into
her memory, knowing they might very well be the most exquisite
of her life.

She contented herself with watching Michael's eyes deepen
with desire as she lightly traced her fingers along the faint ridge of
collarbone, dipping into the small hollow above, then running her

fingertips down the soft slope of Michael's chest. The other
woman's small sounds of pleasure and the fine tremor flickering
through her muscles fired Sloan's blood. She heard the rasping
sounds of her own ragged breathing loud in the hushed space.

"You have wonderful hands," Michael murmured, feeling as if
her bones were melting with each gentle caress. She rested her
palm on Sloan's waist, content to let Sloan undress her. "I've
never been so...never felt like...this...before."

"Are you sure?" Sloan asked, wondering how she would stop
now if Michael asked her to.

"I've never been more certain of anything in my life."

They stood only inches apart, both of them resisting the urge
to press closer. Time hung suspended—each second might have
been an hour, filled to overflowing with wonder. Each sensation
was miraculous, unique and singular, yet as familiar as coming
home.

"You are so beautiful," Sloan whispered, her voice unsteady.
She was trembling with the effort it took to contain herself, her
vision narrowed until all she knew were Michael's eyes and
Michael's mouth. She was no longer conscious of anything beyond
the heat deep inside, the pounding in her head, and the ache in her
chest. Still, she moved carefully, sliding her hands under the edges
of Michael's blouse, parting the cloth as if unveiling a priceless
treasure, lifting the material away and letting it drop to the floor.
Only then did she lower her gaze.

"Oh God." The muscles in Sloan's abdomen clenched and
desire spiraled along her spine. If there had ever been anything to
equal what she saw now, she could not remember. A light sheen of
perspiration covered Michael's skin, accentuating its pale perfection, highlighting her full breasts and taut nipples in shimmering
moonlight. "Perfect," she breathed, still not touching her.

"I'm dying for you to touch me," Michael urged breathlessly,
reaching for Sloan's hands and drawing them to her. She swayed
slightly as all in one quick, possessive motion, Sloan lifted her
breasts, captured her nipples, and squeezed lightly. Michael
moaned, her eyelids fluttering closed. It was too much, too *good.*

"Michael," Sloan gasped, thirsting for Michael's passion, "let
me see your eyes."

With effort, Michael opened her eyes and met Sloan's,
stunned by what she saw in those violet depths—a ferocious intensity, as if Sloan's entire being were focused on her. "No one has

ever looked at me like you do," she said brokenly, cascades of
need rippling through her. "You make me weak, I want you so
much."

"I have to see you...all of you," Sloan insisted. Still fully
clothed, she stepped closer and, with one hand, reached between
them to open Michael's jeans. She pushed them down while sup-
porting Michael with an arm around her waist, and the other
woman stepped free.

For a long moment, Sloan's gaze roamed over Michael's body,
memorizing each wondrous curve and contour. Then she pulled
her close, chest pressing tightly against Michael's breasts, stroking
her back and buttocks and the outsides of her thighs—all the while
kissing her lips, the underside of her jaw, the base of her throat.
She wanted to devour her, to satisfy her consuming hunger with
the sight and sound and feel of her.

"I'm going to fall," Michael warned desperately. Even with
both hands clutching Sloan's shoulders, she was shaking too much
to stand. A fearful pressure was building between her legs, a pleasure so intense she doubted she could contain it for long. "I need
to lie down. I need you to touch me. I'm afraid I'll co—"

"Easy," Sloan whispered soothingly against her skin, stilling
her caresses. Ever so gently, she nuzzled her face between
Michael's breasts, closing her eyes, breathing her in. Then she
turned her cheek, carefully running her tongue over Michael's
tightened nipple. Michael uttered a strangled cry and jerked in
Sloan's arms. Holding her firmly, Sloan guided their bodies
together in a slow sensuous dance. "I want to go slowly. I *need* to
go slowly. I want this night to last a lifetime."

"Please...I don't think I can wait," Michael pleaded. Her head
was spinning, and every drop of blood in her body seemed to be
pulsating between her legs. She had never felt such urgency, had
never sensed such longing, had never needed another's touch so
badly. "I'm going to come apart if you don't do something soon."

Sloan laughed, a wild victorious laugh, and half-carried
Michael to the bed. "Sit down on the edge," she urged, kneeling
on the floor in front of her. Then, throwing off restraint at last,
she cupped Michael's breasts, raised them to her lips, and drank of
her—sucking and biting, one to the other, back and forth, guided
only by Michael's sharp cries of pleasure. Michael's hands were in
her hair, pressing her face into the hot yielding flesh.

"Sloan, Sloan, Sloan," Michael intoned, her neck arched,

head flung back, hips thrusting forward against Sloan's body. She tugged at Sloan's shirt, crazed for the feel of her skin. She gasped at the first unfamiliar, yet oh-so-familiar, softness of smooth skin over tight muscles, awed by the tender strength under her fingers. Dimly, she heard her lover groan.

Sloan stood, pushed Michael back onto the bed, and hurriedly lay beside her, leaning on one elbow so that she could look down the length of her. She ran her hands and then her tongue over the curves, the prominences, the flesh and muscle and bone of her. It was a landscape as known to her as her own body, and yet a world so new she felt the wonder of first discovery all over again.

"I could touch you forever," she said with a sigh. Indeed, she might have been happy simply with caresses, at least until the hunger rose again, if it hadn't been for Michael's escalating whimpers in response to each stroke of her fingers. Those sounds—Michael's need—inflamed her and drove the last shred of reason from her mind. When Michael's fingers went to her fly, pulling at the buttons, searching relentlessly for her clitoris through the wear-softened material, she twitched, dangerously close to explosion.

"Careful," Sloan warned through gritted teeth, pulling her hips back. "Not yet."

"Touch *me* then," Michael begged, grasping Sloan's hand, her pupils so large her eyes seemed to be dark lakes of molten fire. She drew Sloan's fingers down between her thighs, to the place she most desperately needed her, crying out at the first light contact. "Yesohyes."

Sloan convulsed with a low, deep groan, the sweet wet warmth of Michael's welcome so intense that her heart nearly stopped. That simple sign of Michael's desire was more precious than anything she had ever felt. All she knew was the need to please her, and in an instant the flame in her stilled to pure crimson embers, all the more hot for its containment. With gentle fingers, she parted swollen tissues, stroking along, beside, and under the pulsating prominence, never quite touching the heart of the fire.

"Inside, please inside," Michael begged, her fingers boring into Sloan's shoulders as every muscle strained toward release. The terrible sweet tension strummed through her limbs, making her shiver helplessly.

Gasping, Sloan lowered her forehead to Michael's, her eyes

closed. She drew Michael close to her chest with one arm around her back and eased into her. She withdrew almost completely only to return, deeper, again and again, until she filled her. Then she remained motionless and let Michael lead.

Hips thrusting, Michael rocked in time to the surge of her blood and the hum of her nerves and the coiling ache in her belly. Devouring Sloan's mouth, alternately kissing and sucking at her lower lip, she rode Sloan's fingers ever faster, following the primal rhythm thundering through her soul.

Sloan's arm ached from holding back. Barely managing to contain the wild urge to drive into her, she ignored the pain of her rigid muscles and clenched her jaws against the thundering pressure moving relentlessly through her own body, demanding satisfaction. This was for Michael, and she would follow her wherever she needed to go.

"Almostalmost," Michael whimpered frantically, her movements erratic—shorter and harder—her hips jerking wildly. "Need...your fingers...on me."

"Soon...soon, love," Sloan murmured, sensing Michael's muscles tightening for the final surge. As she waited for the peak, she circled the flat of her hand over Michael's clitoris. When she felt Michael's breath stop and body poise on that timeless edge of abandon, she stroked the shaft once, twice, and drove her over.

Michael cried out and gripped Sloan so hard that there would be bruises in the morning. The force of the contractions drew her body bowstring-tight, and she arched in Sloan's arms, shuddering.

"Michael," Sloan gasped, completely lost. *Too beautiful, you are too beautiful to bear.*

Beyond words, Michael floated somewhere, deaf and blind, reduced to only quivering flesh and spasming muscle. How long she hung suspended on that crest of sensation escaped her, but eventually she was aware of her body again—the air moving in her lungs, her heart pounding in her chest, her blood coursing beneath her skin. She felt more alive than she ever had before and more supremely content than she had ever thought possible.

Releasing her hold on Sloan's shoulders, she collapsed back against the pillows. With effort, she opened her eyes and found Sloan's face, discovering there a look of tenderness, wonder, and something else. Something feral seethed in her hazy eyes and flickered just beneath the surface.

"You are exquisite," Sloan declared, her voice hoarse and

choked.

Michael heard the hunger and felt her shudder violently. She sensed Sloan's need, and suddenly, she wanted to satisfy *her* more than she had had ever wanted anything in her life.

"Take off your clothes. Quickly," Michael rasped, frantically tugging at Sloan's jeans.

Michael's unexpected and undeniable lust drove Sloan beyond the edge of control. Suddenly burning, she tore off her shirt, raising her hips as Michael pulled down her constraining jeans. "Jesus, you make me crazy," she gasped.

"Tell me what to do," Michael cried urgently. "Tell me what you need." Her hands were running over Sloan's back, her chest, her abdomen, trying to feel all of her at once.

"Just touch me. I'll come...I'm so close from touching you."

When Michael's fingers found her clitoris, sliding under and over and back again, Sloan was gone. "Oh...JesusGodMichaelMichael..."

Michael struggled to hold her as she bucked and gasped, helpless—and so, so beautiful. She thought she had known power in the competitive world of business, but that had been nothing compared to this. This, *this* was power so sweet her throat closed around tears of gratitude and wonder.

"Sloan," she whispered, almost a prayer. "Oh, Sloan."

As the first spasms quieted, Sloan sighed and rested her head on Michael's shoulder. "God," she mumbled, "that was so good."

"Uh-huh." Michael laughed softly, stroking Sloan's sweat-soaked hair off her face. "You okay?"

"Mmm," Sloan responded, trying valiantly to rouse herself. It wouldn't do to fall asleep right now. Very déclassé. She pushed up on an elbow and smiled a bit dazedly at Michael. "Beyond okay. Excellent. You?"

"I have never been better in my life." Michael's smile sparkled all the way to her eyes.

"I'm glad," Sloan whispered, kissing her lightly. "Are you tired?"

"I could sleep," Michael admitted, suddenly aware that it was late. She did not know what the morning would bring. All she knew was that she did not want the night to end. "But I don't want to."

Sloan grinned—slow and easy and just a bit dangerously—and kissed her again. "Good."

Chapter
Fifteen

At 5:45 p.m. the next afternoon, Michael turned from her drawing board as a soft knock at the door interrupted her. "Come in."

The door swung open and Sarah peeked around the corner. "Hey," she called, a wide smile on her face. "Are you holding up okay?"

Michael leaned back from the table and sighed. "Seem to be. I have a million things to do and only a couple of days to do it, but everything is up and working at the moment." She watched as Sarah crossed the room and sat down on one of the sofas.

"Excellent," Sarah said. "I just talked to Jason, and he said it's looking good. Sometimes these things can take forever to get straightened out. Apparently this time you were lucky."

"I know," Michael agreed, moving over to join Sarah. "Most of the network is functional again. At least everyone will be able to access it when the work week starts tomorrow. I owe Jason and Sloan more than money. They've been incredible."

"No, they're just doing the job they love to do. You shouldn't feel like you put them out, because you merely provided them with an interesting game to play. I'm amazed that either of them stopped long enough to get any sleep last night." She didn't add that she had noticed both Michael and Sloan were absent at the same time, nor did she volunteer that Jason had spent a good part of the evening with her.

"Have you seen Sloan recently?" Michael asked, trying to sound nonchalant. Unfortunately, her heart was pounding just from saying her name. They had parted only a short time before, but it seemed to Michael that it had been days.

"She's in the communications center with Jason, supervising the final system checks and satisfying herself that everything is running okay. Do you need her?" Sarah asked innocently.

Need her? Michael almost laughed out loud at the question. *Oh yes, that seems to be the word for it, all right.*

A few hours earlier, she had been with her, and she could still recall every word they had said and every emotion she had experienced as if it had been etched on her skin and burned into her soul.

She awoke from a light doze, startled in the first moments of awareness to feel someone beside her. She had awakened alone for a very long time. Then in the next instant, she knew where she was and remembered every second of the incredible night in vivid detail. The memory stirred an avalanche of desire, and she was immediately, completely aroused. It was such a foreign sensation, this wanting, that she didn't know what to do. Opening her eyes, she found Sloan lying quietly beside her, gazing at her with a look of such tenderness it stole her breath.

"I'm sorry, I fell asleep," Michael whispered.

"I think that's supposed to happen when you've been awake all night." Sloan smiled, a gentle smile that melted her heart. "Especially when you've been awake all night making love."

Michael blushed, partly because it was all so new to her, and partly because she wanted to do it all again—immediately. She asked quietly, "Did you sleep?"

"No. I didn't want to miss a moment with you."

"I can't decide if your words or your touch is the more beautiful," Michael confessed, leaning close to find Sloan's lips with her own. Her physical arousal had seemed so powerful just a moment ago, but the feelings evoked by Sloan's tenderness were even more compelling. Michael's kiss was part wonder, part gratitude, and part simple appreciation for the affectionate attention and careful way Sloan had loved her over the past hours.

"Thank you so much for last night," she murmured, unconsciously pressing closer until her breasts nestled against Sloan's and her thigh rested on Sloan's leg.

Sloan stopped kissing her long enough to respond, "Michael, please don't thank me. This night has been so special to me, and you've been...wonderful."

"It was more than special..." Michael whispered, and kissed her again.

The kiss slowly deepened until they sought more, caressing each other with their lips, their tongues, their hands. Sloan rolled on top, straddling Michael's hips, and pushed up on her elbows to look into Michael's face. Rasping with urgency, she said, "I want you again...so much. I can't seem to get enough."

"I love the way you want me." Michael knew only that she needed her close, and, guided by instinct, she gripped Sloan's hips and pulled her down hard onto her own tensed thigh. She watched in wonder as Sloan arched her back and gasped, her eyes growing cloudy with arousal. "Is that good?"

"Oh, yeah," Sloan said with a laugh. "That's good."

Michael pressed upward, thrilling to the sensation of Sloan thrusting back, and the rhythm grew between them as naturally as breathing. Michael kept one hand on Sloan's hips as she explored Sloan's breasts with the other, cupping each one, losing herself in the soft flesh and firm muscles, glorying in the heat of her. Sloan's movements became erratic, harder, just a bit frantic, and Michael felt her, wet and hard, against her own thigh. "Can you? Like this?"

"Yes...want to...bad..." Her voice was tight as if she were straining to form each word as she braced herself on her arms to look into Michael's eyes. It was an image of such intensity, and such intimacy, that Michael ached.

"Do it," Michael urged, but she wasn't sure Sloan could hear. "Let me see you."

"I'm coming," Sloan managed, her face intent, her eyes hazy, unfocused, as she slipped toward the edge. Then her lids fluttered closed, her arms stiffened, and her legs tightened around Michael's thigh. She held herself upright as her body rippled with tension and then convulsed sharply, one sharp cry wrenched from her.

Michael's heart surged with something as close to ecstasy as she had ever known. She gripped Sloan's hips tightly and shouted, triumphant. "Yes! Yesyesyes!"

She forgot to breathe for long moments as she gazed in absolute wonder at Sloan's face. She was dimly aware of her own passion surging a path from her pelvis down her legs, but nothing she was feeling could equal what she saw. "What you make me feel... Oh, Sloan."

At last, Sloan dropped her head, her arms finally relaxing, and she lowered herself to lie on Michael's body, trembling, heart-breakingly helpless. Michael held her, stroked her damp hair, her neck, her back, suddenly experiencing a fierce protectiveness she had never before imagined. She understood in that moment what it meant to want someone more than life—to need someone in the deepest reaches of her being.

Sarah's words echoed in her mind. *"Do you need her?"*
Oh yes, I need her.
"Michael?"
Michael jumped, abruptly aware of her surroundings again. Sarah was looking at her with an expression of perplexity and mild concern.
"Are you okay?" the redhead asked gently.
"God, I have no idea." Michael laughed shakily, running a hand through her hair. "I have only the faintest idea of who I am or what I'm doing these days."
Sarah studied her, thinking that she looked tired. Somehow, though, she didn't think Michael's distraction and disorientation were due to fatigue. This was something else, something power-fully emotional, something—
"What's happened? It's Sloan, isn't it?"
"Yes, it's Sloan, but—"
"What's she done now?" Sarah asked, immediately protec-tive, thinking that if Sloan had done something to wound Michael's feelings, she would have to kill her. Michael was too kind and too innocent for Sloan to treat her in the casual way she did most women. Not that she believed for a minute that Sloan was cold-hearted or indifferent about her romantic partners, but she knew that Sloan studiously avoided any real emotional attach-ments, and Michael deserved much more than that.
"*She* hasn't done anything," Michael said quickly, recogniz-ing the edge of concern in Sarah's voice. "It's *me,* too. So many things have changed so quickly lately."
"But *something's* happened between you two, hasn't it?" Sarah persisted.
"Yes."
"You slept with her, didn't you?" Sarah asked, suddenly real-izing that Michael was manifesting all the signs of a woman totally lost in love.

Michael colored, but nodded affirmatively.

"Well." Sarah sighed softly. "I guess I don't have to ask you how it was."

"No." Michael laughed and blushed even deeper. "There wouldn't be any point. I don't even have the words to describe it."

"Great," Sarah said with resignation, although she was smiling. "Things are even worse than I thought."

"Sarah," Michael said, suddenly serious, "Sloan was not responsible. In fact, if I hadn't literally chased her down, I think she would have done anything to avoid sleeping with me. I just wanted her so much."

"And she...gave in?"

"I didn't give her much choice." Michael grinned, heady with the memories still.

"Amazing." Sarah didn't think Michael understood how significant her words were. If Sloan had been avoiding a sexual relationship, it could only be because Sloan had real feelings for Michael. She had no idea how Sloan was going to react to a woman she cared about, but she had a feeling that it wasn't going to be simple. "So, are you okay with that? Sleeping with her, I mean?"

"Am I okay with that?" Michael repeated the question, her voice pensive. "I'm as okay as I can be, I guess. I had an incredible experience with her. I felt things I've never felt in my life. I can't stop thinking about her; I can't stop wanting to be with her again. And I have no idea what this means for me *or* what it means to her. For all I know, she might consider it a one-time thing."

"Well, *I'm* certainly the last one to give advice," Sarah said quietly, thinking that she had been the one surprised when Jason had whispered *not yet* last night when she had reached for him. "But I will tell you that I know what a good person she is, even if she does try to hide it. I love her, and I would trust her with my life. Be patient with her, Michael. This might be hard for her, too."

"I can be patient, as long as she lets me. I've got time. It's taken me fifteen years to understand what I really want."

"And you think it's her?"

"I can't imagine anyone else making me feel what she has," Michael replied softly. "And that's about all I know."

She remembered the look on Sloan's face when they had parted that afternoon in the hall outside Michael's office. For a moment, she thought Sloan had been about to say something, and the look on her face had been one of longing and desire. Instead, Sloan had reached out and stroked her cheek, leaning finally to kiss her lips in a soft caress.

Only then had Sloan whispered, "No matter what happens, last night will always be precious to me."

Michael had merely nodded, afraid that what Sloan had really meant was *goodbye*.

Sloan found Jason in the communication center in very nearly the same place she had left him the night before. He had showered, changed his clothes, and somehow managed to look fresh after what couldn't have been much sleep. She avoided contemplating where *he* had spent the night and steadfastly ignored the image of him and Sarah grappling on the sofa.

"Have we got it fixed?" she asked as she crossed the room and pulled a chair over next to him.

"More or less—given the time frame. It will do for the short term."

"Is it secure?"

"As much as it can be without installing iris or fingerprint recognition devices," he muttered, not taking his eyes off the symbols on the screen.

Sloan looked at him with interest. "Do we have that?"

"No, but the Pentagon does," he answered with a grin.

Sloan grinned, too. "We still have some friends in that neighborhood, don't we?"

Jason turned, giving her a stern look. "We do, and I think we should work on keeping them for a while. Pirating national-security-level toys probably isn't the best way to do it...not until we really need them, at least."

"Probably a good point." She nodded in agreement. "I've told Michael she can go ahead and start working. She has to get into the system to finish what she needs before her meeting Tuesday."

"She should be all right. I'm just giving it a final run-through. I think everything is as clean and tight as we can make it. I still have back-checking on the virus origins to do, but that shouldn't interfere with what she's doing. I made copies of the code to analyze on the guinea pig machine back at the office."

"Good. The sooner we know what it is and where it came

from, the better. With these meetings of Michael's coming up, I don't trust someone not to try this again. If it's someone on the inside, especially someone with *help,* she's still vulnerable."

"You think it's Burke?"

"I do," she said grimly. "And maybe Mayfield. He's been less than forthcoming with assistance. Once we're fully operational, I'll stop in after hours when he's not here to run the internal traces." She paused, then added, "Let Michael know that you'll be available day or night if something else comes up."

"Is there some reason *you* won't be available?" Jason shifted his concentration from the monitor, studying her curiously. "Incident response *is* your department. After this weekend, I'll be more than happy to get back to the office. I don't mind backing you up with tech support in an emergency, but the business end of things is easier on my social life."

Her expression was unreadable and her violet eyes so dark they approached black. "Just do it, please, Jason," she said in a tone of voice that brooked no argument.

She wasn't sure what, if anything, she was going to do about Michael. She hadn't expected last night to ever happen, and she surely had not anticipated her reaction to it. She had learned to accept the comfort of another in her bed as a momentary surcease from loneliness and a temporary antidote to isolation, but she had never again expected to be really touched by someone. That had been just fine, because she never again wanted to be vulnerable to the vagaries of another's affections.

But Michael...Michael is different. She's so open and so totally guileless. She's so easy to care about...so easy to need.

"Did you two fight?"

"What?" Sloan laughed humorlessly. "No, we didn't fight."

It's just that she's touched me...touched my heart. And now those places ache. For her. Sloan flinched without meaning to and tried to put Michael from her mind. "I'll leave you to finish up."

Jason wanted to say more, but there was something about her expression that warned him off. Usually, he did not hesitate to take Sloan to task for what he considered her uncivilized behavior in personal relationships.

This time, however, he sensed her still unhealed wounds very near the surface. Her eyes were haunted with old hurts. As much as she knew about his past, he knew about hers. They had both been betrayed by someone they believed had loved them, and that betrayal had led to their professional discrediting. They rarely spoke of the past, but he knew firsthand how long the pain could linger. Whatever the situation with Michael, he had a feeling it was far more serious than Sloan wanted to admit.

Until a short time ago, he would have agreed with her reluctance to become seriously involved, her resistance to take that risk again. But meeting Sarah had changed everything about how he viewed matters of the heart. Sarah was teaching him that it was possible to be safe, even while exposing his deepest secrets. He hadn't been ready for sex the night before, and he had worried that his reluctance would be seen as rejection. But Sarah had understood even that. She had left a note with his car keys on her way out of his apartment—*Ask Jasmine if she'll go out dancing with me Saturday night.*

It had taken Sarah and her singular sensitivity to lead him to the point of trust. It didn't seem so impossible to him now that someone could do the same for Sloan. In fact, having watched Michael and Sloan together over the past weeks, he had glimpsed an entirely different Sloan. When she was around Michael, there was a tenderness and vulnerability about her that he had never seen before. It was almost as if Michael, without even realizing it, had awakened those parts of Sloan that she had kept hidden from everyone, including herself.

"Sloan?"

She turned at the door and looked back, a question on her face.

"Michael will wonder why you don't call," he said, unwilling to let her go without trying to change her mind. Loneliness was a heartless companion. He knew.

She stared at him, wondering if by some strange sixth sense he knew just how significant that statement was. She wasn't thinking about business but the night that she and Michael had shared as she answered quietly, "I know, Jason. But maybe it's the best thing."

Chapter
Sixteen

Wordlessly, Michael walked past Angela and pushed through the door into her office. She crossed to her desk and slumped into the tall leather chair behind it. Two minutes later, a knock sounded. Sighing, she said tiredly, "Come in."

"So? Tell," Angela demanded, crossing the room to lean against the front of Michael's desk. She peered at her for a second, then asked gently, "You okay? You need anything?"

"No, I'm fine," Michael replied, resting her head against the back of the chair and allowing herself a few seconds of respite. And a few seconds was all she had. There was so much to do. Forcing herself upright, she smiled wanly. "We're still in the running."

"Congratulations," Angela crowed, smiling broadly. Hastily, she added, "I never doubted it."

"Well, that makes one of us." Michael pushed both hands through her hair, then shrugged her shoulders, still tight with tension. "That was the longest morning of my life."

"Was Nick there?"

"Oh, he was there."

"Was he—"

"*Polite* was what he was," Michael said with an expression of distaste. "Polite, condescending, and suggesting—ever so subtly—at every opportunity that *what* we had to sell wasn't nearly as important as *how* we sell it."

Angela snorted. "The old development-versus-marketing argument."

"And in this case, my expertise versus his." She rubbed her

temples, trying hard to forget the thinly veiled loathing in his eyes. It shocked her still to realize how much he had changed, or maybe it had been her. *Both of us, probably.* Rationally, she knew that he felt threatened by the divorce, not personally, but financially, and perhaps that really did account for his animosity. No amount of soul-searching now was going to answer that question, and she had neither the time nor the inclination for it. She had moved on, moved beyond *him.* Sighing again, she added, "Today at least, I had an answer. I presented the prospectus for the automotive project, and I had preliminary bargaining points already ironed out."

"Ha," Angela cheered. "Covering *both* sides of the field. I'll bet he was surprised."

"I think he was surprised that I was able to put it all together in time for today's managers' meeting," Michael mused, remembering the look of astonishment on his face when she'd begun her presentation. "I have a feeling he expected me to have been delayed by *technical* difficulties."

"Like a network failure, maybe?" Angela asked astutely. "You don't really think I believed that Sloan's crew slept here all weekend for nothing, do you?"

Michael looked at her sharply. "Who else knows?"

"No one. I sent out the memo on Friday like you requested about the routine system maintenance and then a follow-up bulletin yesterday saying the *upgrades* were complete."

"Thanks. I didn't think of that."

"You were a little busy," Angela said gently.

"Yes. And now I'm *a lot* busy. I'm sure Nicholas is not going to just walk away after one small skirmish."

"What next?"

"You mean in addition to the open accounts I've still got to work on and finalizing the agreements with Nicholas about the divorce and the business?" She smiled ruefully. "I want to get back to what I do best—design. But before I do that, I'm going to need you to pull some personnel files." At Angela's questioning expression, she added, "It's time to start looking for Nicholas's replacement."

"Just say the word," Angela replied as she turned for the door. "I'll gladly work overtime free of charge for that."

"Angela..."

Angela turned expectantly.

"Has Sloan called?"

"No messages. Do you need me to get her for you?"

"No," Michael said quickly. "If she—" *If she had wanted to talk to me, she would have called.* "Thanks, Angela. But don't bother."

The door closed behind Angela and she was finally alone. Eyes closed, it wasn't her morning's victory she considered. It was the sound of Sloan's voice and the memory of making love with her.

One night. One night to live on—for how long?

During the first five minutes of the match, Sarah managed to land two respectable blows solidly on Sloan's jaw, then executed a leg sweep that knocked her definitively on her ass. Subsequently, she stepped back out of fighting range, dropped her hands, and stared at her friend.

"Would you care to tell me where your mind is?"

"It's nothing." Sloan shook her head, getting slowly to her feet. "Come on, let's spar."

"Uh-uh. Not so fast." It was Sarah's turn to shake her head. "Sloan, you know how much I love any opportunity to beat up on you, but it's just no fun when you're defenseless. What's wrong?"

Sloan's first impulse was to deny any problem. She didn't want to think about anything, let alone try to explain her state of mind to Sarah. But her old friend was too damn perceptive and too damn persistent to let anything go. The moment Sarah noticed the slightest bit of inconsistency or evasiveness, she worked away at it until the whole damn barricade fell, and every secret Sloan ever had was laid bare for her inspection. *Granted, she's always given me just the support I need, but this is one time I do not want to hear what Sarah has to say.*

"If you don't want to spar, let's just lift for a while," Sloan grumbled, turning toward the door that led into the weight room. She was surprised when she felt Sarah's hand on her arm, restraining her gently. She sighed and looked over her shoulder at the redhead. Sarah's eyes were affectionate and reassuring. "What?"

"Come on, Sloan. I know damn well something's going on, and I'm pretty sure I know what it is. It's Wednesday night, and you haven't been into the office all week. Jason told me this morning that you've been AWOL since Sunday afternoon. Want to tell me what's going on?"

"Not especially." Sloan spoke more sharply than she intended, and realizing it, added, "Do I have a choice?"

"You always have a choice, but sometimes you're too pigheaded to see it," Sarah retorted, a slight smile on her face.

Sloan took a long, deep breath, crossed to the side of the room, and flopped down on a pile of exercise mats that had been stacked along the wall. Sarah joined her and waited expectantly.

"It's nothing as dramatic as you're imagining," Sloan said at length. She was lying on her back, arms behind her head, staring resolutely at the ceiling. "We've been running at a fast pace all spring, and after this latest thing with Michael, I just wanted a little break." She was amazed that she could mention Michael's name without stumbling, because thinking about Michael made her pulse jump, and saying her name out loud brought a lump to her throat. She had, in fact, spent the better part of three days trying not to think about her.

That had been largely unsuccessful, since there were only so many things she could find to occupy her mind, and even then her concentration was sketchy. At least a dozen times a day she would glance at the clock, wondering if Michael was in a meeting, or how her project presentations were progressing, or if Nicholas had appeared on the scene to cause more problems. At least twice an hour, she would find herself with the phone in her hand, ready to call Jason at Innova for an update. But then Michael might answer, and if she heard her voice...

Each time she had gently placed the phone back in its cradle, realizing that if she took one step in Michael's direction, she would not be able to stop. And she wasn't sure that was a good idea at all. The problem was, she wasn't sure of anything, and that was as confusing to her as anything else that had happened since meeting Michael. She ran her hands through her hair and closed her eyes.

"Why can't I just take a little time off like anyone else?"

"Uh-huh," Sarah responded agreeably, choosing not to comment on Sloan's obvious distress. "A break. I could buy that if it were anyone but you. I can't remember the last time you voluntarily took a break. Does this have to do with Michael?"

Sloan blew out a breath, too exhausted to keep up pretenses when Sarah would eventually get it out of her anyway. "Most of it."

"Look, sweetie, I'm not trying to pry into your personal life, it's just that I really care about you. And Michael, too. You're one of my oldest friends, and I've loved you for a long time. I haven't known Michael very long at all, but it's easy to care about her. Sometimes when you get thrown together with someone during a crisis, you get to know them better than people you've known for years. You find out pretty fast what they're made of. She's special."

"I know."

"If it makes it any easier, I already know that you slept with her."

Sloan jerked her head around. "She told you?"

"She didn't have to," Sarah said with a soft laugh. "It was pretty obvious that something major had happened to her, and I guessed. She has feelings for you, old friend, and I have a suspicion that it's reciprocal."

"That's the problem. She's not like the other women I've been dating. She doesn't have any experience with this kind of thing, and I'm afraid..." Sloan's voice trailed off as she tried to analyze what she had been avoiding for so long. *What exactly* am *I afraid of?*

"I agree that she's *inexperienced*, but I don't think she's naïve." Sarah nudged Sloan's leg with her foot affectionately. "She's an extraordinarily intelligent, successful woman, and she has been remarkably calm during something that would throw most of us completely off balance. She has managed to deal with her husband's threats, still do the work she's needed to do, *and* handled all of her feelings for you, too. That's an amazing accomplishment, and I think you're doing her a disservice to think she doesn't know *exactly* what this means."

When her comments were met with silence, Sarah continued quietly, "Don't try to second-guess her, Sloan. I can understand how hard it must be for you to trust her. I know how hard it's been for me with Jason, and I haven't experienced the kind of horrible betrayal that you have. But do you plan to spend the rest of your life having casual sex with women you don't really care about?"

"What the fuck do you care?" Sloan eyed her angrily, her temper dangerously close to meltdown. She was about to object further when she realized that her friend was only stating the truth. "Some people aren't meant for relationships," she said flatly. "I seem to be getting along fine the way things are."

"Fine. Uh-huh." Sarah shrugged dismissively. "Maybe you're right, but somehow I don't buy it. I know you, and I know how tender and caring you can be. If you weren't, I don't believe Michael would have fallen in love with you."

"In love...with me?" Sloan started as if struck. "Did she *say* that?"

"That's my reading of the situation, but you'll have to ask her." Sarah stood, offering Sloan a hand up. "I invited her to go out with Jasmine and me on Saturday night. I decided that if I'm ever going to get Jason to believe I'm crazy about him, I'll have to prove it to Jasmine, too. We're all going dancing at Chances. You know where it is, and if you want to know the answer to your question, come by and ask Michael yourself."

Sloan followed her wordlessly into the weight room, thinking about the cost of dreams and the price of passion.

Chapter
Seventeen

Sloan sat in her car across the street from Chances, watching Saturday night revelers come and go. She'd been debating whether or not to go inside for at least twenty minutes. She knew what the problem was and wasn't particularly proud of herself. If she went inside, she would see Michael. She would have to speak with her, and there was no way that she could see her and talk to her without acknowledging what had happened between them.

And then what? I can't even think it through, let alone talk about it.

That was the wall that she had run into over and over again for the last six days. Every time she got close to admitting what she felt, something approaching terror welled up inside and threatened to choke her. She recognized it, even understood it, but could not seem to control it.

I'm sorry I ran out on you, Michael, but basically, I'm just running scared. Right. That will definitely clear it all up.

Nothing about Michael reminded her of Elise. True, there were similarities—on the surface. They were both successful, intelligent, and professionally accomplished. But there the similarity ended. Where Elise had been icily sophisticated and emotionally remote, Michael was approachable and amazingly sensitive. Michael had captured Sloan's attention from the very first moment they had met, and before long, had claimed her heart as well.

Nevertheless, she was afraid. Afraid of caring, even though the ache of missing Michael these last few days had been worse than any pain she could remember enduring, including that humiliating weekend of incarceration. But the scars were still sensitive; so here she sat, paralyzed. She wanted more than anything to see Michael, yet feared the instant when she looked across the room and knew with certainty that Michael was the key to her happiness.

Watching women walk arm and arm into the bar across the street, feeling more and more alone with each passing second, she thought about something Jason had said just that afternoon.

"Jason, can you get the semiannual financial reports together so I can review them?"

"First thing Monday morning. I'm about to knock off now. Jasmine and Sarah have a hot date tonight."

"Yes, I know." Trying to sound only moderately interested, she asked, *"Isn't Michael supposed to be going with you?"*

"Last I heard," he answered, exasperatingly secretive. *"And I hope I won't be doing anything remotely resembling work the rest of the weekend."*

Sloan struggled not to ask for details. "How do you feel about Sarah and Jasmine going out?"

There was silence for a few seconds, and then Jason's quiet voice replied, "A little scared. But too much of me wants this not to take a chance. Sarah is special, and I don't expect anyone like her to come along again. I can't afford not to trust her."

Sloan stared across the street, believing in her heart that she would regret it for the rest of her life if she didn't take a chance. *Michael is special, too. She was brave enough to tell me how she felt about me—in spite of convention, despite the risk of rejection. I can't afford not to trust her.*

Taking a deep breath, she pocketed her keys and pushed open the car door. As she stepped out, someone called her name. Crossing the street, she scanned the crowded sidewalk. She finally spied Claudia Carson, who stood waiting for her beside the entrance to the club. Making her way to the brunette, Sloan nodded in greeting. "Hello, Claudia. How are you?"

"Better than the last time we met." Claudia smiled ever so slightly. "Still looking for Ms. Right, but I haven't made an ass of myself in at least a couple of weeks. I do owe you an apology."

"No, you don't. I wasn't exactly innocent in the whole deal

either. Sometimes it's easy to fool yourself into thinking you have
no responsibility for the way other people feel, but I think that
might just be a convenient excuse. I'm sorry for the way things
turned out, too."

"Are you?" Surprised by the remorseful tone in Sloan's voice,
Claudia studied her curiously. It would be much easier to forget J.
T. Sloan if she weren't so attractive standing there in her black
jeans and crisp white shirt, maddeningly sexy in her utter disre-
gard for external trappings. "Sorry enough to give it another try?"
Claudia asked lightly, resting her hand on Sloan's forearm to con-
vey she was still quite serious. "No strings attached this time. I
promise."

"I don't think that would be a very good idea," Sloan said,
knowing that she could never go back to casual affairs. No matter
how hard she tried to set boundaries, people still got hurt, and
some of that was her responsibility. Beyond that, she knew that
after what she had experienced with Michael, nothing would ever
reach the places in her that needed to be touched. Michael had
awakened those needs, and after their night together, anything else
would be an empty charade. Anyone else would be a pale substi-
tute.

"Well," Claudia said with a wry grin. "I had to ask."

Sloan reached for the door. "Can I buy you a drink for old
time's sake, though?"

Claudia smiled in gracious defeat and took her arm. "I think
one is about my limit these days. But thanks, I accept."

From across the room, Michael saw Sloan for the first time
since the weekend they'd made love. The last six days had been an
emotional roller-coaster ride. The first few times the phone had
rung, she'd answered with near-breathless anticipation, eager just
to hear Sloan's voice, her skin alive with the memory of her touch.
With each passing day that Sloan stayed away, her excitement
turned to confusion and finally coalesced into a hard ache of
rejection. She remembered Sloan's words the first time they
kissed. *"We'll both regret this in the morning."*

Perhaps Sloan regretted it, but she didn't. God, she could
think of nothing else. She'd tried to keep busy with meetings and
the last-minute details of her projects, and for a while she had
been able to relegate her disappointment to the back of her mind.

As the week wore on, however, all she could think of was Sloan. If that weren't bad enough, her entire body seemed to be reacting to their night together in a fashion completely foreign to her. It was as if some hunger, held at bay for years, had suddenly been awakened. It took only a fleeting memory of their night together to arouse her. She was besieged by an almost insatiable need to see Sloan, hear her voice, feel her touch. She'd had to restrain herself from picking up the phone and asking Sloan what the silence meant.

Seeing Sloan now, her pulse pounded with excitement. In the next instant, her heart plummeted in disappointment.

Well, that explains why she hasn't called. She's with Claudia. I guess a one-night stand is exactly what it was between us. Of course, she never suggested otherwise.

She looked at Sloan standing with Claudia and reminded herself that she had practically begged for the one night they *had* shared. And then she had assured Sloan that she knew what she was doing, had promised that one night would be enough. God, how stupid she'd been. That one night was like a single drop of rain in the desert—sweet, sweet torture—and not nearly enough.

This torture was not sweet; it was agony. She turned away, unable to watch as the stately brunette pressed close to Sloan in the crowd at the bar, draping one hand casually around Sloan's waist as she reached for the drink the bartender offered. *I've got to get out of here.*

She glanced anxiously over the crowded dance floor for her friends, needing to tell them this was a mistake, that she had to leave. She couldn't stay here, not with Sloan so near and her own emotions so out of control. It had seemed so harmless when Sarah suggested she go along to Chances with the two of them—something to get her away from the office and out of her hotel room. Sarah had even hinted that she would appreciate the company on her first *date* with Jasmine.

The one thing that Michael hadn't considered was how painful it would be, surrounded by women holding each other, dancing together, sharing small caresses. It was unbearable. Even seeing the first hesitant touches between Sarah and Jasmine was bittersweet. She was happy for them, but at the same time, their intimate glances made her acutely aware of her own deep longing for Sloan. She might have managed to contain the pain if Sloan hadn't actually appeared. Now, seeing her, she was afraid her agony would turn to tears.

Sloan turned her back to the bar, beer in hand, and surveyed
the crowd. She hadn't thought about going out to a club since the
day she had walked into her office and found Michael Lassiter
waiting for her, because after that she hadn't been interested in a
casual encounter.

Looking around at the familiar mating rituals, she found
them unexpectedly devoid of meaning; what had once filled a
need now seemed pointless. She couldn't help thinking that her
affairs had only been an excuse to avoid her own despair, to deny
just how very much it had hurt when Elise left her.

Pretty cowardly, now that she thought about it. That was one
of the things she loved about Michael, how she refused to run
from disappointment, no matter how hard it was.

Jesus. What am I saying? Love her?

"Did you say something?" Claudia shouted above the din of
voices and music.

"No. Nothing."

She had come to find Michael, and she began to search the
crowd for her, but found another familiar figure first. Slender,
long-legged, unashamedly seductive as always in a short leather
skirt and black Lycra top, Jasmine moved on the dance floor with
the same sensuous grace that had first attracted Sloan's attention
years before in a similar smoke-clouded club. Watching her, she
suddenly realized why Jasmine had been able to fool her so successfully the first time they met. When Jasmine wasn't performing, her appearance was subtly different. What make-up she wore
was carefully applied to highlight her eyes and sculpted cheekbones and to accentuate her lips, but it was far less than the stage
make-up that she wore professionally. Out of costume in normal
clothing, Jasmine appeared unquestionably female.

Sloan watched with just a tinge of envy as Jasmine and Sarah
danced. The beat was heavy and fast, an undercurrent of pulsation
to match the barely contained sexuality seething through the couples pressed close on the dance floor. Jasmine and Sarah's eyes
were locked as their bodies met, melded, then parted—surging
seductively to the evocative tempo. Sarah wore jeans and a tight
cotton T-shirt, and anyone looking at them would've thought her
to be the butch and Jasmine the sleek, sexy femme. Sloan smiled

faintly to herself, thinking how often perceptions could be wrong. Thinking, too, that very often the truth could not be known, only experienced.

She continued her surveillance and finally spied Michael on the far side of the room, threading her way through the mass of people toward the door. It was difficult to tell in the dim, hazy light, but it looked as if she might have been crying.

"Excuse me," she said abruptly to Claudia as she set her beer back on the bar. She shouldered away from the throng at the bar and made it to the exit only a minute behind Michael. Once outside on the sidewalk, she hurriedly looked up and down the street and saw her nearly half a block away.

"Michael!" she shouted, breaking into a run. She caught up quickly and stopped her with a hand on her arm. "Michael," she said gently. Being so close brought an ache to her chest. *I've missed you so much.*

Michael turned, quickly brushing the last of her tears from her cheeks. "Hi," she said softly.

"Hi," Sloan answered, her throat dry. She peered into Michael's face intently, noting the wounded expression she was struggling to hide. "What is it?"

"Nothing," Michael replied, smiling ruefully. She wasn't going to embarrass them both again. She had nearly begged her once, and that was enough. "I just had a bad moment there. It's been a tough few days."

"It's been a tough few *weeks,*" Sloan agreed, gazing deep into Michael's eyes. She didn't notice the people stepping around them as they stood in the center of the sidewalk, bathed in the streetlight's pale golden glow. All she could see was Michael. "But it's been an amazing time, too." She gently slipped her fingers down Michael's arm and into her hand. "For me, at least."

"What do you mean?" Michael asked, surprised by how hard it was to speak, and how hard it was to concentrate on Sloan's words. She was mesmerized by the feel of her so near, the faint tantalizing smell of her, and the heat that poured from those fingertips as they lightly brushed her own. Gazing at Sloan's lips, she imagined them on her skin. Remembering their kisses, she longed for more.

Sloan sensed Michael waiting for an answer, knowing that she owed her the truth. Until now, Michael had been the one to take all the chances. It was time to match her courage and take a risk for her.

"*You* happened to me," Sloan whispered, stepping near, her lips a breath away. "You swept into my life and stole my heart."

"Really?" Michael heard the words and wanted to believe her. Her body didn't care—she was already aching for her. Taking a deep breath, she asked quietly, "What about Claudia?"

Claudia? For a second, Sloan couldn't understand the question. She was having a hard time thinking around the buzzing in her head. Michael was so close she could see her pupils flicker.

"That's been over a long time, Michael," she finally said, slipping both hands to Michael's waist, shaking slightly as she surrendered to the truth. "There isn't anyone but you."

"What about tonight? In there?"

"I didn't know she'd be here. We ran into each outside—I just bought her a drink. There hasn't been anyone else since the moment I saw you. I swear." Lightly, she stroked Michael's cheek. "I can't think about anything except you. I'm *crazy* for you."

"Is that why I haven't heard from you all week?" She swayed slightly, leaning into Sloan's body almost against her will.

"I—" *No excuses. Not with her.* "I wanted to call. I was...scared."

"Sloan," Michael murmured, her voice hushed with desire. "Oh, Sloan. Why?"

"Because of this." Sloan did kiss her then, a long careful kiss—just their lips tenderly exploring, their bodies bending to one another but not quite touching. It was as if they both knew that any further contact and they would forget exactly where they were.

"Way to go," someone cheered as a small crowd of women shouldered past on their way to the club.

Sloan finally broke the kiss. Michael smiled up at her tremulously and said, "We seem to be making a spectacle of ourselves." But she made no move to step away.

"Mmm," Sloan agreed, thinking that she wanted to taste Michael's lips again. Had anything ever been so sweet? "We should...talk."

"You might invite me back to see the view from your loft," Michael whispered, her fingers trailing along the edge of Sloan's jaw. Sloan shuddered lightly, and Michael felt a lightning surge of desire. "Say yes. Hurry."

"Oh God, yes," Sloan grated, grasping Michael's hand and

pulling her toward her car.

"Sarah will wonder where I am," Michael declared urgently, even as she hurried across the street to keep pace with Sloan.

"It'll be all right," Sloan replied, fumbling her keys out of her pocket. "She'll be too busy tonight to worry."

Michael didn't answer; she simply slid into the seat, slid her hand along Sloan's thigh, and leaned over to kiss her neck. "So will I."

Chapter
Eighteen

Fortunately, Chances was only a few short blocks from Sloan's loft, and traffic was light. If she'd had to drive any further, Sloan feared she would wreck the Porsche. Michael's hand was like fire on her thigh. She slammed into the garage, hit the remote to close the double doors behind them, and keyed the sequence to bring the freight elevator down to the ground floor—all before she'd turned off the ignition. In a matter of seconds she vaulted around the front of the car and grabbed Michael's hand.

"Come on. I've got a great view."

Michael laughed, but when they reached the loft, she hesitated on the threshold, letting Sloan go ahead. Sloan turned back, a quizzical look on her face.

"What is it?" she asked softly. Michael looked uncertain and terribly vulnerable, and Sloan's heart ached to see it. She wanted to reassure her, to kiss the fear from her eyes.

"What does this mean? Our being here tonight?" Michael asked, her voice catching on the words. It was hard to expose her heart again—the pain and loneliness of the last week with no word from Sloan lingered still. Searching Sloan's face, she found tenderness there, and caring. She remembered Sloan's gentle touch and knew that she wanted it again. But she had to know if she was alone in her desire.

"If this is just...a night, I can't. Because I don't think I'd ever be able to forget you after this."

Standing very still, Sloan struggled with the words she had never expected to say again. "It means..."

She stopped, aware of lingering fears, hammering at her. Aware, too, that those fears were from a different time, and the betrayal another woman's. Not Michael's.

"It means I want you and I...need you. It means I'll do anything I possibly can never to hurt you." She swallowed, then took a step closer to the woman who had captured her heart. "It means I love you...more than I will ever be able to tell you."

Michael smiled faintly, a shimmer of tears in her eyes. She closed the remaining space between them and threaded her arms around Sloan's waist, nestling her head against her shoulder. "How is it you always know what to say?"

"I don't...always." Sloan gently stroked her hair and laughed a little unsteadily. "For some reason, being near you makes it easy to say the things I feel. Even when they scare me to death, I can't stop them from coming out." She kissed the top of Michael's head, then reached gently to lift Michael's chin in the palm of her hand, gazing deep into her clear blue eyes. "I love you, Michael Lassiter. So very much."

"I love *you*, J. T. Sloan." Michael smiled again, a full smile now that illuminated her features with hope and happiness. She brushed her lips across Sloan's and echoed softly, "So very much."

In the truth of one another's arms, they had no need for words. Michael pressed close, caressing Sloan's shoulders, her chest, her back. Their lips met as Sloan freed Michael's blouse from the waistband of her skirt, running her hands over the soft bared skin. Her mouth on Michael's, she raised her hands to Michael's breasts, starved for the feel of her flesh.

In turn, Michael eased back enough to get her hands between their bodies and pulled at the buttons of Sloan's fly. She stroked Sloan's abdomen, running her fingers along the edges of the quivering muscles, desperately pushing at the tight jeans, trying to touch more of her. They twisted together, thrashing on twin hooks of desire, their kisses voracious, their hands greedy—hot, hungry, and wild.

Sloan pulled away first, her stomach knotted with a need so heavy she could barely stand. They were nearly naked in the middle of her living room, clothes in various stages of disarray. Her hands shook where they lay on Michael's desire-dampened skin. "We should...slow down..."

Michael, face flushed, blue eyes cloudy with lust, moaned when Sloan's lips left hers. "No," she protested, sliding her fingers down the front of Sloan's jeans.

"Michael," Sloan gasped. Her knees buckled and she almost fell. "Michael, wait. Bedroom—now, or we'll end up right here on the floor."

"I don't care." Michael was on fire. The only thing she wanted was to feel Sloan, taste her—consume her until the famine of a lifetime was satisfied. And then she wanted to feel it all again. "I want you so much," she implored. "Hurry."

They half-stumbled across the floor, still embracing, shedding the rest of their clothes as they went. At the edge of the bed, they toppled onto the covers in a tangle of arms and legs. They couldn't seem to get close enough—tumbling over one another—claiming one another with lips and hands and desperate caresses until the air grew thick with the heat of their passion.

"I can't stand it," Michael moaned. "I want...more...all of you. Everything." She reached between Sloan's thighs for what she craved and found her hard and wet. Stroking through the swollen tissues, she entered her deeply, then eased slowly out, tantalizing her with light touches and teasing caresses.

"Let me touch you," Sloan protested, catching Michael's wrist as she tried to roll onto her, wanting *her* more than she wanted to be pleasured. Michael stopped her, far stronger than Sloan had imagined.

"No," Michael murmured, sliding inside again, reaching some place beyond the physical with her hands, her eyes, and her pure selfless desire. "No, I want you. I want *you*. Trust me, please."

Sloan fell back, surrendering, giving her body and letting go, finally, of the pain. "Yes," she whispered, the word ending in a small choked cry. Then Michael's mouth—biting lightly—was at her throat, then moving lower—over her breasts, down the center of her abdomen, pressing into the soft skin at the base of her belly. Her hands found Michael's hair, then her cheek, and she lifted her hips in silent offering. Breath still in her chest, she waited, blood poised to burn for the touch that would set her free.

Awestruck, Michael paused as Sloan arched and grew taut on the precipice of exploding. Eyes closed, heart full, she told Sloan with each tender touch of her lips how very much she loved her. And when Sloan grew full and hard in her mouth, the bands of her restraint breaking with a deep groan, Michael continued to glory in her until all that existed in that room was the perfect harmony of their blood, and their breath, and the beat of their hearts.

Sloan awoke in darkness, streetlights casting pale flickering shadows over the bed. Michael's head lay on her shoulder, and the soft weight of Michael's breast filled her palm. Even in the faint light, Michael's hair shone golden against her luminescent skin, giving her the look of a sleeping angel. Sloan ran her fingers through the silken strands, thinking about miracles and second chances. She realized that even in the first blush of infatuation with Elise she had never felt so connected, or so damn lucky. Maybe the lesson was that it took losing to understand what it meant to win. She sighed without knowing it, pulling her lover closer.

Michael lay quietly, listening to the comforting, steady rhythm of Sloan's heart, basking in the tender attention of Sloan's caresses. When she heard Sloan sigh a second time, she asked, "What's bothering you?"

"Did I wake you?" Sloan murmured, kissing the tip of her ear.

"No." Michael snuggled a little closer, one hand resting lightly against Sloan's abdomen. She smiled when the muscles jumped at her touch. "And don't change the subject."

"I was just thinking," Sloan replied, her voice still tinged with regret, "that I almost didn't let this happen. I was too stubborn to see that what I thought was love years ago never was at all."

"Don't torment yourself." Michael shifted until she lay on Sloan's welcoming body, raising up on her elbows and gazing into her lover's face. "You were young and you were innocent, and there's no blame in that. We're here together now, and that's all that matters."

"I love you," Sloan whispered, liking the sound of it.

"That works out well then," Michael responded as she brought her lips close to Sloan's. "Because I love you, too."

It was slower this time, but no less powerful. When kisses weren't enough, they traded languid strokes and caresses designed to torment, staring into each other's eyes—watching passion rule. When desire deepened to overflowing, Michael arched her hips to take all of Sloan inside, murmuring, "Soon."

"Uh-huh," Sloan agreed hoarsely, the pressure building, pounding, in the pit of her stomach. She clenched her jaws and said through gritted teeth, "I'm ready to go."

Michael began to tremble lightly, her eyelids fluttering closed for long seconds as her teeth caught at her lower lip. Then her eyes opened wide as her hips jerked hard into Sloan's hand. "Ohyes," she cried just before her head snapped back and her voice tripped over the sudden gripping spasm.

The sound of Michael's pleasure was all it took to drive Sloan beyond her limits, and she surrendered with a sharp cry as tongues of fire swept through her muscles and along her nerves, burning a white-hot path into her brain. She was molten, dissolving, destroyed.

Eventually, Michael found her voice and whispered, "I...I've never felt anything like that before."

"Neither have I." Sloan brushed at the tears on her own cheeks.

With a sigh, Michael tucked her head under Sloan's chin, fitting herself into every curve of Sloan's body. "That's all right then, isn't it?"

"Oh yes," Sloan murmured on the edge of sleep. "Just right."

When next they awoke, still wrapped in one another's arms, it was fully light. Sloan smiled at Michael, a slow easy smile of undisguised satiation. "Good morning."

"Morning," Michael responded, amazed to find herself where she had scarcely dared dream she would ever be. Hearing the warmth in Sloan's greeting and feeling the heat of their bodies pressed close together, she realized it was better than any dream. "Is there any particular morning-after ritual I should know about?"

"Well, let's see." Sloan's contagious grin widened. "There's the part where we shower together—taking a little extra time to get reacquainted, of course. And then there's the part where we fix breakfast, and, between clearing up and reading the paper, we come back here for a bit more intimate activity, and then maybe, just maybe, sometime later we get dressed."

"Sounds lovely." It was Michael's turn to grin. "However, I think we need to do the breakfast part before the shower and those other wonderful activities because I'm starving."

"I think we can arrange that," Sloan said, kissing her lightly, enjoying the prospect of sharing the morning routine with her.

Just as they were about to get up, the phone rang. Sloan

stared at the annoying intrusion and debated answering it. She couldn't think of anyone important enough for whom she would interrupt this moment, but she didn't want to chance it ringing again at an even more indelicate time either. *Better now than later.* She reached for it.

"Sloan," she said distractedly, captivated by the way the sheet outlined the curve of Michael's breast.

"Ah, Sloan," Sarah's familiar voice responded. "Am I interrupting anything?"

"Actually, yes." Sloan pulled Michael close and nuzzled her ear.

A soft laugh came to her through the line. "I thought I might be. I saw you come into the bar last night, and the next thing I knew both Michael and you were missing. I hope that means something."

"Oh yes, it definitely means something," Sloan murmured, her eyes on Michael's lips. They were full, slightly swollen from their kisses the previous night, and the sight reminded her of how those lips felt on her skin. Her heart stuttered in her chest. She glanced away because she didn't trust herself to form words while viewing any part of Michael.

"Something good?"

"Definitely."

"My, my," Sarah continued with her teasing. "People will talk."

"Jasmine looked quite stunning last night," Sloan managed, ignoring the taunt and giving Sarah some of her own medicine. She was willing to bet that she and Michael hadn't been the only ones to raise eyebrows the night before.

It was Sarah's turn for silence. Then, her voice husky, she responded, "Yes, she was...amazing. Beautiful, every step of the way."

"Hmm...is there a follow-up to that statement?"

"None that I can share."

"No fair to tease."

"Sorry," Sarah said softly, replaying those first moments alone with Jasmine. They were in her bedroom, a little after midnight.

They were hesitant, shy, still clothed as they kissed—both of them shaking. She wasn't sure which of them was more nervous.

Sarah felt Jasmine's body, female, but somehow...not, pressed to hers, and the allure of boundaries blurring excited her. "I love the way you feel."

Wordlessly, Jasmine removed the short black wig, and Sarah ran her hands through the slightly shorter golden hair beneath, amazed at the subtle shift from wholly feminine to androgynous just with that simple act. "I love the way you look."

When she reached under Jasmine's tight black top to release her bra, she thought for an instant that Jasmine would stop her, a swift tightening of muscle and sharp intake of breath warning of her fear.

"It's all right," Sarah whispered, running her tongue lightly up Jasmine's neck as she lifted the top and undergarment off together. "I want this. I want you. All of you."

In the faint glow of the bedside lamp, the chest she exposed was smooth and hairless, starkly muscled, and shimmering with a light sheen of sweat—the female become male. As she ran her fingers over the clearly defined contours, Jason quivered.

She was so intent on watching Jasmine become Jason, she scarcely noticed his gentle hands removing her blouse until their skin met. She gasped at that first touch of her nipples against his. Glancing to the side, she saw them in the full-length mirror on the wall, both nude from the waist up—naked breasts pressed to bare chest, one in jeans, the other in skirt and stockings—images not only reversed but completely exchanged. She watched their reflection as she lifted the leather skirt, slid one hand beneath and found the sheer thong. She clasped the fullness there, her knees weakening as Jason groaned and thrust himself against her palm.

When their bodies merged, Sarah gazed up into Jasmine's tender eyes and felt Jason, strong and deep, filling her. She welcomed them both with her passion.

"Sarah? You there?"

"Huh? Oh, sorry," she repeated with a self-conscious laugh as she shook off the last of the memories. "Trust me, though. Jasmine was lovely, and Jason was rather outstanding, too."

"I'm glad, Sarah. Really." The caring and wonder in Sarah's voice was impossible to miss. "I couldn't be happier. Jason is special, and so are you."

"Thanks, Sloan. You're a friend."

"Listen, friend," Sloan said good-naturedly, smiling at

Michael, who waited patiently. "I've got business to attend to."

"That's okay, so do I. Very pleasant business," Sarah said with another laugh. "I just called to satisfy my curiosity. Tell her I said hello."

"I'll do that." Sloan put down the phone and turned so she and Michael lay face to face. "Sarah says hi."

Michael didn't seem to be paying attention so Sloan kissed her, a kiss that lengthened until she felt herself edging past the point of stopping. She pulled away, whispering, "I'm having a bit of a problem."

"Hmm?" Michael said absently. She was circling her hand over Sloan's chest, brushing across her nipples with her palm. It was fascinating, the way they hardened at the first faint touch. She grasped one, squeezing steadily, and grinned when Sloan made a noise that sounded like pain, but wasn't.

"Jesus." Sloan shifted on the bed, arching under Michael's fingers. "You're making me awfully hot." She was a little breathless, and her hips had begun rocking of their own accord. *So crazy, so fast.*

"Is that bad?" Michael asked innocently, running her lips over Sloan's ear as she moved her hand lower.

"Uh. No. Only if you stop," Sloan gasped, praying that she wouldn't.

Michael loved doing this to her. "Can you wait?" She kissed her softly. "Until after breakfast?"

"Oh my God, I can't believe it," Sloan exclaimed, her eyes narrowed with a combination of lust and surprise. "You're a *tease.*"

"I've just discovered how much fun it is," Michael agreed, taking pity on her and moving her hand up to her shoulder. "But I've heard that it's better if you have to wait."

"No, it's not," Sloan declared in mock aggravation, swinging her legs out from under the covers and sitting up. "It's better if you just do it a lot."

"I'll remember that." Michael got up, brushing her fingers lightly along Sloan's arm. It was so hard to stop touching her.

"Good," Sloan muttered, still throbbing. "Because otherwise you'll kill me." She glanced at her and added, "You need to put some clothes on because I don't trust myself around open flames if you're naked."

Michael merely grinned and padded toward the bathroom, a

satisfied look on her face. Sloan found sweatpants and a T-shirt for her and pulled on sweats of her own. They took turns in the bathroom, then met in the kitchen to peruse the contents of the refrigerator together.

"Omelets?" Sloan inquired, reminded as she surveyed the paucity of food that she hadn't had a woman stay overnight in her apartment for a very long time. Her nights of carefully controlled intimacy had never included anything so intensely personal. She couldn't imagine now how those sterile encounters had sustained her for so long. Michael had reminded her of what it meant to hunger—and to be filled.

"Mmm, omelets sound perfect." Michael wrapped her arms around Sloan's waist from behind and stood on tiptoe to kiss the smooth skin on the back of her neck, then peered around her to look at the selection. "Is that orange juice I see?"

"Yep." Sloan shivered at the light caress and tried to ignore the quick twist of want in her stomach. This woman was going to drive her nuts. She gathered things from the refrigerator and stacked them on a nearby counter. "And I believe there's some blue cheese and mushrooms, too."

Somehow they managed to construct breakfast and still remain within touching distance of one another the entire time. As if by unspoken agreement, they sat side by side at the breakfast bar with the Sunday paper, which Sloan had retrieved from the front steps, spread between them. Sloan held her coffee cup in one hand while resting the other lightly on Michael's thigh. Michael, in turn, toyed with Sloan's fingers absently as she turned the pages of the paper for them.

"Have you got the tech section?" Sloan asked, relinquishing her empty cup.

"Yes, here." It occurred to Michael that she had never been so comfortable with anyone in her life. How something so simple could feel so exciting—and so very right—was quite beyond her experience. Even as she sat in contented silence, she was very conscious of the faint echoes of desire still whispering in her depths. She couldn't forget the way Sloan's eyes had darkened and grown hazy when she'd stroked her. Finally, she admitted to herself that she was not concentrating on anything she was reading. All she was aware of was Sloan. The heat from Sloan's hand on her thigh and her faint sweet scent aroused some primal response quite beyond her control. She wanted her.

"Sloan?" Michael inquired softly.

"Yes?" Sloan replied quietly, most of her attention on the slight press of Michael's leg against hers that was adding to the already distracting heaviness between her thighs, a persistent stimulation that had never completely quieted since they left the bedroom. She needed to be touched.

"Is it at all normal for me to want to make love to you twenty-four hours a day?"

Sloan swung toward her on the stool and raised one hand to lightly stroke her cheek. "Oh, I hope so," she whispered, her throat tight with renewed urgency, "because I feel the same way."

Michael placed her hands on Sloan's waist as she leaned forward, laughing. She kissed her, nibbling gently on her lower lip for a second, then slid down off the high breakfast seat. She moved closer and straddled Sloan's thigh, slipping her hands under Sloan's T-shirt to caress her back and then lightly stroke her stomach, running just a fingertip under the waistband of her sweats.

Sloan sighed with the pleasure of it. "Absolutely, completely normal," she gasped. "Oh man..."

"Well then," Michael murmured, tugging her by the hand toward the bedroom. "I'm all for doing what comes naturally."

Chapter
Nineteen

Late Monday morning, Sloan walked into her reception area and was greeted by Jason, a knowing smirk on his face. She stopped just inside the door and looked at him with raised brows and a wry grin.

"So?" she asked defensively. "You have something to say?"

"How was your weekend?" he asked sweetly.

She eyed him steadily, then answered smartly, "Probably a lot like yours. Spectacular."

He blushed and had the good grace to look mildly embarrassed. "My weekend was most satisfactory. Thank you."

She turned and headed toward her office, commenting as she went, "Well then, I'm sure you're more than fit for duty. Perhaps I can have that six-month fiscal report sometime before the next century, hmm?" She closed her door before she could hear his scathing response—and before he could hear her laugh. *Man, it is going to be awfully hard to work today.*

Through a supreme act of will, she managed to stop thinking about Michael and spent the next several hours sorting through files, reviewing accounts, and contemplating the order in which she wanted to deal with the most recent requests for her services. Her phone rang as she was studying a rather unusual application for a security check at a local police station. It wasn't the kind of work that was usually sent out to non-municipal agencies, and she wondered if someone suspected internal tampering. For a moment, she thought of the last time she had become embroiled in the politics of governmental intrigues and what it had cost her. It surprised her to find that the memory didn't hurt quite as much as it once had, but she tossed the file aside anyhow. *Let the police sort out their own mess.*

Glad for the distraction, she grabbed the receiver and said perfunctorily, "Sloan."

"Sloan, it's Michael."

Sloan sat up straight, catching the edge of alarm in Michael's voice. "What is it?"

"I just received a message that Innova's board is convening in four days—an unscheduled review of the quarterly financial statistics and *supposedly* to vote on next year's proposals."

"Who told you?"

"E-mail."

"Nice," Sloan seethed. "What do you think?"

"That this must be due to Nicholas's instigation. We've always taken care of these things at the end of the fiscal year. There's not much I can do about it, I guess, but I *had* hoped to have a little more time. The presentation last week went well, and if I could just delay this board meeting, I think I would have a better chance of convincing them of my competency." Michael sighed. "Of course, Nicholas knows this, too, which is why he's making his move now."

Sloan cursed powerfully under her breath. When she could speak calmly, she responded, "From what you've told me, your accounts are in good order, and, like you said, you've done well with the recent projects. Even if Nicholas pushes things toward a showdown with your board, you should be fine."

"Yes, I do know that, and I'm probably as ready as I can be. Just the same, I wish I knew exactly what he had planned."

"Maybe we can find out," Sloan murmured almost to herself.

"I don't want you to compromise yourself because of my situation," Michael said firmly. "But I am grateful for the offer."

"Don't worry, I'll stay far away from anything that might turn into a problem," Sloan said, already silently considering possible avenues of inquiry. "I'm sorry about this, Michael. I think that what you've offered him as settlement is more than fair. I'm sure some of this is prompted by the fact that you're leaving him."

"Well, that's one part of this debacle that I have absolutely no regrets about. It's something I should have done a long time ago." She fell silent, thinking of the magical weekend they'd just shared. She recalled a vivid image of Sloan, leaning across the front seat of her car that morning, stroking her cheek for an instant as she whispered goodbye. The look in Sloan's eyes had made her feel as if she were something precious. It was a feeling she hoped she would never lose. "The other part is you. I love you."

Sloan smiled, the husky tone of Michael's voice instantly arousing her. "I love you, too."

"Is there a chance I might take you out to dinner tonight? I'll have to work nonstop for the next few days, but we both have to eat, right?"

"More than a chance. You can count on it," Sloan said with certainty. "Hey, I know you can handle him. Just do what you do best and don't worry too much, okay?"

"I'll try," Michael answered. Since Sloan was practically all she could think about, that might not be too hard. "I'll see you tonight then."

"I'll be waiting for you."

As soon as Michael hung up, Sloan buzzed Jason, stating without preamble, "It's time to get everything we possibly can on Nicholas Burke. How are you doing with the virus trace?"

"Getting there. What's the rush?"

"Michael's getting ready to take him on, and if there's anything we can offer her as ammunition, we need it now."

"I've got some things working," Jason said. He didn't think Sloan needed to know exactly how much time he had spent perusing the files at Innova while repairing the damage from the virus. Nor how easy it had been to backtrack into Nicholas's personal logs.

"Make it fast, because Michael doesn't have a lot of time."

"Don't worry. I'm on it."

"Good," she said, setting the phone down, thinking of all they needed to do. She stared at her desk, trying to quiet the surge of rage she felt for Nicholas Burke.

"I don't really care, you know," Michael mused, running her fingertips slowly along the edge of Sloan's rib cage. They were tangled together, partially covered by a sheet, still languorous in the aftermath of their lovemaking. Their clothes lay scattered across Sloan's living room.

"You don't really care about what?" Sloan stretched and settled her arm more comfortably around Michael's shoulders, holding her possessively close.

"Whatever Nicholas is planning," Michael murmured. She was much more interested in the way Sloan's breasts rose and fell gently with each breath and in the faint flush of her skin that lingered after her passion was spent and in the muted echo of desire that still tingled in her own limbs. "At this moment, I feel invincible."

"Well, you conquered me."

Smiling, Michael ran nails down Sloan's abdomen, watching the muscles flicker. "I noticed." She added seriously, "Besides, nothing is as important as this."

"I understand." Sloan kissed the top of her head and said with a mixture of contentment and worry, "You matter more to me than anything else, too. But this is your work, Michael. This is a huge part of your life. There's no way he's going to take that away from you."

"Tomorrow I'm sure I'll agree." Michael pushed up on one arm and shifted until she was lying on top of her lover, whose legs parted automatically to accept Michael's thigh between them. Their breasts fit together effortlessly. Resting on her elbows, her hands framing Sloan's face, she whispered adamantly, "But right now—if it were impossible to ever leave this room, I wouldn't be sorry."

Sloan had no doubt that she meant it, because a part of her longed for exactly that—to be only with Michael and to know nothing else. But tomorrow would come, and eventually they would need to face the world.

"You'll work this out," she said softly, forgetting her resolve to be rational as she ran her hands lightly down Michael's smooth back to the round firm swell of her buttocks.

"Yes," Michael whispered, lowering her head to capture a nipple as her fingers pressed between them, seeking the tantalizing welcome of Sloan's body. "Yes, I will."

"Oh jeez, here I go again," Sloan confessed, feeling herself grow heavy and damp with desire. She groaned softly with the first promise of that exquisite pressure.

"This is getting to be fun." Michael grinned, all thoughts of Nicholas and business forgotten. Nothing stirred her quite like watching Sloan succumb to desire. It was a heady sensation knowing she could steal Sloan's control in these private moments. She thought pleasing Sloan was even more satisfying than being pleasured by her, and *that* was more satisfying than anything she had ever known. She closed her eyes, murmuring, "I love you," as she gave herself over to passion.

Nicholas strode angrily toward Angela's desk and demanded harshly, "What's so important it couldn't wait another few days? I don't appreciate being summoned by my wife like an office boy."

"Just a moment, I'll see if she's free," Angela replied with an icy smile.

It wasn't often that she saw Nicholas Burke out of control, and she had to work to hide her pleasure. She reached to her console to inform Michael that Nicholas had arrived, but he continued past her, sputtering, "Don't bother to announce me. I don't intend to wait."

He pushed open the door and marched across the plush carpet to confront Michael, who was seated behind her desk. "Do you mind telling me what's going on? I've got meetings scheduled and—"

"Yes, I know." Michael rose and came around to the front of her desk to face him. "And an important board meeting to prepare for as well. I assume there'll be more on your agenda than the budget. Like who will be running Innova this time next year?"

"That doesn't have to be an issue," he said quickly.

"Really? How is that?"

"Look at the proposal from *my* attorneys. It's fair—and suited to your talents. You could stay on as head of design—"

"I don't think so."

"If you challenge me for control of the company, I've got the support of the division heads. You'll lose." He didn't bother to disguise his contempt.

"You've overlooked something." At his sudden expression of confusion, Michael reached beside her and pulled over a folder, then flipped the cover open and extracted several pages. Glancing at it, she began reading what she knew by heart. "Ramos—design, Conklin—advertising, Villanueva—research, Davis—marketing." She looked up at him. "This is *my* list. There are more, Nicholas. I have a team ready to go—men and women with proven track records who the board will recognize and trust."

"You think I don't have a list of my own?" he asked condescendingly.

"Ah, but Nicholas, *you* don't have *me.* "

For the first time he looked nervous. "We could avoid all of this if you'd just see to reason."

"See to reason?" Michael asked quietly. "You mean ignore the fact that you attempted to sabotage my work? The very same work that is essential to the success of several major projects for some very important clients? Do you think that the board members will appreciate that?"

"I don't know what you're talking about," he said confidently. "But if you make a statement like that in public, it's slander. And my attorneys will have a field day with you."

"Nicholas," Michael replied softly, "I realize that you don't know me very well any more, but surely you remember that I'm not given to flights of fancy." She leaned over to the phone and punched in Angela's extension. After a second, she asked, "Is she here? Good. Ask her to come in, please."

Nicholas looked in the direction of the door as it swung open. He lifted his chin perfunctorily. "Who's this? I assumed this was a private matter."

"No, Nicholas, this is business," Michael answered. "Nicholas Burke, J. T. Sloan."

The two of them stood a few feet apart, visually taking each other's measure. A muscle twitched in Sloan's jaw. Nicholas' shoulders stiffened.

"I've heard the name," he said. He didn't extend his hand.

"Mayfield probably mentioned me," Sloan replied, her eyes winter cold.

"Can't recall."

"No reason you should." She moved away, because she had an overwhelming urge to punch him. That probably wouldn't help Michael, but it sure would make her feel a whole hell of a lot better. It was difficult knowing that this man had been intimate with Michael for so many years and had clearly never appreciated how fortunate he had been. That he was trying to hurt Michael now made Sloan crazy.

"Sloan is the head of a computer security company I asked to review our network. We had a major intrusion last week—one directed primarily at me."

"A computer glitch? And I should care...why?" Nicholas looked annoyed, staring from her to Sloan. Then he shot his cuff and made a show of looking at his watch. "Look, I've got—"

Michael nodded to Sloan.

"Have you ever heard of 18 USC 2511 and 18 USC 1030?" Sloan asked conversationally.

"What?"

"They're federal statutes protecting against computer hacking and electronic eavesdropping. Conviction can carry prison time."

Nicholas's eyes narrowed slightly, but his face remained expressionless. "It seems to me that that's more Mayfield's concern than mine. I'm sure he can straighten out any...irregularities. Now, I have proposals to review before our board meeting." He said pointedly to Michael, "If you change your mind, call my attorneys."

"I think you might find what Sloan has to say of more interest than anything you are preparing for the board meeting," Michael replied.

She left the statement hanging in the air unqualified and knew as he stopped, turning slowly back to them, that everything Sloan had presented to her early that morning was true. There was a wary look on his face and something close to panic in his eyes. How she could have been so wrong about him she would never understand. She could only believe that, over the years, they had both changed and that this was not the man she had once thought she loved. None of those feelings showed in her face as she met his gaze evenly.

"You've got a problem, Nicholas. One I might be inclined to help you with."

"What are you talking about?"

She glanced at Sloan. "Sloan?"

"I'll be brief," Sloan said with a glint in her eye. "Hackers—even the very best hackers—leave fingerprints. Programming platforms have something called a history file, a kind of log of user commands. You can tell what a particular user does—where he goes—what files he opens, or downloads, or institutes."

Nicholas looked bored. Sloan just smiled.

Leaning back against Michael's desk, her arms folded loosely over her chest, she continued smoothly, "Usually a malicious user will disguise his or her identity—create a false user ID. If they gain root access—programming capability—they can erase files, and in a company like this, where data is product, they could cripple the company. Or immobilize just one department. Or just one individual. Depending on the target."

"That's all very interesting, but—"

"It is," Sloan agreed, her smile predatory now. "Because once you identify the user ID of someone who has injected a malicious virus or deleted files—even someone with a false ID—you can backtrack through the firewall logs to the IP address, and then eventually to the e-mail address. Now, a clever hacker will reroute through several different servers and direct e-mail tools to more than one account address, but a good cyberforensics person can sort it out."

Nicholas sighed and looked at Michael. "Really, I can't see where this concerns me."

Her voice steady, Michael answered, "It does if it's you."

"What!"

"It's all right here, Mr. Burke," Sloan said, extracting a thick file from her briefcase. "All the logs, all the traces. Right back to your private e-mail address. The time logs from your office computer match perfectly the periods of the malicious activity."

"That's ridiculous," Nicholas barked defensively. "There's no way you could have legally accessed any of that information. This is nothing but technological blackmail."

"On the contrary," Michael informed him calmly. "All of this involved the corporate network, and as such, the security company I hired has a legitimate right to it. You forget, Nicholas," she added softly, "this is *my* company."

He took one swift step forward, a sound very close to a growl resonating in his throat. Michael didn't flinch, not even when he began to raise a tightly clenched fist.

"Don't," Sloan said quietly. She still looked relaxed, but was poised for the move. *Please, just give me the reason.*

"Calm down, Nicholas." Michael spoke before he could move further, angling her body between him and Sloan. She didn't doubt Sloan could handle him, but she had no intention of letting him anywhere near her lover. "I'm not interested in putting you in jail."

"It isn't true," he insisted, but his voice had lost its earlier ring of conviction. "Besides, you'd never be able to prove any of it."

"On the basis of what I have," Sloan interjected, "I could have the FBI here with a warrant to seize your computer, all of your personal records—everything—by this afternoon. Who knows what else we'll find in your e-mail?" She already knew what they'd find. Burke hadn't been very circumspect with his messages to Mayfield. He obviously had never anticipated anyone checking.

"God damn it, it wasn't me," he seethed. "It was *Mayfield.*"

"*If* it was," Sloan said, and she believed it had been, "he was clever enough to leave the breadcrumbs at the door of the person giving the orders. The trail leads undeniably to you, Mr. Burke."

"What do you want?" he asked, staring at Michael. Casting an angry glance at Sloan, he added quickly, "Assuming any of this is true."

"I have no interest in dragging this mess into court," Michael said. She reached for another document and regarded him with a mixture of anger and private sadness. "On the other hand, you tried to destroy not only my work, but also my position within the company. I don't feel that Innova has any obligation at this point to continue a financial association with you in the future. I have instructed my attorneys to withdraw all monetary incentives and compensation to you once the partnership is dissolved. Given the information I have regarding your activities, I consider that more than fair."

Nicholas's jaw muscles tightened and bunched as he struggled to contain his wrath, staring at the documents she held out to him. He looked from one woman to the other and knew with certainty that he had no bargaining power. It was a simple decision to make. He could not afford the adverse publicity that an investigation into his and Mayfield's tampering would entail, even if he could somehow prove he didn't actually *do* it. He'd ordered it done, and that was all it would take to destroy any future he might have in the corporate world. Now was the time to accept this small defeat in order to preserve his future opportunities. He nodded once.

"All right."

"I'll expect the signed agreement returned by the end of the day, Nicholas."

"You'll have it," he grated, turning to leave.

"And—"

"What else could you possibly want?" he snarled, looking over his shoulder.

"I've convened the board." She glanced at her watch. "They're waiting for us now. It's time to end this."

"You're so sure that they'll accept your plans to dissolve our partnership and institute *your* new team?"

Michael knew she was ready. "Yes."

"We'll find out," he barked as he flung open the office door. "I'll see you in the board room."

She watched him leave, feeling a chapter of her past closing as the door shut resoundingly behind him. She turned to look at the woman who would forever occupy the heart of her future, smiling softly.

"I should get in there."

"Yes," Sloan said. "I'll wait."

"It could be a while."

"I'll be here."

"Thank you."

Sloan shook her head, stepping close and resting her hands gently on Michael's waist. "There's no need to thank me. I love you."

"I still appreciate all you did. I don't intend to bring any of this up at the board meeting. I can win this one on merit. But at least now I know that he won't contest their decision and tie me up in court for years."

"I didn't do all that much, but we both owe Jason and Sarah a night on the town," Sloan said, laughing. "He missed another date while we put all this together."

"Absolutely," Michael agreed, raising her arms to Sloan's shoulders and pressing against her. She kissed her neck and leaned back so that their eyes met. "We'll take them out—anywhere they want—but not right away. As soon as this is over, I intend to keep you busy with personal matters for quite some time."

Sloan chuckled and kissed Michael hard enough to make her gasp with sudden pleasure. When she drew away, Sloan asked teasingly, "Personal matters, huh? Is that right?"

"That's very right," Michael said emphatically before she gently stepped away. "You can trust me on that."

"I can trust you in everything," Sloan whispered, "and that's all I'll ever need."

Honor Bound

Secret Service Agent Cameron Roberts made a promise to Blair Powell, the President's daughter--not to place her own life in danger protecting Blair--but a request from the Commander in Chief forces her to break her word. In this sequel to *Above All, Honor*, Cameron places duty before love and accepts reassignment as the chief of Blair's security detail, despite knowing that this decision may destroy their tenuous new relationship. As the rift between them widens, more than one woman is happy to offer Blair the company that Cam cannot. Amidst political intrigue, an escalating threat to Blair's safety, and the seemingly irreconcilable personal differences that force them ever further apart, these two unusual women struggle to find their way back to one another.

Available at bookstores everywhere.
ISBN: 1-930928-80-7

available from
Quest Books

Shield of Justice

Special Crimes Unit investigator Detective Sergeant Rebecca Frye is attempting to solve a series of sexual assaults and running into dead ends at every turn. Finally, she has a break in the case—a witness—one person who may help her bring a madman to justice. But, the witness is a victim herself and Rebecca must convince the injured woman's physician, Dr.Catherine Rawlings, to assist her—a task that will force both women to confront their own personal demons. Amidst professional conflicts and a growing mutual attraction, the two women become reluctant allies in the battle to stop the perpetrator before he strikes again.

Available at bookstores everywhere.
ISBN: 1-930928-41-6

Other books also available
By Radclyffe

Love's Melody Lost

Victim of a terrible accident, famed composer and pianist
Graham Yardley loses her sight, her heart, and her soul. Wealth
and fame mean nothing after the devastating loss of her beloved
music; her life is reduced to silence, darkness, and bitter regret.
In a bleak mansion atop windswept cliffs, the blind woman
withdraws from the world, her once consuming passions now a
source of anguish and fear. Then Anna, a lost woman seeking a
place in the world, comes into her life and awakens feelings she
thought were dead forever. A fragile melody of love is played
between these damaged souls, a song made sweeter and stronger
by the day...but will their blossoming romance be destroyed by
an outsider's greed or will it succumb to the discord of Graham's tormented heart? Can she find happiness with Anna,
caught up in the fiery overtures and darkly gothic strains
of...Love's Melody Lost?

ISBN 0-9716812-7-9

Above All, Honor

Single-minded Secret Service Agent Cameron Roberts has one mission—to guard the daughter of the President of the United States at all cost. Her duty is her life, and the only thing that keeps her from self-destructing under the unbearable weight of her own deep personal tragedy. She hasn't counted on the fact that Blair Powell, the beautiful, willful first daughter, will do anything in her power to escape the watchful eyes of her protectors, including seducing the agent in charge. Both women struggle with long-hidden secrets and dark passions as they are forced to confront their growing attraction amidst the escalating danger drawing ever closer to Blair.

From the dark shadows of rough trade bars in Greenwich Village to the elite galleries of Soho, Cameron must balance duty with desire and, ultimately, she must chose between love and honor.

ISBN 0970887426

Other Books from
RAP

Darkness Before the Dawn
By Belle Reilly
ISBN 1-930928-06-8

Chasing Shadows
By C. Paradee
ISBN 1-930928-49-1

Forces of Evil
By Trish Kocialski
ISBN 1-930928-07-6

Out of Darkness
By Mary D. Brooks
ISBN 1-930928-15-7

Glass Houses
By Ciarán Llachlan Leavitt
ISBN 1-930928-23-8

Storm Front
By Belle Reilly
ISBN 1-930928-19-X

Retribution
By Susanne Beck
ISBN 1-930928-24-6

Coming Home
By Lois Cloarec Hart
ISBN 1-930928-50-5

Madam President
By Blayne Cooper and TNovan
ISBN 1-930928-69-6

And Those Who Trespass Against Us
    By H. M. Macpherson
        ISBN 1-930928-21-1

Restitution
    By Susanne Beck
        ISBN 1-930928-65-3

You Must Remember This
    By Mary D. Brooks
        ISBN 1-930928-57-2

Bleeding Hearts
    By Josh Aterovis
        ISBN 1-930928-68-8

Jacob's Fire
    By Nan DeVincent Hayes
        ISBN 1-930928-11-4

Full Circle
    By Mary D. Brooks
        ISBN 1-930928-25-4

A Sacrifice For Friendship
    By DS Bauden
        ISBN 1-930928-30-0

Broken Faith
    By Lois Cloarec Hart
        ISBN 1-930928-40-8

The Road to Glory
    By Blayne Cooper and TNovan
        ISBN 1-930928-27-0

These and other
Renaissance Alliance titles
available now at your favorite booksellers.

Radclyffe is the cyberpersona of an author/surgeon who lives and writes in the Northeastern United States. She admits to a life-long love affair with fictional romances of all persuasions, and, after discovering lesbian fiction at the age of twelve, she has collected it, written it, and finally, one career later, published it. Her works range from romances in both the classic and modern tradition as well as several action/mystery series. The common theme throughout is a celebration of the power of love between strong, valiant women. In addition to writing, her passions include the martial arts (she holds a black belt in Ju Jitsu and a brown belt in Aikido) and everything about the life she shares with her partner, Lee.

A Matter of Trust is her seventh published novel. More information on these works can be found at www.radfic.com.

Printed in the United States
39046LVS00003B/117